LETHBRIDGE-STEWART

BLUE BLOOD

Chris Thomas

CANDY JAR BOOKS · CARDIFF
2022

ISBN: 978-1-913637-96-5

Range Editor: Andy Frankham-Allen
Editor: Shaun Russell
Editorial: Keren Williams
Licensed by Hannah Haisman
Cover by Paul Cooke & Will Brooks

Printed and bound in the UK by
4edge, 22 Eldon Way, Hockley, Essex, SS5 4AD

Published by
Candy Jar Books
Mackintosh House
136 Newport Road, Cardiff, CF24 1DJ
www.candyjarbooks.co.uk

PROLOGUE

A **STEADY** electrical hum permeated the air. Luminescence from equipment displays provided the only light in the darkened room. Electronic beeps came at regular intervals. And several beds lined each wall of the room, all containing completely motionless bodies. Not a flicker of movement among them. If they were breathing, it was imperceptible to the human ear or eye.

The room was old, as if it had many stories to tell. Part of a larger building. A salty spritz in the air and sound of the sea nearby gave away the coastal location. But it wasn't originally designed for medical purposes, that much was certain. There was a military sense to the place. Possibly an old naval base, abandoned after the war? It definitely had stories to tell... probably ones best to tell in the dark. The place definitely had that sort of feel.

Given the lack of light, secrecy was obviously paramount. The copious amounts of equipment connected to, and monitoring, the bodies also meant someone wanted them preserved. Alive, but definitely without anyone knowing they existed. The question was why.

He was drawn from his thoughts by a voice in the room.

'You needn't look surprised. We know this is your doing.'

The words were left hanging in the air, almost taunting him. It wasn't clear where exactly they were coming from.

'How did you do it?'

A poker face was the best way to play this situation – but it wasn't needed. He had no idea what the man was talking about. But he had to sit tight to find out what was going on. And why he was involved.

'The silent treatment will get you nowhere. You caused what you see before you. Tell us what you know. How they came to be this way.'

There was nothing more frustrating than someone insisting you knew something when, in fact, you didn't know anything at all. But he knew better than to say that. Any denial would seem feeble and make it sound even more like he *did* know something.

'You may think I'll grow weary if you say nothing for long enough, but I'm willing to take whatever time is necessary. After all, the people here have been waiting more than twenty-five years. But you know that already.'

Again, he was in the unenviable position of someone making demands while he remained clueless. Whatever had happened there was a puzzle. One neither his captor, nor anyone else, could quite piece together. That was clear: why else had he been brought here? For some reason, it was believed he was part of the jigsaw.

The voice echoed around the room again. 'Both you and I know what happened during the war. Don't think I don't know. The experiments you chose to forget. The orders you were supposed to follow. Remember the cover-up? Look around. You're looking at the consequences of those experiments. The past may have been forgotten by some but, for others, it is simply a waiting game.'

It sounded as if the man knew more than was being let on and was deliberately taunting him. Had they met before? The tenor of the voice definitely gave that impression.

This time he couldn't help himself.

'What are you talking about?' He tried pulling on the chair's restraints, to no avail. It was unlikely he could have broken free and escaped; it was just a natural instinct when placed in such a position.

The accusatory voice continued, this time almost taking pleasure in whatever discomfort he could cause. 'Do I detect a twinge of guilt? Or shame? That's not why we're here. Perhaps you should be proud. They're still alive, at least. In a sense.' There was a pause. 'If you can call it living.'

There was nothing for it. He had to play along and bluff his way through. Perhaps he would discover something about what was going on. And that information might be useful to his contacts, if they ever found him. Hopefully someone had cottoned on to the fact that he was missing.

'Your knowledge would be extremely helpful to our cause.'

Cause? What cause? There was a certain undertone to the word he didn't like. There was an association he couldn't quite place.

Whatever it was, he knew it wasn't good. Either for him or the unconscious men in the room.

The voice echoed around the confined area once more.

'So, tell us… What's the secret, Professor Travers?'

CHAPTER ONE
Thankful Distraction

'Is all this really necessary, Fiona?'

Alistair Lethbridge-Stewart had been trying to humour his fiancée in relation to their wedding plans, but he was getting tired of the trivialities. Given his military background, he was all for a well-organised event, but surely the tablecloth colours and calligraphy on the invites were much of a muchness? He sighed internally, knowing there was little he could do about it. Just grin and bear it, he supposed. However, Alistair couldn't help but think there were rather more things a man of his stature and command should be worried about.

'Alistair, don't be like that. You promised you'd be part of this. It's your wedding too, you know.' Fiona had given him a reprimanding look, holding up two pieces of fabric he was supposed to choose from. One was pale apricot, the other a mild aqua.

'As I've said before, when it comes to these details, I'm quite happy for you to make the decision.' Knowing his comment might be taken the wrong way, Alistair then quickly added: 'You're more than capable. I'm sure I'd only mess it up.'

'That's not the point and you know it. Part of being married involves making decisions together.'

Alistair shook his head. There was no way he was going to win. 'Fine, then. The orangey-looking one. But I doubt very much our guests will care one way or another.'

'Of course they'll care! They'll care that everything looks nice and complements each other on our big day.'

Alistair arched an eyebrow. 'Really? Do you remember the colour of the tablecloths at other weddings you've been to?' Fiona didn't dignify him with an answer. She simply rolled her eyes and walked her petite frame out of the room.

It wasn't that Alistair was trying to be difficult. He did want the wedding day to be a success; he really did. For Fiona's sake, as much as his. She deserved the best. But given everything they'd been through, especially him, it was hard to focus on the mundane. Some people found these things a welcome relief after traumatic experiences, but not him. He hated admitting it, but everything that had happened over the past few years had made him even itchier for action. So, the contrast between unexplained encounters and wedding invites was a gaping chasm for him.

Fiona came back into the room. 'I know this isn't quite running through a field, dodging bullets and chasing after goodness-knows-what, but it's just a bit of give and take.' She now had a more conciliatory tone, twirling a lock of blonde hair as she spoke. 'Your work means a lot of secrecy and things remaining hush-hush and I have to accept that. But you have to accept you need to play a part in the little things as well.'

'Of course.' Alistair knew she was right. Perhaps he needed to relax a little more. Or just understand what made Fiona happy. The little things in life were important to her. He needed to make more of an effort. 'Have we decided on the main course yet?'

The cushion just missed his ear. It had been tossed in playful frustration.

'Does chicken Marengo ring any bells?'

Somewhere at the back of Alistair's thoughts there was a vague recollection… He must have just agreed to it at some point. 'Ah yes… Sorry, slipped my mind.'

As the moment hung between them, the phone rang. Welcoming the distraction, Alistair went into the hallway to answer it.

'Lethbridge-Stewart.' He listened intently. Finally, he replied. 'Surely it should be a matter for the police, Sergeant Maddox? Sounds fairly routine to me. They have a missing persons' department; I don't see why the Support Group needs to be involved or, indeed, even the military to be honest.'

Fiona stuck her head around the corner. 'Trouble?' she mouthed. Alistair tried shooing her away while listening to the sergeant. He knew it was probably nothing. Or that one of his senior officers could deal with it. He really should be reprimanding Maddox for wasting his time. But the alternative was more wedding planning with Fiona and probably getting into trouble for not remembering whether it was trifle or pudding for dessert.

'I must say it's highly irregular, Sergeant. But if your

judgement says to call the highest-ranking officer, then I'm sincerely hoping there's something in this worthy of my attention. I'll be there soon.'

As Alistair hung up the phone, he saw Fiona in the doorway with her arms crossed.

'Really, Alistair? You just said it sounded routine.'

'You know better than to eavesdrop. Sometimes it's better you don't know things. Just for your own safety.'

'I'm a big girl, I can look after myself. Or have you forgotten our engagement holiday so easily?' Her defiance radiated through the room. 'All I heard was that some people had gone missing. Happens all the time. Call back and tell them to get someone else to deal with it until they have something more interesting to tell you.'

'I'm sorry, Fiona, but Maddox wouldn't call me unless it was a highly irregular matter. There's only so much information that can be conveyed over the phone. You never know who might be listening. My men know not to bother me if it's not important. There must be something else they need to tell, or even show me.'

Fiona scowled. Alistair thought he sounded plausible but felt guilt nevertheless. She saw right through his excuse for leaving. But even if it was a false alarm, Alistair knew he would welcome the brief respite. No harm in checking everything was in order at the Madhouse.

Eventually, Fiona spoke.

'Oh, go on, then,' she said, waving her arms at him as if he should leave. 'You'd only keep on grumbling about our wedding plans.'

Alistair couldn't help but smile. Just a small one. It was like she finally understood.

'Very well, then. I'll be off shortly. Not sure how long I'll be. Depends what's up.' He went up to Fiona, embraced her, and kissed her before turning about.

'I love you too, Alistair,' she called after him. 'And I want your opinion on what font the calligrapher should use on the wedding invites when you get back.'

Staring at the pot of tea on the table, Anne Travers was miles away. She was going over and over things in her mind while absent-mindedly holding the teacup to her lips. Despite her thoughts, she was in a daze.

'Are you going to drink that or just soak up the aroma?' Bill Bishop looked at her from the other side of the table, grinning. Playful yet sensitive. Anne knew Bill loved teasing her.

'Sorry. A lot on my mind.' She quickly sipped up a mouthful of tea and placed the cup back onto its saucer.

'Really? A lot or just the enormity of one subject?' Bill picked up the teapot and poured his own brew. Adding a dash of milk, he paused. 'It's pretty obvious what you're thinking about. I could almost sense your mind ticking over from the other room.'

'Should Uri Geller be worried?' Anne half-smiled at her fiancé. 'Or should I be more worried that it now appears you can read me like a book?' She hated the idea she had become that predictable. Given both of them had experienced such extraordinary things in recent times were they now thinking alike?

'It's hardly surprising,' Bill said, interrupting her train of thought. 'It's a lot to take in. Even after almost two months. It took you a long time to come to terms with your dad's... passing, it's only natural this...' He smiled again, before he said too much.

'Okay, then yes, I am thinking about...' She found it hard to say the name. '...Ted.'

Their eyes met at the mention of this moniker. They both knew Ted wasn't his real name – even Ted himself knew that. He had adopted the name to try to make things a little easier.

Bill put his tea down, went around the table and started rubbing Anne's shoulders. 'He's not your dad. You know that.'

Anne glanced upwards, appreciating his efforts at trying to relax her. 'No, but he's the spitting image of my father and goes by the name of Professor Edward Travers, except when it comes to me. Completely identical to the father I know but he hasn't experienced the past thirty-five years the same way. How can I not think of him as my father? That's all I see when we're in the same room together.'

'Can you not think of him as some long-lost identical twin? Or a triplet, at least,' Bill added, remembering Edward Travers already had a (deceased) twin. 'Would that help?'

Anne shrugged Bill off and half-rolled her eyes. 'I never said my thoughts about this were rational.'

'Can I quote you on that?' Bill asked as he walked back to his seat and cup of tea. 'The logical scientist admitting she's not being reasonable?' He looked at her mischievously.

'I *am* being reasonable, Bill! If the positions were reversed, what would you do? Come to think of it, what if an identical version of me turned up and you had no idea who she was? Would you be analysing the situation with coherent, common sense thoughts?' Anne knew she was coming across as feisty but, despite her scientific background, her feelings played a part in this, too. Bill almost laughing at her didn't help. She took a breath and had another sip of tea. 'Sorry, just venting.'

'Perfectly understandable.' Bill gulped half his cup. 'I'm not saying the situation isn't strange. But it's the situation we now have, and have to deal with. Besides, one of you is more than enough for me.' He added a little wink at the end.

Cheeky... But why does he have to be so understanding? Anne smiled on the inside. That was part of Bill's appeal, she knew. He wasn't just a military man – she couldn't be with someone who was just brawn and had no mind of his own. Bill was a good soldier, but also had a caring nature, which made him stand out from the rest. And a good scientifically curious mind. *Plus*, he had an amazing ability to make her laugh when she was worried and even when she was angry – somehow it defused everything.

'Do you believe his story?' Anne wanted his support now and valued his opinion. 'It's all a bit far-fetched, if you ask me.'

'Says the woman who can understand any alien language courtesy of a translation matrix coded to her DNA. And let's not forget all the other things we've experienced since joining the Fifth. Including time travel.'

'Yes, yes... but, come on – time-travelling with HG Wells, the man who wrote *The Time Machine*? It's like Agatha Christie trying to solve a real-life murder-mystery, rather than writing about them, or Charles Dickens being visited by ghosts at Christmas.'

Bill chuckled. 'You don't believe in ghosts.'

Anne shot him a look back. Bill finished his tea. A pause lingered between the two, allowing them a moment with their respective thoughts.

'Have you heard from him lately? Ted, I mean.' There was genuine curiosity in Bill's voice.

Anne shook her head. 'Not for weeks. I never know what to say or do when I'm around him. Kind of glad about that, in a way.'

'That silence from him may not be a good thing.'

Anne could see Bill's military instincts springing to life, suspicions raised and ready for anything. She could almost see the prickles on the back of his neck.

'And why is that?'

'We don't really know anything about this version of your father… er, I mean Ted. We don't know what he may be capable of, or what he gets up to.'

Anne looked into the bottom of her now-empty teacup and focused on the few tea leaves that remained. 'For all intents and purposes, he's still the same man. Loathe as I am to admit it.'

'Is he? We don't know how long he was out there travelling these parallel worlds he mentioned. We don't know what he had to do to survive. People can change; be influenced by others. A bad experience can cause them to go off the rails. We just don't know enough about him to trust him completely.'

Anne considered what Bill was saying. All sounded reasonable. She wasn't sure she trusted Ted herself. Up until now, she had put it down to her mixed emotions upon seeing a father who didn't really know her.

'Hmm… That reminds me…' Anne stopped. *Why am I being so suspicious?* Her own doubts and insecurities about the whole situation could be making her look for things that weren't there.

'Go on.' Bill's prompt made her voice her concerns.

'I didn't think much of it, but Ted's been in touch with an old friend of my father's. Professor Watkins.'

'Do you know why?'

'Not really. They've been exchanging postcards. The thing is—'

'What?'

'I'm pretty sure Professor Watkins is under the impression Ted is really my father.'

'You mean he's corresponding as Professor Travers? Why would he do that?'

'It could be nothing. Maybe he doesn't want to complicate things any further. How could Watkins possibly understand what's happened, even with his scientific background? Look at how weird it is between Ted and me. I'm not even sure how to approach it with Alun.'

Anne tried not to picture it. Telling her brother that, somehow, their father was still alive. And he looked a good thirty-five years younger…

Bill stood and started putting the teapot and empty cups on the tea tray, ready to clear away. 'But if he goes around claiming to be the real Professor Travers, I'd say there's potential for him to run into trouble at some point, wouldn't you?'

Anne looked at Bill, blankly.

'Think about it — your real father was privy to highly top secret information, based on his experiences. This version hasn't had the benefit of those experiences.'

'What are you saying?'

'If Ted claims to be the real Professor Travers, even to just a select few, he could get himself into a terrible mess.'

CHAPTER TWO
More than Meets the Eye

AFTER AN uneventful drive, which allowed Lethbridge-Stewart a little peace, he arrived at Dolerite Base (the secret HQ for the Fifth Operational Corps hidden beneath Edinburgh Castle) primed and ready for whatever was in store. Sergeant Maddox had given him rather limited information over the phone, and he hoped there was something more to these missing persons' reports. Flashing his security pass as he went through the gates, the junior officer gave him a salute. Once he parked his car, Lethbridge-Stewart marched through the New Barracks and into the lift that took him beneath the castle. He emerged and headed directly for the briefing room. Regimental Sergeant Major Samson Ware was waiting for him.

'This better be good, Samson. Missing persons?'

'Better than wedding planning,' Samson said, once the door was firmly closed behind Lethbridge-Stewart.

He'd wondered why Samson was here giving the briefing, when it should have been either Captain Miles or Captain Bishop. Now he knew.

'Quite.' Lethbridge-Stewart allowed a small smile and indicated Samson ought to continue with his report.

'Well, it certainly started out as a simple missing person. People have been disappearing all over London and other parts of Britain. Here in Scotland, too. All over the UK, in fact.'

'How are they different from normal missing persons' cases? Anything strange or unusual that would warrant the Fifth investigating?'

Samson shuffled through some files and pulled out various documents and photographs. 'Not originally, sir. The reports have been filed over the past six months. There's been a bit of a spike in the numbers, though.'

'Still sounds like a police matter.'

'That's what we thought. Until this happened…' Samson handed Lethbridge-Stewart the files. 'Very unpleasant viewing.'

Lethbridge-Stewart leafed through the papers and looked at the photographs thoughtfully. He'd seen plenty of horrific injuries and dead men in battle over the years. But the corpses shown in these pictures were horrendous. They had been viciously torn apart; their organs and insides hanging out. Lethbridge-Stewart was glad he hadn't eaten recently.

'What in the blazes would have caused those injuries, do you think?' He chanced another glance at the pictures and winced. 'Some sort of wild animal?'

Samson shook his head. 'That's just it,' he said. 'Nobody knows. The police consulted some wildlife experts but it's like nothing they've ever seen before. A lot of these people were also found in metropolitan areas, so an animal attack is highly unlikely. And I've checked – there have been no reports of any zoo escapes in the timeframe we have for this. It's all completely unnatural.'

'Hence us becoming involved.'

Lethbridge-Stewart eyed Samson up and down. Their acquaintance dated back a good two decades. Indeed, it was Lethbridge-Stewart himself who had convinced Samson to return to the military, after a brief stint as a stuntman. He was a good, reliable man and knew far better than to call Lethbridge-Stewart in on a wild goose chase.

'If it's as widespread as you say, then we're going to need our men out and about to investigate all the areas mentioned in the reports,' Lethbridge-Stewart said. 'Is there any one place that has a greater number of missing persons than the others?' He didn't want to stretch his men too thin, and it seemed logical to start with the location where the majority had disappeared.

'Quite a few missing in the Northumberland area, sir. Several corpses found there as well.'

'Right. Bring Bishop in on this, if he isn't already.'

Samson took the hint. 'Of course, sir. He's due in shortly.'

'Good. I still want men in the other locations, so allocate your resources accordingly. The right ratio of men to disappearances, that sort of thing.'

'Yes, sir.'

'I'll coordinate things from here and will expect regular updates.'

*

Captain Bishop wasn't that familiar with Newcastle. He'd had no real reason to visit it in the past and was only here now because of his current assignment.

Wandering the streets, he realised he knew very little about the place, other than it used to be a coal-mining town. There was still a shipping industry, it seemed, given the yards on the River Tyne but, looking at the youthful faces (and long hair) passing him by, it was definitely a hub for students now. Hardly surprising. The scant information he'd managed to glean before arriving told him there was a university and polytechnic on hand. He was glad of Samson's suggestion to dress in mufti for this particular investigation. A military uniform would have made anyone they were trying to get information from clam up immediately. Still, Bishop wasn't exactly comfortable with the choice of attire.

'You look fine, Bill, I don't know what you're worried about.' Samson grinned at him.

'Is that so? Despite what's supposedly in fashion these days, I really don't feel "groovy" or whatever the word is. And I feel too old to be "hip".' Bishop looked himself up and down and couldn't help but feel slightly ridiculous. He didn't know why his normal out-of-uniform clothes couldn't have sufficed.

'Too old? You're barely a quarter of a century. Besides, you look good in bellbottoms.'

Bishop gave a reluctant nod and took in Samson's outfit. 'You look fine, Sam, but I think you could pull anything off. It's just the way you carry yourself. Anne couldn't stop laughing when I left the house.'

'I hope this isn't along the lines of all black men being able to dance?'

Bishop thought about what he'd said or accidentally implied.

'Not every cliché you hear is true,' Samson noted.

Bishop noticed the cheeky glint in his eye. Time to change the subject.

'What are the other men up to?'

'Christiner and Miller are asking around, trying to find people who might have been friends with those who went missing.'

'I suppose we better do the same. What have the local police said about it all?'

Samson pulled some papers from inside his jacket pocket. 'Not a lot. Their leads turned up nothing.'

'Not surprising. I can't imagine students or anyone young in this town really wanting to talk to uniformed police. Scared of getting caught being spaced out, I imagine.'

Two long-haired youths brushed past them awkwardly in the main street. Bishop hated to admit it, but he did have trouble telling which one was male and which was female. Sign of the times, he guessed.

'We probably should start poking our noses about. Best place might be a pub or two, eh?'

'Isn't it always?'

The Horse and Hound was no different from any other pub Bishop had been to, complete with rowdy arguments coming from different ends of the bar. Except the Geordie accent was far more prevalent, of course. And there was an incongruous amount of young people in there; something he didn't expect. It wasn't until he saw the Student Discount sign that it made more sense.

Jostling through the crowd, the two men made it to the bar. The barman nodded at them from the other end and, after finishing his pour and serving his customer, approached the pair.

'Right, lads, what'll it be?'

'Two bitters. Pints,' Bishop said. 'Whatever's popular around here.'

'Coming right up.' The barman grabbed the glasses and deftly poured two perfect pints.

'Always this busy?' ventured Samson, looking around as Bishop paid his sum. The place was packed, people continually squeezing past each other to get from one place to another.

The barman considered the question. 'S'pose so. Hard to say. Trade's finally picked up since those disappearances.'

Bishop's ears pricked up immediately. 'What disappearances?'

'Where have you been? It was in all the local papers. Lot of young'uns going missing. Few turned up dead, may God rest their souls. People were scared to go out for a while, especially the students.'

'And now they're back?' Samson swigged his beer. 'Is that because it stopped happening?'

'Nah, it still happens from time to time. Hard to say if people have really gone missing or if they're running away from something. You just can't tell, can ya? People just got on with their lives… A man needs a drink. Can't stay home all the time. Plus, I've been offering the student discount, which helps a bit.'

Samson and Bishop exchanged knowing glances. They didn't

want to push too hard on the questioning. But before either could say another thing, the barman put an end to the conversation.

'Sorry, lads, you can see the bar's heaving and I really ought to be lending Emily a hand with everything.' He gestured towards a young, attractive woman who had emerged to help out at the bar.

Raising their glasses in acknowledgement, Bishop and Samson struggled across the room to find a seat. Miraculously, a group was leaving a small booth in the corner.

'So, what now?' Samson asked as they sat down. More people elbowed past.

'We should at least finish our pints.' Bishop grinned. 'We'll keep an eye open here for a bit, just in case we can learn any more beyond what the barman told us.'

'We probably need to find a student or two willing to talk.'

'There are plenty in here.'

At that moment, a man in head-to-toe denim bumbled into their table, almost causing himself to fall.

'Sorry about that, fellas,' he said, his north London accent standing out in a room full of Geordies. As he steadied himself, Bishop and Samson took in his bushy beard and mop of curly hair – along with the camera around his neck. 'Gary Merrin, student photographer,' he offered, holding out his hand. The two soldiers responded in kind, unsure what to do next. Fortunately, their new acquaintance made the next move by sitting down with them. 'Hope you don't mind me joining you?'

'Sure, why not?' Bishop said.

Gary smiled. 'Another Londoner, eh?'

'Mitcham. Originally.'

'Nice,' Gary said.

'What do you photograph?' Samson asked.

'Oh, anything! Mainly for the student paper. Whatever concerts I can get to; they're always fun to do. But I'm also trying to break into the big press, so I dabble a bit in that.'

'Aside from bumping into our table, what made you join us, Gary?' Bishop wondered.

Gary looked from side-to-side, then leaned in, trying to whisper against the background noise. 'You're not from around here.'

'Clearly,' Bishop said. 'But, you know, I could be a student. They're from all over the place.'

Gary smiled. 'Suppose you're young enough. Just about. But

you two carry yourselves completely differently. Spotted it as soon as you walked in. A bit stiff, even slightly awkward. You're missing the relaxed "don't care" posture of people from around here. The rigid way you carry yourselves makes me think you might be military?'

Bishop's shoulders slumped. *I used to be better at this. Has the Fifth really aged me up?* Despite their best efforts to blend in, they had been spotted a mile away. It was hard to shake years of military training and experience in one fell swoop. He decided to play Gary's game.

'And if we are...?'

'Then I would wonder what the military is doing in Newcastle. Especially given all the missing persons in recent times.'

'What makes you think the two are connected?' Samson eyed him suspiciously.

'You seemed particularly interested in what the barman had to tell you.'

Bishop wondered why they hadn't spotted Gary earlier. He kind of stood out in his denim jacket, denim jeans and white trainers. Plus, he was lugging a large camera around his neck.

'If you know we're military, then you'd be smart enough to know we're unable to reveal things to civilians,' Bishop said pointedly.

'Is that so? What if I said I had some information that would interest you? Would that change your mind?'

'Depends on what the information is. And reporting of what we're up to – if anything at all – could see your efforts slapped down with a D-notice. Had you thought of that?'

Gary considered it for a minute. 'Finish your beers. It'll be easier if I show you.'

A short while later, Bishop and Samson were being led by Gary into a warehouse. It seemed fairly innocuous, but Bishop would have preferred it if they had been armed.

He wasn't sure what to expect – Gary had mainly talked about some of the recent concerts he had photographed, including the Plastic Ono Band. Apparently, Eric Clapton was on stage with them the night he attended. At least Bishop had Samson as backup; a good, strong and solid fighting man if the situation called for it.

Peering into the dim light, Gary led them through the

warehouse into a large room full of beds and equipment. Despite the absence of people, it looked like there had been recent use.

'What are we looking at here, Gary?' Samson tried to take it all in.

'It's where the students come. For the experiments.'

'What experiments?' Bishop asked.

'There are signs up around campus, asking students to take part in experiments for a research project. There's an incentive for them to do it – they get paid a small amount.'

'And the experiments happen here?' Bishop looked around. The warehouse didn't appear to be a particularly legitimate place for proper research done by a tertiary institution. 'Surely those sorts of things are usually done on campus?'

Samson nodded his agreement. 'You'd think so.' He looked around again. 'What sort of experiments are they?'

Gary's tone became grave. 'Not exactly sure, although the signs around campus have some vague descriptions about "sleeping less". I can see how that would appeal to some students when they're cramming for an exam – coffee can only do so much. Don't know much beyond that, except some•students have disappeared after taking part. A couple have been found dead.'

Bishop wandered around the room, looking at the equipment. He wasn't sure what everything was or its purpose – it was something Anne would have been much better at identifying. He'd been doubtful about Gary bringing his camera, given its bulk was so noticeable, but the eager student had done his best to conceal it.

'Can you fire off a few photos, Gary? We know someone who might be able to tell us what all this stuff is for.'

As Gary took his shots, the flash illuminating the room vividly, Samson spoke. 'How did you come to uncover all this, anyway? And why haven't the local police made this connection before?'

Gary stopped to consider Samson's question. 'The missing students are usually the desperate ones. That's why they need the money.'

'You mean drugs?'

Nodding, Gary explained. 'That's what the deaths have been put down to. As for those who've gone missing, people are just saying it's the transient nature of students. The ones who really take on the hippy lifestyle.'

'You'd still think the police would have checked this place

out,' Samson said, looking around. 'If you've made the connection, Gary, I can't see why they wouldn't do the same.'

Gary shrugged and went off to take another photo. Shortly after he'd meandered off away from them into another section, Bishop and Samson heard a blood-curdling scream. They both bolted in the direction of the noise. Passing through a dilapidated doorway, they could see Gary cowering in the corner of the room. Looming over him was a woman, screaming into his face.

But that wasn't the strangest thing. She seemed to be in pain, screaming both for herself and at Gary. As she turned to face the two new arrivals, Bishop's stomach lurched.

Half her intestines were hanging out, ripped from her by goodness-knows-what.

Despite the danger, Gary fired off as many shots as he could on his camera, the flash going off in unison. The woman was temporarily dazed. A hush fell over the room as Bishop and Samson contemplated their next move. Gary stood rooted to the spot, his face as white as a sheet.

Unfortunately, the momentary quiet was short-lived. The woman screeched even louder this time – so much so, Samson and Bishop had to cover their ears. Despite the noise, Gary didn't respond and simply stared at the horrendous sight before him.

Before anyone could respond, the woman moved quickly and was suddenly clawing at Gary's beard, seemingly angry he was the source of light that blinded her. It was enough for him to move out of his paralysis and try to push her away. But the force was too strong. Gary had been caught by surprise and was doing his best to stay upright.

Bishop nodded at Samson, and both charged into the woman with all their might.

As she flew backwards from the sheer brute force, Samson called out. 'Run, Gary! Run now!'

The denim-clad photographer didn't need to be told twice. He picked himself up and high-tailed it out of there. Bishop was quick to follow. Samson elbowed the woman in the face, stunning her again and providing crucial extra seconds to allow their escape. Screeching sounds came after them as they exited the building.

The three men re-grouped a couple of streets away, panting from the exertion.

'I knew we should have remained armed,' Bishop said.

'While undercover?' Samson shook his head. 'We had no idea we'd encounter something like that.'

'Yet we did,' Bishop countered. 'We need backup and we need it fast. Call the Madhouse and report in.'

'Got it.' Samson hared off to find the nearest phone box.

'Gary,' Bishop said, 'we're going to need to commandeer your camera.'

'No chance.'

'We need those photos.'

'So do I. These photos are gold. Perfect for the big press.' Gary clutched at his camera, moving it away from Bishop.

'Not this time around. This is now a military investigation. Please hand over the camera. Or the film, at least.'

'But I only just started this roll! It'd be a waste.'

Bishop sighed. It always came down to money. 'We'll buy you new film. Look, surely you can see that woman is a threat to the public. And probably herself. The situation needs to be contained. Plus, you have all those photos of the equipment back there.'

Reluctantly, Gary started winding back the film.

INTERLUDE 1

Brock University
1812 Sir Isaac Brock Way
St Catharines
Ontario, ON L2S 3A1

Dear Mom and Dad,

Just a short letter to let you know how I've been settling into campus life. I know how you worry and, even though I tell you that you shouldn't, I know you still do. So you'll be pleased to know I'm alive and well and seem to be doing okay. I was a little hesitant at first, because I'd heard life can be tough for a freshman, but that hasn't been the case at all. I'm really loving university life (even the study!)

Have joined the ice hockey and lacrosse teams – you know I couldn't resist – and seem to be fitting in well. Both teams have lost and won a game. Mom, don't worry, I *am* using my mouth guard on the ice rink. At the first sign of trouble, the referee stops play. So I'm not going to get hurt.

My roommate is a swell kind of guy. I could have been stuck with a real keener or beau cave but Samuel's a great person to hang out with and he also gives me quiet time to study or just be by myself. He's usually out on a date, anyway. (No mom, I haven't started dating anyone yet but there are plenty of cute girls on campus. Let's give it some time, eh?)

Actually, Samuel told me a story the other day, obviously designed to scare freshmen (and women.) But it sounds like an urban legend to me.

Because some students are on a tight budget (thanks for your help with this, by the way,) they're always looking for anything free, especially food. If you're one of the 'chosen ones,' your doorknob rattles around midnight. By the time anyone opens the door, whoever rattled it is no longer there. But it's the signal to meet behind an old, unused shelter shed near one of the playing fields. If you go there, a large barbecue is supposed to be taking place with all sorts of meats and other things on offer. There's no way you could go hungry.

These students always seem to disappear. It's usually put down to low grades or the fact they found university life wasn't for them. But no one ever really hears from these people again, even people who were good friends or couples who were dating. It's like they disappear off the face of the Earth.

But, as the story goes, there was one student who managed to come back. When he did, he wasn't the same. He behaved like some kind of wolf-man, howling and screaming all the time. It was believed he was acting that way for a bet until he started attacking other students. Campus security was called and he was taken away in a straitjacket, never to be seen again. No one has ever been able to name the student or even pinpoint the year it took place, which leads me to believe it's just a tall tale. I think it's so other students can go around rattling doorknobs in the middle of the night just to scare each other.

I'm writing about it simply because it's of interest, not to worry you in any way. At the end of the day, it's just a story. Nothing more. Lots of students drop out in the first year, statistically. Don't fret, I'm not planning to be one of them.

I hope you are both keeping well – and Dad, maybe start using a bit less maple syrup on your pancakes so your pants still fit when I get home. Mom, maybe also make a few less pancakes for him in the morning.

Your loving son,
Logan Tremblay

CHAPTER THREE
Experimentation and Investigation

IT SEEMED like a good idea at the time. Hugh needed some cash and thought he could handle a little pain. He didn't know much about these kinds of experiments, but it sounded like a good deal to him. Go in, be poked about a bit, maybe get the odd needle or two and then walk away with a tenner. He was surprised more people didn't do it. Maybe they did; he was the sort that remained blissfully unaware of what was going on around him. That's just how he went about life, falling into things as they cropped up instead of methodically planning ahead.

Arriving at the address, Hugh pulled a crumpled flyer from his pocket. He'd taken it down from one of the polytechnic's noticeboards, just in case he couldn't remember all the details. 'Earn £10 – volunteer for science!' it read. 'Lie down and help us uncover the mysteries of sleep. Research explores lessening the need for sleep without becoming tired.' Aside from the address at the bottom, it was fairly vague otherwise. But a tenner was a tenner and that meant a lot to a struggling student, no matter what was involved.

He was met with a fairly nondescript building. An old warehouse of some sort. He wasn't too clear on why this wasn't done on campus. *Maybe it isn't big enough for everything that needed to be done?* One day the polytechnic might expand and become a university but, for now, they made do.

He walked in through the main doors, made himself known to the dolly-bird at the makeshift reception and was led into a jury-rigged medical room. It certainly looked like a ramshackle affair, put together rather hastily. Hugh had been to see doctors before; *should I strip off?*

Before having a chance to embarrass himself, two men walked in. Hugh presumed they were the ones conducting the experiment, given they had smocks over their clothes and facemasks on. It gave them a slightly ominous appearance, but Hugh knew there was nothing to worry about.

'Right, up on the bed,' the slightly taller, blond one said. 'I'm sorry, but we do have to restrain you for the purposes of the experiment.'

'Well, as long as you *un*-restrain me afterwards, right?' Hugh laughed, expecting some sort of response. Not even a smirk was forthcoming. Trying to recover from his failed attempt at humour, he added, 'Whatever it takes to get my ten quid.' Still nothing.

He clambered up onto the bed and let them go about their business. Once he was strapped in, the other man spoke.

'We just need to give you a few injections to start with.' No apologies about the forthcoming needle-pricks.

Hugh wondered what had muted the personalities of these men. Or was that just what scientists were like? He braced himself and felt several jabs in quick succession.

Not too bad, he thought. *For a tenner. And quick, too.*

The two men nodded at each other and made their way to leave.

'Hey, where are you going?' Hugh called out. 'Aren't you going to untie me?'

The blond man stopped. 'We haven't finished yet. You need to stay here so we can see what reaction you might have.'

'What?' Hugh tugged at his restraints. They were far tighter than was necessary. 'Nobody said that! In and out, that's what I was told. You can't leave me here! I've got things to do.' The men walked out. 'C'mon, I've got a date tonight! A real babe.' He thrashed and writhed about. 'Her name's Angie!'

He stopped for a moment.

Maybe part of all this is psychological, to see how I'll react?

'Okay, I get it! You wanted to see what would happen if you just left me. Well, you just saw it – I panicked and protested. That's what you wanted, isn't it? Come on… Joke's over!'

Despite Hugh's pleas and protests, there was no longer anybody there to hear them.

Lethbridge-Stewart was unavailable, so Samson spoke to Colonel Douglas, who promised he'd take care of things. Once done, he decided he should go back and deal with the deranged woman. But he was having a hard time convincing his captain.

'Look, I admire the gallantry, but without backup, the risk

to you is just too great,' Bishop said. 'We don't know what else might be lurking about at that warehouse.'

'We can't wait for the Brig to send reinforcements,' Samson said. 'She's a major public threat. If we both arm ourselves, I'm sure we can contain the situation.' He was a man of action – decisions needed to be made; things needed to be done. Sometimes it verged on being rash, but he was a disciplined soldier and knew how far he could stretch any leeway he was given.

'What about me?' piped up Gary. 'I've never fired a gun in my life.'

Bishop wasn't sure what to do about Gary. Samson had recommended ditching him but, on his own, he could have done more damage than good. Samson wouldn't put it past the young photographer to make his way back to get more pictures. And he'd soon set about selling them to the highest bidder.

Bishop considered Samson's pleas and eyed Gary.

'You need a licence to carry a firearm. But maybe you could be our man on the ground, looking into other strange goings-on. But all hush-hush, you understand.' He tapped the side of his nose to emphasise the point.

'What's in it for me? You've already threatened to take action if I do anything with any photographs I take.'

Fair point, thought Samson. *What is Bill's game here?*

'We'll make sure you have a story or photos at the end of it all. It just has to be approved by us. Some things can be made public; others can't.'

Gary snorted. 'I'll have to take your word for that.'

'Look, you know the area. We want you to ask around – subtly, mind you – to see if anyone else has been involved in these experiments. You might start with the homeless.' Reaching into his pocket, Bishop offered him a five-pound note. 'For more film.'

After a moment, Gary nodded his agreement, checked on where they would meet up, and went on his way.

'You sure that was wise?' Samson asked. 'We have no way of keeping an eye on him now.'

'Did you really want to go back and tackle that howling woman with him in tow?'

Samson was now in the unenviable position of wanting to do two things at once – deal with the woman and follow Gary to make sure he kept up his end of the bargain.

'Round up Miller and Christiner. Four of us should be enough. And we need to get Gary's film developed as soon as possible, just in case the photos can help us.'

*

Lethbridge-Stewart sighed. Fiona had called him and, not unreasonably, was suggesting he go home, given nothing immediate was happening. With Miles allocating resources for investigation and handling that side of things, Lethbridge-Stewart was essentially just shuffling papers until something of note was reported. Still, he wasn't too keen on the idea of going back to discussing wedding plans, either. He preferred to stay put and work on various admin tasks he'd been putting off, however dull they might be. It was a more efficient use of time, somehow. Endless talking about wedding minutiae without landing on a decision just wasn't in his nature. But he also had to be fair to Fiona while managing his own reticence about such matters.

'You know how unpredictable this job can be,' he told her. 'Anything can happen at any time.' Lethbridge-Stewart felt guilty as soon as he said it. It wasn't that he didn't want to spend time with his fiancée – but he wanted it to be quality time, not trivial wedding nonsense.

'I know that, Alistair. I think you've given me that lecture at least a hundred times now. And I know full well you have some very capable troops under your command who can handle things when you're not there. If a crisis emerges, you're just a phone call away.' There was a slightly irritated tone in her voice. 'I know you're married to the military, but you're also almost married to me. You need to show me the same level of commitment.'

Deep down, Lethbridge-Stewart knew she was right. She'd already given him some space by letting him come into base; now she was expecting nothing more than her future husband having dinner with her. And he knew if he couldn't manage that, despite the responsibilities of his job, the foundations of their marriage would be rocky at best.

He had obviously paused too long. Fiona spoke again; this time with concern.

'Alistair? Everything *is* all right, isn't it?'

'What? Er... yes.' Lethbridge-Stewart fumbled, looking for the right words. 'There's definitely something for us to look into. Not sure what it's all about yet.'

'Then come home! Sausages, mash and peas, smothered in gravy. Better than what you'd get in the mess any day of the week.'

25

When Fiona put it like that, how could he resist? Comfort food, cooked with loving care by his loving partner. Surely that was worth a bit of chit-chat about wedding nonsense?

'All right, then.' He grinned. 'I'm not made of stone.'

'Finally! And if you're especially good,' Fiona teased. 'I might even run you a bath.'

Corporal Sanford had been sent to Cardiff to look for *anything unusual.* That had been the instruction relayed from Captain Miles. Which hadn't been particularly helpful. A man standing on one leg with a pint on his head in the pub could fill that brief.

He'd been sent with two privates, and they'd made the decision to split up to cover as much ground as possible. Sanford tried to remember his training from Captain Younghusband. 'Always keep an eye out; be ready to notice anything,' he had been instructed. That meant remembering a lot of things he wouldn't need down the track. Sanford found that sort of thing tiresome. He knew not everything would be served up on a silver platter but, similarly, he felt he was always the one being sent on wild goose chases.

The decision had been made to remain out of uniform. Tensions were high, given the miners' strike, and the locals were resistant to any sign of authority. That suited Sanford – he liked to look inconspicuous but, deep down, he knew he was less confident without his fatigues on. He felt he was respected a little more when people saw him as a soldier. But he also hated confrontation.

Making his way out of Caerau, Sanford came to St David's Church and decided to cut through the graveyard and onto Cowbridge Road. He took in the gravestones as he passed.

'Hello, can I help you?'

Sanford turned to see a man in a black cassock and white collar. Given his surroundings, he realised this had to be the local priest.

'Oh. Hello, Father. I was just... It's okay to cut through here, in't it?'

'Of course it is, son. Beautiful day,' the priest said, looking skyward. 'Our Father has truly blessed us.'

Sanford gave a non-committal nod. 'I guess so.'

'Is there anything I can help you with?'

'Erm, I dunno, is there?' Sanford hadn't been expecting to talk to anyone right at that moment, let alone a priest.

The priest beamed a radiant smile. 'Sorry, I didn't introduce myself, did I? I'm Father Robert Riggs.'

'Pleased to meet you. I'm Kian Sanford.'

Father Riggs inhaled a deep breath, and then looked thoughtfully at a nearby grave. 'Some people come here to be alone, they do, which I understand completely.' His voice became gentler, more considerate. 'But then there are others who are at a crossroads and don't know how to reach out. A silent cry for help, you might call it.'

There was something utterly endearing about the old man. He was the better part of seventy; robust with rosy cheeks. Bald and overweight, he appeared a man with a life well-lived and seemed to exude kindness. Sanford knew he could be extremely negative but, for once, here was someone he felt he could reach out to and trust. At the very least, maybe he could ask the priest a few questions. Cogs ticked over in Sanford's mind. Churches were the hub of many communities, so he felt it was worth exploring.

'Thinking about it, maybe you can help me.'

'I hope so, my dear boy, I truly hope so. Perhaps we could retire to the vestry for a cup of tea? I'm always happy to lend an ear, I am. Poor is the fellow man who cannot help that of another, eh?'

Sanford managed a weak smile and, accepting the offer, followed the priest past an old hut as they made their way to the church. Along the way, Father Riggs pointed out various items of interest, whether religious, botanical or historical. With a captive audience, he made polite chit-chat and embraced Sanford's presence with exuberance unlike that of any septuagenarian the lance corporal had seen before.

Eventually inside, sitting with a pot of tea between them, Sanford decided it was time to start probing for information. He knew he better at least make a stab at it, or he'd be mocked yet again when he returned to base. Father Riggs poured the two cups and offered the sugar bowl.

Stirring two teaspoons into his brew, Sanford began. 'Cheers.' He took a sip. 'Bloody lovely. Oh, sorry.'

The Father waved away the mildly offensive word.

'I'm trying to find out something, and I reckon you might be able to help. Has there been anything unusual happening of late?'

Father Riggs stared over the top of his cup, steam rising past his eyes. He seemed surprised and mildly disappointed at the question. 'Well. I guess it depends on your definition, doesn't it?' He slurped at his tea. 'Are you certain there's nothing bothering you, Kian?'

'That's what I mean, in't it? Place like this, you see all sorts, don't you? Anybody come here all troubled?'

The priest smiled sympathetically. 'I open my heart to all sorts of troubled souls. The ill, the meek, the unwanted. I share God's love and His wisdom in the path to helping people, whether they need redemption, direction or just a helping hand.'

Sanford was getting nowhere. He had to be more specific. 'Well... Look, what I mean is, have you come across anything outside... of your normal religious guidance?'

For the first time since they met, Father Riggs frowned. 'Sodom and Gomorrah.' He whispered the comment through clenched teeth.

'What's that?'

'Young men and women being led astray for what can only be immoral purposes, Kian. It's easy to prey on the vulnerable, isn't it?'

Putting his teacup down, Sanford leaned in. 'That's it! What purposes, though?'

His question was met with a glare. Sanford wasn't sure, but it looked like the man was hiding some pain as well. Something about his face – as if whatever pain others had endured, Father Riggs had felt it, too.

'Listen, young man, why you asking all these questions then? You're best staying clear of these things, you are.' The friendly tone from before had completely gone. 'I would hate for you to suffer the same fate, son.'

'That's why I'm here, in't it?'

'Oh really? Why didn't you say so before?'

'I was... ashamed.'

'God will forgive you.'

'I don't want to fall into the same trap as the others, do I?' Sanford had no idea what he was talking about but was hoping to eventually elicit something from the priest so he could run with it.

Father Riggs reached out and patted Sanford's hand. 'You're safe here now, Kian. Don't do the experiment. Don't be lured into something that goes against God's plan. It's abhorrent.' He shook his head. 'So many of my flock have gone missing, they have. Please don't be another.'

Experiments? People missing?•Now Sanford felt he was onto something.

'I won't.' Sanford took a sip of tea and then looked at Father Riggs. 'But I need to know what's been happening, to avoid it. Some people can be very convincing when they want to be, can't they? I don't want to fall into that trap.'

'When people fall on hard times, they grasp at anything. And people take advantage of that.' Father Riggs closed his eyes and recited to himself. 'How dangerous be the poor angry man,' he mused, then looked wide-eyed at Sanford. 'You've heard of these experiments, but they are abominations, if what I'm told is true.'

'Oh yes? And what is that, Father?'

'They pervert the true course of what God intended, Kian. Man was meant to sleep; not spend every waking hour at toil. That's why we have a day of rest. It was meant to be.'

Another sip of tea, another thoughtful pause. Sanford was doing his best to rise above himself. He found the priest talked in religious riddles and it confused him. But he felt he was doing something that was actually useful. Gaining intelligence; being a good soldier. Sanford didn't get that feeling very often.

'Listen, Father, if people have gone missing, how do you know about this? What happened to them?'

Father Riggs now wrapped both hands around his teacup and took a shallow swig. 'I fear the worst, son. Friends of some of these people have come to me. They've seen unimaginable horrors, they have, as if they had been smote by Beelzebub himself.'

'But where are these experiments being conducted? What about the police?'

'All they can do is take a missing persons' report. No one has been able to track down where any of this is actually happening.' Father Riggs' face saddened. 'It's just not right.'

'No, it's not. But what are they experimenting *for*? That's what I want to know, I do.'

'One young boy came to me, he did. Just couldn't sleep any more. He thinks they tampered with his body somehow. As days went by, he became more and more agitated. He ran away. Never saw him again, I didn't.'

'You think they're trying to keep people awake? Why?'

Father Riggs nodded, knowingly. 'It's definitely unholy. People need some peace in their lives. As to why, I put it down to one of the seven deadly sins. Greed, son. If you make things more efficient, the more money there is to be made. I just never thought I'd see the day where they applied that principle to man himself. And women, too, of course.' His smile returned a little. 'We are living in a more enlightened age, after all. *Ecclesia semper reformanda est.*' Noticing Sanford' puzzled face, Father Riggs quickly explained. 'The church is always reforming itself.' He picked up the teapot and went to pour Sanford another cup.

The corporal waved it away. He was excited at the information he'd managed to glean, and couldn't wait to report back to Imber. Once it was relayed back to Captain Miles, he was sure he'd be pleased.

'Thanks, but I think that's enough for me. Gotta sleep meself at some point, haven't I?' Sanford stood. 'You've been really helpful, you have.'

'Thank you. Please be careful out there, Kian. Remember what I said. Do not fall prey to the evil that lurks in the hearts of other men.'

Gary was somewhat affronted that his camera film had been confiscated. He was fairly confident it was a violation of some right, but not sure what. He'd have to ask someone at the polytechnic later. Or at the pub. At least Ware and Bishop had given him some money for more film, which was probably more than most would do.

For now, Gary had to return to his affable, jolly self if he was to get some decent pictures out of this. The way Bishop had been talking, it sounded like he might even be able to write the story to go with his pictures!

But he was getting ahead of himself. Gary didn't mind a wild goose chase – there was always something to learn and maybe use later on – but he already knew he was onto a decent lead, given the experiments, maniacal woman and military involvement. It was time to find out more.

Bishop's suggestion seemed a reasonable one, so he made his way to the local skid row.

Gary knew Tyne Bridge was a good bet. Or anywhere down that way along the river. It offered a little bit of shelter when it rained and people who had fallen on hard times were generally left alone. There was the odd dust-up between vagrants, but police rarely bothered to attend. Police were like that around here. Not surprising they didn't cotton onto the fact the missing students and paid experiments might be connected. Vastly understaffed, they could barely catch a cold.

Trudging his way down the footpath to Quayside, Gary looked at the massive arch stretching across the water. Ships meandered their way along the River Tyne while cars came and went with their usual clamour of noise. As he got closer, he could see all sorts of nooks and crannies where homeless people might hole up and make a space for themselves. He'd hidden his camera as best he could under his denim jacket – anyone down here was bound to be suspicious at the best of times, but even more so if he suddenly stuck a Miranda Sensomat in their face.

'Giz a snout, mate?'

Gary had only been down near the river ten minutes, the stench of fish and pollution enveloping him completely. He turned and saw a wizened scruff of a man – what the locals called a gadgie – draped in hessian bags, holding his hand out from underneath. Gary had already passed a couple of old blokes, prostrate and unconscious, probably sleeping off whatever cheap booze they'd managed to lay their hands on the night before. This was a bit more promising. At least this chap possessed the power of speech.

'Don't actually smoke,' Gary replied, although on this occasion he wished he did, if only to further engage the man.

'I'm clamming for me bait, can you help?'

Gary was at a loss. But he decided to attempt a conversation despite his lack of tobacco.

'I guess you live down here?' He vaguely motioned to the area around him with his arm.

'Aye. From the toon are you?' He gave Gary the once-over, making an assessment. 'A right nebby bugga, I'd say.'

'I just want to ask some questions.'

'Reet, like I said.' He ventured out further from under his sacks. Absolutely caked in dirt and grime, Gary noted. He didn't like to think of the last time this man might have had a bath, but he guessed it wasn't at any stage in the past six months.

'Has there been anything odd happening down this way?' Gary kicked himself over the phrasing of his question. Everything was relative once your life had ended up like this.

'Howay man! Are yee daft? Yee wanna come down here at night; many a strange thing been going on. Especially for the right amount. Whatever yee fancy.'

Gary didn't like where this was going, so he thought he better spell out what he meant.

'It sounds like what you're talking about happens on a regular basis. I meant anything that doesn't usually happen.'

'Like you turning up?'

'I suppose so. But before now.'

'Whey aye man. Few months ago. A real smooth operator. He was giving us hackies.'

Gary had been living in Newcastle long enough, but every now and then the Geordie phrasing got the better of him. He had to rack his brains to figure out what the man was talking about. Despite the stench, Gary moved closer.

'So, there was a suspicious looking man down here? What did he want?'

'Offering money to people to go up to toon. I divvent want to; somethin' didn't seem reet about 'im. But others did. Nowt seen 'em again.' The man picked something from his teeth with blackened nails.

Gary steadied himself and contained his disgust.

'Do you know where they went? Or what they offered the money for?'

'Nowt really. Most of 'em were drunks so if there was a chance of gannin' on the hoy, they'd follow the money. Although I hear from someone that all they were being asked to do was lie doon somewhere for a bit. Most around here would've thought that was purely belta.'

'They liked the idea, eh?' Gary quickly clarified. During the conversation, he was unaware his jacket had flapped open and the man had spotted the camera inside.

'Giz a deek at that.'

'Oh, it's just a camera. Nothing special.'

'Whadja bring it here for? Looking for new models?' The old man guffawed then broke into a huge grin. His wrinkles scrunched up into even more wrinkles. But it was the teeth – or lack thereof – that painted a not-so-pretty picture.

Gary leapt at his chance and fired off as many frames as he could, doing his best to wind the film on quickly between shots.

'Umm, thanks!' he called out, as he scurried away.

'Oi, ya doylem! I want ma' money if you use those pictures.'

As Gary turned for one last look, he saw the man try to get out and shake a fist but fall over backwards into his hessian bags. He didn't have to leg it as fast as he originally thought.

Now, he had to get back to Bishop and Ware – but not before developing the film and making duplicate prints. He wasn't making the same mistake twice.

After driving at a leisurely pace, Lethbridge-Stewart arrived home and found Fiona in the kitchen, hair wrapped in a towel, hovering over pots and pans on the stove. She quickly turned down the heat and ran over to embrace him.

'Alistair! How wonderful you've chosen to spend some time with your fiancée. You know, the person you're going to spend the rest of your life with.' She gave him a cheeky sideways glance, then kissed him on the lips.

Lethbridge-Stewart tasted the wine before noting the open bottle of claret on the kitchen bench. 'Hilarious,' he said, drily. 'I'm here, just like you asked.'

'Yes, but I shouldn't have to beg you. Not when I'm the one slaving over a hot stove.'

Lethbridge-Stewart was about to protest, but Fiona quickly put her finger on his lips.

'Sshh! Get out of your uniform so we can relax over dinner. And help yourself to a glass of wine. I know you saw it. It helps me think when I'm putting things together in the kitchen.'

Arching his eyebrow, as if to question the validity of her claim, Lethbridge-Stewart broke away from Fiona. 'Roger that,' he said, and went to get changed.

While the main focus of the investigation was in Newcastle, Captain Miles had assigned other teams throughout the UK, and for Corporal Louise Jenkins that meant an investigative mission in London. It was nice to get out of the office, so she took the opportunity to doll herself up, in an effort to use her feminine wiles to her advantage. Men were men, after all, and if showing a bit of leg helped her get what she needed, then she had the upper hand.

Jenkins wasn't stupid, of course. She'd had the foresight to ensure that Private Lincoln and Lance Corporal Morgan shadowed her – at a distance – as she ventured further into the East End. She found herself near the Spitalfields Markets where a group of men were trying to keep warm around a fire of vegetable boxes. The area exuded poverty; an intergenerational cycle of no hopes or prospects. Just existing and getting by were achievements in themselves.

By now, the men had noticed Jenkins. Her bright orange scarf and just-above-the-knee skirt certainly weren't the norm around these parts. Inevitably, a variety of wolf whistles rang out.

Jenkins steeled herself. Her aim was to get attention and distract but she knew she had to be careful, too, no matter what backup she had.

Moving closer to the men, she feigned embarrassment.

'You flatter me, boys.'

'Not at all,' one said. 'Don't see your sort around here very often.'

'Oh, I'm visiting my aunty; I'm not from the East End.' Jenkins batted her eyelashes slightly.

'Yeah, we can tell from ya posh accent,' another said.

Looking more closely at him, she could see he had extremely bloodshot eyes. Jenkins put it down to alcohol abuse, or worse.

Without warning, another lumbered over and squeezed her backside.

'Lookin' for a good time, are you luv?'

Much as Jenkins hated to admit it, the uninvited grope caught her unawares and made her cheeks flush.

The first one to speak pushed his lecherous peer away. 'Oi! Hands off! Show some respect, ya mongrel dog!' He bowed his head, in a long-forgotten ritual. 'Some people just don't know their manners. You're takin' your chances with the likes of him and others around here.'

Composing herself, Jenkins took a breath. She definitely had their attention. Now she needed information. She decided to push ahead with the first one who had shown at least a bit of decorum.

'Thank you… um… What was your name?'

'Jim.' He half-bowed again. 'You must be cold in that get-up. Wanna move closer to the fire?'

Jenkins thought better of moving in among them. Instead, she concocted a story on the spot.

'Thanks, but I'm just wondering if you could help me. I was visiting my aunty because of my cousin… He's gone missing.'

Jim rubbed his hands over the fire. 'That's fairly common around these parts.' The others murmured their assent. 'You sure he ain't skipped town? Or shacked himself up with some bird.' A couple of the men guffawed.

'Maybe,' Jenkins responded. 'We just really don't know. So, we're asking around wherever we can. Anyone who might have come across something unusual.'

'Who you calling unusual?' Her groper from before lunged forward but Jim caught him and pushed him back into the huddle.

Glancing sideways, Jenkins hoped Lincoln and Morgan still

had their eyes on things. Jim looked thoughtful for a moment and rubbed his chin.

'Was your cousin into drugs or anything like that?'

Play along, Lou, she told herself. She hung her head in shame. 'My aunty said he'd been hanging around with the wrong crowd. Getting up to all sorts of wrong-doings.'

Jim grunted. 'It's part of life around here. But I will tell ya somethin'. Been hearing about new drugs doin' the rounds. Keeps people awake around the clock. Young ones love it 'cos they can party all night and go on to work. Not me; I love me sleep. When I can find somewhere to doss down, mind you.'

'Do you know anyone that sells these drugs… I mean, they might lead me to my cousin.' Jenkins had almost tripped herself up by jumping on the information too quickly.

'Nah.' Jim grunted. 'Just 'eard about it. Might not even be true. Not much to do around here. People love making up tall tales.'

'I 'eard something about this, too.' The second man – with the bloodshot eyes – had rejoined the conversation.

'What do you know?' Jenkins asked, carefully.

'They inject ya,' he spat. ''Aven't slept for ages.'

'Do you mean…?' Jenkins was suddenly coming to a realisation.

'Yeah, got taken away,' he said, quietly, before bellowing: 'But I escaped!'

At that moment, he let out a guttural, inhuman scream and went to pounce on Jenkins. But her military training stood her in good stead, and she anticipated his movements. Crashing to the ground, he became angrier and started lashing out at the men around him. Somehow, Jenkins managed to extricate herself from the melee and make a run for it. She decided to leave her heels behind to flee the scene more quickly.

Lincoln and Morgan were already running towards her.

'Pull back!' she ordered. She caught up to her colleagues and chanced a quick look at what was happening.

A small riot had broken out. Men were on the ground; blood was everywhere. The fire had been pushed over and one poor soul was trying to extinguish himself. Jim was battling to hold the screaming man, to no avail. The man was scrabbling at his own face, as if trying to gouge his own eyes out. Jenkins didn't want the situation to worsen, so she motioned with her finger as if she was firing a gun into the air.

Morgan and Lincoln caught on quickly. They fired their guns into the sky and most of the rabble dispersed. The trio then hotfooted it away from the markets, not waiting to see what was left behind. It was enough of a public disturbance already; local police were unlikely to believe the cause of what had unfolded.

Once they were well enough away and had regained their collective breath, Jenkins conferred with the two men. She was a little dishevelled after the encounter and knew she appeared slightly pathetic standing there barefoot. Still, they had been assigned to do a job.

'We need to report back to Captain Miles,' she said. 'I'm sure he'll be interested in what we've found out, however it might fit with anything else going on.'

Halfway through their meal, Fiona tried to engage her husband-to-be in the pros and cons of which shoes were best for the bridesmaids – and how that would affect the colour of nail polish they wore.

'Jolly good, Fiona, I must say.'

'You think lilac is best for the nails?'

'No, I meant the meal. Delicious, as always.' Lethbridge-Stewart was hoping to talk about something else for five minutes.

'I'm glad you like it.' Fiona took a sip of her wine. 'But we were talking about the wedding.'

'Hmmm… You were, at any rate.'

'Well, I'm sorry if I'm *boring* you, Alistair.'

Lethbridge-Stewart didn't want to upset her, so tried to explain. 'I understand the wedding is important, but we can talk about other things.' He reached for his wine.

'So, can you tell me anything about what's happening?' Fiona asked. 'You've got that annoying distracted look about you again. The one that says your mind is somewhere else.'

'Part of the job.'

Cutting through her second sausage, Fiona shook her head. 'You need time to switch off, too. I know you've seen and dealt with some terrible things. Burying yourself deeper into your work doesn't help with that.'

'All right.' Lethbridge-Stewart decided to give in. 'Tell me more about the shoes.'

'No.' Fiona's voice was firm. 'I think you need to take your mind off work *and* the wedding. But I can tell you now – you're doing the dishes! Deal?'

'I suspect I don't have an option.'

'Correct.' Fiona re-filled her wine glass. 'And don't think about going back to work tonight. Whatever's going on, it can wait until you go in tomorrow.'

'Yes, ma'am!' Nodding, Lethbridge-Stewart scooped up some of his gravy-soaked mashed potato. He glanced over at the kitchen sink and rubber gloves, glumly.

It seemed he would have to run his own bath.

CHAPTER FOUR
Not Enough Sleep

SAMSON WAS ready to go back to the warehouse straight away, so felt a bit miffed he had been sent on a boy's errand to drop off Gary's film. He had to find someone who would develop it privately and wouldn't ask too many questions, given they were away from base. He knew what was likely to be on the negatives, so Samson was quite pleased with the cover story he'd come up with – they were photos of special effects used on actors in a student horror film made at the polytechnic.

Fortunately, the private photographer was happy to do the job for the right price and didn't ask any further questions. But it would obviously take time to develop both the negatives and photo prints.

Samson liked to be ready for anything; it was something he'd psyched himself for many years ago as part of the Cyprus insurgency. Although he'd hated it at the time, the experience had shaped him into the man he was today. Just like everything else in his life – working as a boxer, bouncer and stuntman – had honed his skills, reactions and thought processes, leading him back to the soldier's life. It was odd how cycles were created like that. Once a soldier, always a soldier, no matter what else you did. Plus, he had to admit, he enjoyed the adrenaline.

Time hadn't been on their side the day before, so Bishop got them all to stay in a cheap B&B for the night. The experience hadn't been pleasant. Together with the two privates, they'd all tucked into a breakfast of bacon and egg sandwiches and coffee before Samson went on his photographic errand. The others were headed back to the warehouse, ostensibly for reconnaissance, promising not to take action until Samson re-joined them.

Happy he was finally able to sink his teeth into something other than breakfast, Samson tried to be subtle as he strode down the street towards the warehouse. Which wasn't easy, given his stature and, of course, the brown hue of his skin that seemed to worry everybody (except the photographer he'd met earlier). He found Miller and Christiner easily enough, but where was Bishop?

'I thought we weren't going to tackle this until I got back?' Samson was mildly annoyed. If anything, he should have been the one going boldly ahead, alone into the unknown.

'It was pretty boring just standing around, sir,' Christiner said.

'Nothing was happening,' Miller added. 'So the captain decided to go in and have a bit of a poke about.'

Samson looked across at the warehouse. After what happened to him in September last year, Samson would have expected Bishop to be a bit more cautious. Still, Samson reflected, he had to admire the man. Not letting such a traumatic experience change how he soldiered. In truth, Samson knew he'd be much the same himself if the positions were reversed.

'Anything to report since he went in?'

'No sign of him, sir. We've been keeping watch.' Christiner seemed proud of what they had been doing, despite the fact it amounted to nothing.

Samson tried not to glare. 'I also meant anything else. No other comings and goings, strange noises, shadows passing by the windows?'

Miller shook his head, suitably admonished.

It's like extracting teeth, thought Samson, groaning inwardly. 'So how long since the captain went in?'

'About an hour, sir,' Miller said, promptly.

A lot could have happened in an hour.

'Didn't it occur to either of you that the captain could be in trouble?'

Miller and Christiner looked at each other.

'We better get in there, then!' Samson barked. 'Look sharp. Know you have a weapon, but only use it if you absolutely must,' he cautioned them, reminding himself that they were still pretty green. New recruits to the Fifth went through training down at Salisbury, but there was nothing as instructive as being on the battlefield. As it were. 'First, we find the captain, and then hopefully we carry out our original plan. Any other intelligence gathered at the same time is a bonus.' He paused to let them digest his orders. 'In other words, don't blunder in and make a meal of it.'

The privates nodded their understanding and made their way

across to the warehouse. The front entrance seemed as good a place to enter as any. It had worked the previous day.

Samson knew he shouldn't have expected anything after going through the front door, but still felt let down when there was nothing. It was exactly the same as the day before.

He wasn't sure if they should spread out or not. Usually, it was a good idea because it helped to cover ground more quickly. He just had a nagging feeling at least one of the privates would get themselves into trouble. Still, they were soldiers in the Fifth and had to toughen up to be ready to face anything.

Ultimately, he decided it best if the privates flanked him on either side.

Samson couldn't figure this place out – if they were conducting experiments here and paying people to take part, why did the place seem abandoned? Perhaps there was another entrance or, given the nature of what was going on, they'd set up deeper into the warehouse. Or maybe they just set up and made themselves known when they knew for sure someone was coming. Anything was possible, he supposed.

As the three went further into the building, their anticipation grew. Bishop had to be in here somewhere. *And that awful beast of a woman from yesterday*, Samson reminded himself. Plus, the beds and all the experimental gear. He thought that was the best place to head; although the more they moved through the building, the more a rabbit warren it became.

After what seemed an eternity (in reality, only about ten minutes), they finally came across the makeshift medical room again. Samson didn't know how else to describe it.

'Be on your toes, lads. This is where we encountered the...' Samson wasn't sure how to describe her, either. But he made an attempt. '...distressed woman yesterday. Consider her dangerous.'

The trio now had guns in their hands, ready in case they were set upon.

'I haven't seen her again,' a voice whispered behind them.

It was all Samson could do to contain a visible jump, as his thoughts finally caught up with recognition of the voice. The privates, on the other hand, had let out audible gasps. Christiner scrambled to pick up his dropped weapon, a rather sheepish expression on his face.

Turning to look at the new arrival, Samson replied. 'Glad you're okay Captain. Why didn't you come back out so we could all go in together?'

'Too good an opportunity to snoop around and see if I could learn more.'

'But what if that woman had attacked you?'

'I was armed, so the risk seemed fair, Sergeant Major.'

'Of course, sir,' Samson said, taking the silent reprimand in his step. He had to remember the privates with them.

'I thought you said they did experiments here, sir?' Miller asked.

'That's what we were told by a photographer.' Samson realised it sounded a bit lame when he said it out loud like that. Fortunately, Bishop came to his rescue.

'And we encountered what we suspect is a result of those experiments.'

Thoughtful for a moment, the private then countered, 'So why is the place empty, sir?'

It was a good point, Samson conceded. Especially coming from Miller. But there hadn't really been time the day before to have a good look around to see if they could uncover anything. The screaming woman had put paid to that.

'We need to explore more,' Bishop said, decisively. 'Time to split up. RSM Ware, you're with Christiner. Miller with me. Two armed men should be able to tackle trouble, should we run into any. A thorough search of this room might be the first point of order, so Miller and I will stay here for the time being. If we don't turn up anything useful, we'll start exploring further.'

Samson was happy to start actually doing something, but he wasn't keen on babysitting a nervous private. But then again, that was his job. If he didn't like it, he shouldn't have accepted the promotion to RSM. He gritted his teeth and started walking. 'Fall in, Christiner,' he commanded. 'And be ready.'

Bishop would rather have explored with Samson, but he knew better than to keep the two privates together. He'd never seen men who were quite so wet behind the ears. Not even Lance Corporal Evans had been this bad. Evans had his shortcomings, that was true, but he wouldn't have achieved his rank if he hadn't shown some merit. Miller and Christiner would probably end up shooting each other in the feet at the first sign of trouble.

As Bishop made a systematic search of each bed (with little luck), he called out to Miller at the other end of the room, rummaging through a drawer.

'Found anything, Private?'

Miller turned to face him, a roll of Sellotape in one hand and a ball of string in the other. His weapon was on top of the bench, away from him. Bishop sighed internally. It was like spoon-feeding a baby.

'Private, if you don't find anything useful or unusual after a minute or so, move on to search something else.' Miller looked back, his cheeks flushed red with embarrassment. 'We don't know how much time we have.'

'Just trying to be thorough, sir.'

'You also need to be efficient.'

Miller nodded in acknowledgement and moved onto a cupboard to explore.

'Forgetting something, Private?' Bishop was met with a blank stare. 'Over there, Miller, where you just came from. Your gun. You might need it.'

Miller scurried back to retrieve his weapon and nodded at Bishop. 'Sorry, Captain, I…'

Bishop raised an eyebrow, and Miller blushed, glanced down, and gathered himself. *And that's why the Brig learned to do that,* Bishop thought, glad he'd practiced the solo eyebrow raise.

'Shall I try those cupboards over there, sir?'

He was obviously trying to show initiative so Bishop kept his thoughts to himself, thinking it was obvious that each and every part of the room should be searched. Instead, he gave a curt, 'Yes, Private.'

Silence descended upon the room as they searched fruitlessly, bar the odd door or drawer being opened and closed. Until Miller knocked over a tray of medical equipment, each surgical tool making a thunderous clanging sound as it hit the floor.

Bishop immediately reached for his gun and readied himself. If someone else was in the building, they would have surely heard the noise. He glared at Miller, who went down on all fours to pick up the dropped items. Bishop shook his head furiously. The private got back up and primed himself, mimicking his captain's stance.

As Bishop backed up to the door and peered over his shoulder, he couldn't help but wonder how this setup worked. How did they get people in and out and then suddenly nobody was around? Was it that smooth an operation? If so, it was the sort of thing that needed a certain precision, which made him wonder if there was some sort of underlying military background to it all.

Focusing on the corridor, Bishop paid little attention to

Miller. He just hoped the private was flanking him the way he'd been trained.

Unfortunately, with their focus on the outside of the room, both had completely dismissed their search inside. With a piercing, inhumane scream reverberating around the walls, Bishop heard the sound first, before turning back to see a man on top of Miller, scratching and gouging away. Miller was doing his best to wrestle with his attacker, but he was no match for the strength holding him down.

Instinctively, Bishop aimed his gun.

Three shots rang out into the air and the screaming man fell back. Injured but not dead.

Miller scrambled up and joined Bishop, his face now white as a sheet. Bishop looked at the man, spread-eagled on the floor. At least he'd stopped that awful scream. There was a crimson tide of blood everywhere. With his gun still trained on the man, Bishop ventured closer. And that's when he noticed it.

The blood wasn't just from his bullets. The man's insides were torn apart and had been trailing along with him. Bishop couldn't fathom how he could possibly be alive, even without the gunshot wounds. Taking another tentative step forward, he could see there was no way it could be an animal attack. Unlikely, anyway, unless something had escaped from the zoo. Self-inflicted, it seemed, although not with a sharp instrument.

Had he butchered himself with his own hands?

Bishop's train of thought was interrupted as the sound of another bullet being fired pierced the air. The man slumped dead, a pellet of lead to his head. He turned around and saw Miller behind him, two hands on his gun. Even paler than before, sweat ran down his face.

'What are you doing, Private?' Bishop seethed.

'To stop it attacking again, sir. Look at its guts.' Miller's voice wavered as he spoke. 'It was going to die anyway.'

'That may be so, but we may have been able to learn something in the meantime.'

Frightened soldiers with guns didn't mix well. Miller hadn't exactly disobeyed orders, but it should have been clear that, unless under direct threat, he shouldn't have discharged his firearm.

'What happened here?'

Bishop looked around to see Samson and Christiner at the doorway, panting. They'd obviously heard the previous gunshots and bolted back, ready to join the action.

'All over now, Sergeant Major.' Bishop turned his head and nodded at the corpse on the ground. 'He attacked Miller from behind. No choice but to take the most affirmative action.'

Samson joined Bishop and they both moved closer to the dead man, doing their best not to step in the tsunami of blood that had pooled before them.

'Any idea who he was?' Samson was taking in the man's injuries and Bishop knew he was internalising his revulsion. He'd been doing the same.

'I would suggest someone who took part in the experiments Gary was telling us about yesterday.'

Christiner suddenly spoke. 'Lack of sleep caused this?' Seems he *had* been listening to their quick briefing session last night.

'I don't think it's just a case of insomnia. We're talking about forced or accelerated insomnia, caused by whatever they're injecting into their subjects.'

Bishop reached down into the pocket of the man and extracted his wallet, going through it to find some form of identification.

'Hugh Langford, nineteen,' Bishop read aloud from a student card. 'Attended the local polytechnic.'

'Ties in with what we've been told.' Samson surveyed the room. 'Did you find anything else?'

'We didn't get far until Mr Langford here attacked Miller. What about you?'

'Same. As soon as we heard the gunshots, we came back straight away.'

Almost forgotten in the corner, Miller finally spoke. 'What are we going to do now, sir?'

'We need to get this body back to base and clean up this mess. We need to be quick. I don't trust this place is as empty as it seems. And there's always a chance we could encounter that woman from yesterday. Given this one's brute force when attacking you, Miller, the strength of those affected cannot be underestimated.'

'I'll secure the necessary vehicle so we can clear out,' Samson said.

Bishop nodded his agreement and he marched over to a cupboard to find a couple of mops and buckets.

'Miller, Christiner – start to clean this mess up. And be ready for anything. Someone is behind all this, and we don't know when they'll return. But we do know there's at least another person on the loose in or near this building who might attack in a similar way.'

The two privates looked at each other uneasily. Bishop had had enough.

'You heard me! Now!'

Despite the command, they still managed to bump straight into each other as they went for the mops.

Gary was becoming disheartened. He had been traipsing from newspaper office to the next and was now trying his luck at *the Newcastle Evening Chronicle*. The photographer was tired of explaining himself over and over. Couldn't these newspapers see he had a scoop? And had the photos to prove it? He felt like he was banging his head against a brick wall.

The *Chronicle*'s chief-of-staff had reluctantly granted him an audience and listened to Gary's story while looking at his photographs. He took a puff of his cigar, exhaled the smoke pointedly into the air and leaned back in his seat.

'At the end of the day, Gary, this is just a picture of an old man. I can't fault your technical skills — you know what you're doing there. But it's just a homeless tramp and there are hundreds of those.'

Gary was a little slighted. It wasn't just about the picture. The photograph was part of the story he had relayed about other homeless people going missing. And how it tied in with all the others who had disappeared or turned up dead. He touched on what he had witnessed with Bishop and Ware but decided not to go into too much detail, in case he got into trouble.

'There's something going on, I'm sure,' Gary said. 'These disappearances aren't random.'

The chief-of-staff eyed Gary's double-denim and mop of unruly hair. Gary wondered if his youth or appearance were contributing to this man's dismissive nature.

'Look, how do I know any of what you've said is true?' He stopped to deal with a deep smoker's cough, then continued. 'For all I know, you could be making it up.'

'Why would I do that?'

The chief-of-staff shrugged and sucked on his cigar again, completely dismissing his earlier coughing fit. 'Beats me. Student prank? Wouldn't be the first time.'

'But it isn't,' Gary insisted. 'Don't you want a story?'

'A credible one, yes. And we have our own reporters for that.'

'Why aren't they interested in these missing people? And the deaths?' Gary knew breaking into big press was difficult but he was adamant a decent photo and story would get him over the line.

The chief-of-staff rummaged around his desk, delving into a pile of newspapers. He pulled out a couple of copies and waved them under Gary's nose, pointing to various articles with his cigar. 'We've covered those stories. Even on the front page.'

Gary gave them a cursory glance and skim-read a couple of paragraphs. 'Yes, but you haven't looked at *why* this is occurring or the possible link between them.'

'We just report the facts, Gary. The police are the ones who should be investigating and putting things together. So far they haven't. Which tells us there's no story beyond what we've already published. If you can show us actual evidence, rather than some barmy story and a picture of an old man, then we'd be more inclined to follow up. If you want to be a newspaper photographer, your pictures need to show a… a smoking gun, so to speak. Let me put it this way: pictures of a crime occurring are newsworthy; a picture of the ambulance leaving the scene isn't.'

Bowing his head, Gary had to admit to himself he needed more. If only Bishop and Ware hadn't taken his original film. With the sting of rejection washing over him, Gary mumbled something about 'trying harder' before leaving the man's office.

His only option was to go back to his new soldier acquaintances. At this stage, it seemed they were the only people willing to listen to him.

CHAPTER FIVE
Change in the Air

SAMSON RETURNED with a van; the sort used by painters and decorators all over the UK. He'd considered a military vehicle with a canvas canopy at the back, but they were supposed to be keeping a low profile. He just hoped the Fifth would be able to justify his expenses later on. It wasn't easy getting exactly what you needed at short notice, so Samson had to splash some cash to secure the vehicle. Unfortunately, these sorts of deals didn't exactly end with a receipt, so he hoped his claim would be recognised.

Strange he was thinking about that, rather than the matter at hand. No matter what walk of life you came from, no one wanted to be ripped off. Even when lives may be at stake. Samson thought back to his time as a stuntman. Any number of stunts could have gone awry, but as long as he got paid he'd been fine with the danger. Same now as part of the Fifth. Maybe his perspective would change when he got older. When he had children.

When…? *If,* he told himself. The idea of settling like Bill and Alistair was… It was almost as alien to him as the monsters they seem to fight on a regular basis.

As Samson rounded the corner back to the warehouse, his thoughts were drawn back to his present task. Aside from that unfortunate Langford lad and the screaming woman, they hadn't uncovered much. But sometimes you had to pull a thread for something to unravel.

Parking the van, Samson breathed in and made a quick check to see if anyone else was around. Even though they were yet to find hard evidence of more than two people in the warehouse, he knew he still had to be careful. There was definitely a room where experiments or medical procedures had taken place. Given the reactions of the two people they'd encountered, it likely followed they were a result of whatever had happened in that room. But where were the people running the show? It must have been extremely slick if they could pack up and disappear whenever necessary.

Weaving his way around the now-familiar corridors, he found Tweedle-Dee and Tweedle-Dum wrapping up the body of Langford with some sheets they had found. Bishop wasn't there, so Samson took command.

'You know what to do.' The two privates looked at each other blankly. Samson rolled his eyes. 'Body in the van as quickly as possible.' The two nodded and started lifting the corpse. 'Where's the captain?'

'Went for another look around for anything else that might be useful, sir,' Christiner said, as he accidentally bumped the corpse's head against the doorframe.

'Miller, Christiner… maybe before you move the body you should put those blood-soaked mops away.' Samson shook his head. He was a strong man, but he needed a different kind of strength to deal with these two.

As they made their way back outside, they found Bishop near the van.

'Good work, Sergeant Major,' he said, scratching his chest. 'Hope it wasn't too much trouble finding this motor.'

'Could have been worse. What happened, new washing powder reacting with your scar?'

Bishop looked down. 'Don't think so. Just itchy.'

Samson opened the back doors of the van and moved aside to let Miller and Christiner put the body inside. 'Time to move out?'

'No, we still need to poke our noses around here, I think.'

'But what about the body?'

'Oh, just get Miller to drive back. He's probably had enough action for one day.' Bishop stepped away from the van, his eyes twitching.

'Shall I get him to pick up the photos as well?' Samson asked, eyeing Bishop carefully.

'Photos?' Bishop was clearly more distracted by his itch than he wanted to admit.

'You know, the ones Gary took here yesterday. They had to be developed.' Samson noticed beads of sweat forming on Bishop's forehead. 'You all right? Maybe you should come and sit down in the van.'

'I'm fine, it's just a tad warm today.' Bishop shook his head a little, apparently trying to regain focus. 'Whatever you think best, Samson. Gary's photos, the van, the Brig. Am sure you're more than capable.'

At that moment, Gary came round the corner and ran up to the van.

'I've got some news! The homeless are being taken, too!' He was waving his photos of an old man in the air as he came up to them.

'Gary!' Samson hissed. 'We're supposed to be undercover here. Quiet down!'

Looking around at the motley crew that had formed, he despaired somewhat. They were supposed to be a highly trained group of soldiers attached to a precision investigative unit. Gary was a civilian, he understood, so that random factor couldn't be helped. But it was almost as if the four soldiers present *wanted* to stick out.

'Suggest we all bundle into the van and at least make ourselves a little more inconspicuous.' Samson thought it best to retreat at this point. 'Gary, you can tell us what you've found, and we can coordinate things a little better before sending Miller back to base.'

Gary saw the body in the back. 'Mind if I sit in the front? Not too keen on sharing the ride with him. Your men are probably more used to these situations.'

Samson nodded, although doubted Miller's and Christener's stomach for it.

'I'll stay,' Bishop said.

Samson turned around to him. He looked extremely unwell. 'Are you sure that's wise?'

'That's an order, Sergeant Major.'

Just in the line of his peripheral vision, Samson saw movement. Someone emerging from the warehouse. He didn't have to wait long to find out who.

The woman from yesterday. Screaming and howling, both in menace and agonising pain. More decrepit than before, she staggered forward with her insides torn wide open.

'Captain, in the van. *Now!*' Samson said forcefully. 'Miller, Christiner, arm yourselves!' Samson pulled out his gun and readied himself.

The woman was getting closer.

'Captain! Bill! You need to—'

A scream came from Bishop's mouth, hitting the exact same pitch as the woman. He was trying to resist, shaking his head, but he was losing the battle. Samson had no choice but to make a decision.

Bishop was still several feet away. But he was also armed, and Samson didn't want to wait for whatever had taken hold of his friend to realise that.

Throwing himself in the back of the van, Samson called out to Miller.

'Drive! Now!'

Fortunately, only Christiner had moved to the back previously, leaving Gary and Miller in the front.

'Where, sir?' It appeared all the screaming and general kerfuffle hadn't clued him into the need for a quick exit.

'Anywhere! Just away from here.'

Now was not the time to have an idiot in his ranks. Miller got the van started and set off down the street, only causing the vehicle to backfire once. The back doors remained open, and Samson readied himself to fire. But there was no way of being sure he'd hit the woman and not Bishop. Begrudgingly, he reached out and closed the van doors, then slumped in the back.

Samson wasn't clear on what had happened. He scowled at Christiner as the van turned the corner. No real reason – he was just frustrated.

He looked at the corpse, then Gary and Miller in the front.

It was time to get hold of Lethbridge-Stewart. He needed to know what was going on.

Lethbridge-Stewart put down the phone. Things had progressed out there, and not in a good way. Eviscerated people, Bishop apparently infected by… something. He'd send Samson straight back out, once the body had arrived at the Madhouse.

It seemed whatever was going on in Newcastle warranted much more scrutiny than the local authorities had given it.

A post-mortem was needed, and that meant they'd require the services of their best science expert. Captain Lindsay could handle the actual post-mortem, but Anne had a special knowledge…

Lethbridge-Stewart bowed his head, staring at his boots, dreading the conversation he was about to have. *This is why it's not good to work with loved ones,* he reminded himself, thinking briefly of Sally. True, thus far, there had been little instance of conflict when Bill and Anne worked together, but there was always a first time.

Taking a deep breath, he turned back to his desk and picked up the phone, dialling the number for the Warehouse. He would just have to trust in Anne's professionalism.

'Corporal, it's Lethbridge-Stewart. Put me through to Dr Travers.'

CHAPTER SIX
A Quest for Knowledge

ANNE RESPONDED to Lethbridge-Stewart's call reasonably quickly, although once arriving at base she discovered the body she was supposed to look at had not yet arrived. She was, of course, concerned about Bill, but Lethbridge-Stewart assured her that he'd send Samson back out as soon as the body arrived. In the meantime, he needed her full attention on the job at hand.

Easier said than done. She worried every time her fiancé went out these days, a result of the damage he'd undergone as a result of Vaar's experiments back in September. But she would never stop him; besides, as Bill would remind her, danger was the price they paid for the job they did. Which meant, she had no choice but to let Samson handle it.

So, she went about another task that had been set for her; to go through the files Lethbridge-Stewart's adjutant had put together. Lethbridge-Stewart was certain it all related to what was going on out there, but he wasn't quite sure how.

She read the files, and began to think about the experiments she *did* know about.

Some were pure stunts, of course, such as the American DJ who stayed awake for two hundred hours back in 1959. Scientists believed he was dreaming while he was awake. Some form of hallucinations, anyway. And then his life fell apart afterwards. Anne also recalled an American high school student – it was always the Americans – who was awake for eleven days in 1964. He was moody (big surprise), had memory and concentration problems (who wouldn't?), suffered from paranoia and hallucinations.

With just a desk lamp illuminating her desk, Anne thumbed through the folders. The odd thing of interest caught her eye. A horrible experiment in Russia in the late nineteenth century that killed puppies, after they had been forced to stay awake for several days. A year later, the University of Iowa tried it with three men. They survived.

Not all the reports were about sleep deprivation. Many of the military files highlighted what the Nazis got up to during World War Two. It made for sickening reading. The more Anne read, the more she realised the truly abhorrent nature of mankind.

Bone, muscle, and nerve transplantation experiments; sewing twins together; malaria infections; exposure to mustard gas; forced sterilisation; amputation without anaesthesia; poison injections. Anne's stomach lurched and turned over several times. *Thank goodness they brought in the Nuremberg Code*, she thought. *And the Declaration of Helsinki.*

Her heart sank as she delved deeper. During the 1950s, the CIA embarked on a top secret program (codename MKULTRA) to find drugs, tools and techniques for mind control. It involved slipping LSD to unsuspecting pub patrons, testing electrical shock techniques, tricking heroin addicts into taking a variety of hallucinogens and using sleep deprivation in an attempt to brainwash them. The last aspect piqued Anne's interest.

Anne read with horror but little surprise about Unit 731, a department of the Imperial Japanese Army, that conducted vivisections, dismemberments and bacterial inoculations on infected prisoners, mental health patients and even a large number of infants. Nothing about sleep, though.

It also seemed the British weren't averse to human experimentation, Anne noted as she flipped back through another mound of papers. Ronald Maddison died in the 1950s due to a lack of ethics and negligence. The British Army used hundreds of British and native British Indian Army soldiers as guinea pigs in the '30s and '40s. It appeared the experiment was to determine if mustard gas would cause greater damage to Indian skin compared to British skin. The racism shouldn't have come as a surprise, as it was before partition, but it still bothered her.

Pausing to collect her thoughts, take a breath and keep going, something caught Anne's attention in the flotsam of papers.

'Classified – Never For Release.'

She looked at the papers within more studiously. *Home-Army Fourth Operational Corps Army Experiment – Nature of Sleep.* That alarmed her. She knew of the Fourth, of course, learned about it some time back, and her father's own involvement with it. But experiments on people...? Anne couldn't believe her father would have been involved in such a thing. She wasn't involved in every aspect of the Fifth, so it stood to reason that her father hadn't been involved in every aspect of the Fourth during the '40s.

The majority of the documents were either blacked-out or '[REDACTED]' was repeated throughout. Anne found a year – 1942 – and 'By order General Charles DORNAN'. There was nothing else. But it did tell her a British sleep experiment was conducted during the war. And *directly* connected to sleep, too; it wasn't just a tangential aspect of a larger experiment. It was just what she needed.

Another thing she needed was unlimited access to the file. Or someone who was involved in some capacity. But to do that, she required help. Someone to crack open the tight-lipped military.

Exactly fifty-three minutes had passed since they had left Bill behind. In that time, Samson had made the dreaded call to Lethbridge-Stewart. Somehow, in the middle of the mad scramble away and wash of emotions about his friend, Samson had even managed to send Miller off to get Gary's earlier photos. Just giving an order, even a simple one about photographic prints, made him feel like he was doing something.

Now parked on a nondescript Newcastle side road, Samson tried to take stock. He still had Christiner and Gary with him. Plus, the corpse in the back of the van. Even when Miller re-joined them, it wasn't exactly a crack team. Some sort of backup would be helpful but, by then, it might have been too late for Bill.

Gary had quickly filled him in on his encounter with the homeless man, talking ninety to the dozen. Samson had only taken about half of it in, partly due to the speed Gary was talking and partly due to what he'd just experienced. But he'd managed to relay as much as he'd remembered to Lethbridge-Stewart as part of his report.

Samson also knew he had to make some decisions, and quickly.

'Gary, I need you to drive this van and corpse back to our base. Christiner and Miller are coming with me. The longer we delay, the more at risk Bishop is.'

'But I need to be here to take photos!' Gary looked back at Samson, as if he were a sulking child.

'You've already captured evidence of what's going on. When Miller gets back, you will return this corpse to our base, and hand all photos over to my boss, Brigadier Lethbridge-Stewart. No ifs, no buts. This is beyond some attention-grabbing headline in a paper now.' Samson gave his best 'don't argue with me' glare.

It didn't work.

'I'm not a soldier,' Gary protested. 'You can't give me orders.'

'I actually *can*, under the Emergency Powers Act 1964. This is an emergency, so civilians must follow the orders of defence personnel.' Samson knew he had just told a whopper of a lie. He was hoping Gary would simply respond to him spouting various bits of law that sounded important, delivered in an authoritative tone. The only person who could enable the Emergency Powers Act was Queen Elizabeth II herself – no one else. Certainly not a regimental sergeant major.

Fortunately, Samson's knowledge of this legislation, and his bluff, paid off.

Gary looked at him and muttered something about civil liberties under his breath. 'Right you are then. You better make sure I can actually get into your base, where it is, so directions might be useful. Can't imagine they'd normally let someone in with a dead body.'

Samson smiled. 'Directions are easy enough. Edinburgh Castle. Our base is underneath it.'

Gary didn't get a chance to voice his surprise, since it was at that point that Christiner chose to speak.

'Are you saying just you, me and Miller are going back to the warehouse, sir?'

Turning his head, Samson looked him right in the eye. 'That's exactly what I'm saying, Private.' He could see Christiner's eyes widen and face turn pale. But he said nothing more. 'We'll pick up Miller, check what weapons we have at our disposal, then get Gary to drop us off.'

'Shouldn't we get reinforcements, sir?' Christiner had obviously regained his composure a little. Enough to try and weasel out of Samson's orders.

'We don't have time. Captain Bishop is still out there. I'll call the brigadier again, let him know what's happening. Let him know to expect Gary here.'

Now it was Gary's turn to pipe up. 'Do you really think your boss is going to let you attack or do whatever it is you're planning on doing?'

'Of course he will. We're not amateurs,' Samson said, ignoring Christiner's look of horror at the idea. 'The Brig values his men; he wouldn't let us just leave Bishop out there in the state he's in. The man has been through enough.'

After receiving Samson's second report (and approving his rescue mission), and with a good four hours until the body arrived, Lethbridge-Stewart made himself busy finding out who was funding the experiments. Intelligence operatives around the world also indicated this was something much bigger than a domestic problem. At present, his resources were limited – but if he followed the money trail, that might do the trick.

He also wasn't sure how he felt about a civilian coming back to base with a body that was part of a current investigation. Especially a photographer with journalistic ambitions. He'd had enough of that nonsense with Harold Chorley. The last thing he needed was a nosy journalist *and* now a photographer poking their noses into the Fifth's business.

Captain Miles and his other teams had reported in from other places in the UK. There were definitely similarities in terms of people going missing and mutilated bodies turning up.

With rows of numbers and accounting charts in front of him, Lethbridge-Stewart should have been in his element. He had no problems adding up or even doing basic algebra but, when comparing financial records, the devil really was in the detail. And that detail became somewhat monotonous after a while.

Fortunately, the phone rang to draw his attention elsewhere. He was surprised to hear from Anne so soon but, after putting the receiver down, he was rather glad he could get on with something else. The thought of ruffling a few feathers in authority was slightly bemusing to him. Perhaps just because it was something different. Or the fact that asking questions about their financial status made certain people uncomfortable. Someone was bound to be doing something illegal somewhere along the line, even if it didn't relate to Lethbridge-Stewart's current concerns.

He put the various files away, picked up his baton and went to join Anne.

The Australian Nullarbor held many secrets, told many tales. Just ask the Mirning people, who lived mostly in the south near the coast. Their Dreamtime told of the water serpent Jeedara who was chased by Yugarilya – known by others as the Pleiades – who seized anyone he found in his territory.

Then there were the local wags, who created their own legends, fuelled by one too many beers at the local pub near Eucla. And so the Nullarbor Nymph was born... a blonde, white woman wearing a bikini made of kangaroo skins, allegedly photographed holding a kangaroo by the tail. Seen only from time to time, she supposedly tormented men who dared cross her path.

But the Nullarbor Nightmare was something else entirely. Kangaroo shooters only spoke of it in whispered gatherings around the campfire, sipping their billy tea, as if an increased volume would surely bring it upon them.

'That's the thing, mate,' Darren said to his companion. 'The body didn't look like a dingo attack at all.'

'Then what could it be?' Steve-o continued the hushed tones. 'A fox?'

Wally looked around the treeless plateau. 'Out here? Nah. No one could tell what it was, that's why it was so strange.'

Darren was a solid, no-nonsense bloke. Wally had his moments, but he was fairly level-headed, too. Steve-o couldn't see why either would have any reason to lie. But he couldn't quite get his head around what he was being told.

'How come these mutilated bodies are never reported to police?' Steve-o definitely wanted to know more, even if they were spinning a yarn or a colourful half-truth.

'Too far to come, I'd say,' Darren said, staring aimlessly into the fire. 'By the time they get here every manner of animal would have had a crack. The police would just put the deaths down to exposure – lack of water and survival skills – and there would hardly be any remains to deal with, anyway, by the time they got out here.'

'You're not going to tell me there's a Tassie tiger or two out this way as well?' Almost everyone in the Aussie outback had something to say about seeing the now-extinct thylacine. 'No one believes those stories.'

Wally looked at Steve-o, pointedly. 'The Nullarbor Nightmare isn't just a story.'

'I wouldn't wish it on anyone,' Darren warned. 'And pity whatever created it in the first place.'

Steve-o decided to be quiet for a bit. Darren had told him that other shooters in the area had been found with their insides hanging out. Entrails everywhere. But they were adamant wild animals hadn't been involved. At first they thought the local Aboriginals had rebelled and attacked for some reason, in a typical lack of understanding about their culture. But tribesmen had also been found in the same condition. And this was the part Steve-o was having trouble believing. It appeared the men had died from ripping their own innards from within, as part of a desperate rage.

As the embers popped and clicked, Darren spoke. 'I wouldn't have believed it if I hadn't seen it meself.' His eyes focused on the fire, as if the flickering light gave him something else to think about.

Wally threw his two bobs' worth in. 'It's said the Nullarbor Nightmare never sleeps.'

'What's that supposed to mean?' Steve-o wasn't sure what to make of everything. 'I thought that was just a description… Are you saying it's a man?'

Darren drank the last of his tea and threw the leaves from the cup over his shoulder. 'Not a man. The very opposite. Something inhuman.'

Steve-o enjoyed tall tales around the campfire, although he wasn't sure whether Darren and Wally were pulling his leg just because he was the new shooter in the team. He was originally taking it all with a grain of salt, to let the other two have their fun. But the way they spoke about this Nullarbor Nightmare seemed to come across as fair dinkum.

'Where did it come from? And why hasn't anyone just shot it?' Steve-o thought they were fair questions. Nothing that made him look too much like a drongo.

'You don't think those other 'roo shooters tried?' Wally shook his head. 'There are always spent cartridges near their bodies.'

'And no one really knows the full extent of what happened at Maralinga and Emu Fields,' Darren added.

Steve-o thought about it. 'You think it's some sort of mutation from those atomic tests? They were back in the '50s – ages ago.'

'I don't know what to think. Do you, Wally?' The shortest of the three responded with a shrug.

'Then what?' Steve-o pressed for more, even though the conversation was taking a darker turn and it was high time they all went to sleep.

'No one knows what else happened out there. The government could have done all sorts of experiments and hushed it up. And not just there – look at all the empty land around us. Be easy to set something up beyond the black stump with no one to bother you. Some reckon the Yanks have a secret base just up in the Territory.'

It sounded both far-fetched and plausible at the same time. Steve-o was a simple 'roo shooter, but he didn't trust the government. He always felt like they had something to hide. Like that prime minister bloke... Holt... who supposedly drowned after going for a swim at the beach. There was a certain part of Steve-o that felt he probably *was* a spy, taken away by a Chinese submarine. What had started as a scary campfire tale had left his head spinning.

'So, you're saying this Nullarbor Nightmare is part of some experiment?'

'More likely something that escaped,' Darren said. 'Or was leftover and forgotten somehow.' Wally nodded in agreement.

Eventually, the conversation faded away, the men bunking down in their swags as tiredness overtook them.

Steve-o didn't know what to make of the evening's discussion. He was nothing more than a hunter – he fired his rifle and got a bounty for each red giant pelt he brought back. Sometimes he'd get a little more if the kangaroo carcasses were fresh and the buyer could use them as pet meat. Tales of some wild beast of a man were probably just that... Bush stories whispered among men around campfires, simply because they had nothing better to do. Steve-o's thoughts became more and more vague as he drifted off to sleep.

Wally's screams woke him with a start.

What time is it?

All Steve-o could hear was Darren yelling. 'Grab your shotgun. Fire at it! Whatever you do, just shoot it!'

Steve-o scrambled for his weapon. Before he could get completely on his feet, he was pushed down with a thud. He looked into the eyes of Wally. But the eyes were red and wild – it was not the Wally he knew.

Wally roared and grabbed him around the neck with almost superhuman strength. A hand ripped Steve-o's cheek apart, flesh now hanging from his skull. He had no idea what was **happening**.

Barely able to whisper, he croaked.

'Get out of here, Darren! Stop this!'

And, with that, Steve-o passed out once again, although this time it wasn't sleep.

He was completely unconscious.

But not for long.

CHAPTER SEVEN
Uncovering and Stonewalling

YOU CAN thank me later.'

Anne looked up from her desk; Lethbridge-Stewart was in the doorway, a hint of a smile on his face. She noticed he had a folder under his arm.

'I hope it's good news.'

Lethbridge-Stewart walked towards her and put the file down. 'Depends on your definition. And what you're specifically referring to.'

She gave him a withering glance as she spoke. 'You're becoming more like a crossword every day.' Lethbridge-Stewart indicated he had no idea what she was talking about. 'Far too cryptic.'

'May I remind you, Anne, that just because one investigation becomes a concern for the Fifth, it doesn't mean other issues and situations no longer warrant our attention.'

Anne felt suitably reprimanded. 'So, what have you found out?'

Lethbridge-Stewart nodded at the folder. 'I had to pull quite a few strings to get that file. Although we have access to our predecessors' files, it seems some are more secure than others. Maybe General Dornan was being over-protective of British secrets during the war, but you'd think enough time had passed now. Other intelligence of the same ilk is freely available.' Lethbridge-Stewart paused for breath. 'But I was blocked at almost every corner with this one. Lots of rumbling in the ranks. Seems like someone really didn't want us to see it.'

'How did you get access, then?'

'When soldiers serve and fight together, they form an unshakeable bond. Especially if they save a fellow man's life. So, years down the track, one might call for a favour in return. Help from an old comrade or a person who might be in a position of power now. That's what you can thank me for.' Anne went to speak but Lethbridge-Stewart stopped her. 'No, I'm not going to say who it was. Just know I don't call in those favours lightly.'

Slightly humbled, Anne looked down and focused on the now-uncensored report. It wasn't long before she got to the relevant section that made her look back up at Lethbridge-Stewart.

'Yes, I know,' he said. 'Your father.'

Ten minutes had passed, and Anne still couldn't believe it. She had hoped her father had nothing to do with the experiments, but…

She'd read the report twice, as if the content would magically change the second time she went over it. But the facts had been laid bare.

Her father had been involved in the sleep experiment on soldiers in World War Two. Human experimentation. Something that she abhorred. Father? She just couldn't fathom it. What possessed him to become involved in something like that?

Lethbridge-Stewart was still in the room, trying to exert a calm influence over a visibly shocked Anne.

'I found it hard to believe myself,' he said, matter-of-factly.

Anne rubbed the bridge of her nose and looked Lethbridge-Stewart square in the eye. 'That doesn't change anything.'

'I was going to say *but*,' Lethbridge-Stewart quickly added. Anne paused, waiting. 'All we have is this report,' he said. 'We don't know the circumstances of why your father was part of this. He was involved with the Fourth Operational Corps, that we know. But he would have been given assignments and I doubt he got to pick and choose which ones. It was a time of war, remember.'

'That's no excuse,' Anne shot back. She realised she was being unfair. She didn't live through that time; she didn't know how she might act and respond during the same set of circumstances. So many people were forced to do things they didn't want to do during wartime. 'So, you're saying he was just following orders? As simple as that?' Anne looked at the papers again. 'But, Alistair, these were *British* orders.'

'I get the impression this General Dornan was a no-nonsense sort of fellow. Can't imagine Professor Travers had a choice. Probably thrown in at the deep end, as was often the case.'

Lethbridge-Stewart was right. Anne needed to bring back her objectivity and consider the report from a scientific perspective. But it was chilling to learn that the British were just as bad as the Nazis… in this regard, anyway. And this was just one incident they had come across.

'What else has been covered up, all done in the name of the war effort?' she wondered aloud. 'Makes you think, doesn't it?'

Lethbridge-Stewart didn't respond immediately. And when he did, he switched the conversation onto slightly safer shores.

'What do you make of it?'

Anne flicked through the pages. 'Given what's been happening across Britain and also the world right now, in terms of these missing persons and what may be happening to them… If your reports are true, then I'd say we've found a decent lead.'

Lethbridge-Stewart nodded his agreement. 'Rather unclear in some places, if you ask me, although it was probably deliberately so,' he said, taking the file from Anne. 'I'm amazed any of the detail was recorded anywhere. What it doesn't tell us is the specifics of the experiment. All the report mentions, is that British army volunteers were used for sleep experiments to see if they could develop more stamina. If they removed the need for sleep, they would have soldiers who could operate twenty-four hours a day at their disposal.'

'Yes and no real mention of what the soldiers were given or what ultimately happened to them.'

'Well, we definitely need more information. Or further help uncovering what went on. Should we pay a visit to… Um, the *other one*?'

It was comforting to know she wasn't the only one trying to work out how to fit the younger Professor Travers into their lives.

'Aren't you forgetting something, Alistair? He isn't the correct version of my father. Ted wouldn't have experienced this event. It occurred after 1935.'

'I may have the *military mind*, as you call it, Anne, but I did actually consider that. I was thinking more along the lines of same man, same mind. Even if he didn't experience these events, a man of his intelligence might shed some light on what they used on the soldiers. Particularly when matched with the mind of another academic, such as yourself.'

Anne was so ruffled at the idea of seeing Ted she hadn't considered that line of thinking. But she thought it was a long bow to draw. *Yet a scientific mind needs to investigate all possibilities as they present themselves*, she told herself.

'I suppose there's no harm in asking. Possibly an afternoon

wasted, that's all. But I actually haven't heard from him in a while. No contact in… at least six weeks.'

'I thought that might be the case. He did say he was going to keep his distance.' Lethbridge-Stewart smiled. 'Of course, I've had people keeping tabs on him. Just in case.'

'Smart, but you know what Father was like. Always disappearing somewhere and re-appearing again weeks later without a care in the world. I suspect Ted is probably the same. The last I heard was that he was in correspondence with Professor Watkins. Except…'

Lethbridge-Stewart's eyebrow shot up. 'Except what?'

'Watkins believes he is dealing with the *real* Professor Travers.'

'Well, he is, isn't he?'

'I suppose so. But I mean, Watkins is under the impression he's been dealing with my father. Not a man thirty-odd years out of time.'

'Oh. I see. Careless of Ted.' Clasping the baton at his side, Lethbridge-Stewart added, 'Let's pay him a visit.'

After their third attempt at knocking at the door, Anne was starting to think they may have been on a fool's errand. Which was fine, really, as she didn't want to be there anyway.

'Do you think he may be at home but just not answering?'

'It's possible.'

'I thought you had people keeping tabs on him?'

'Not his every move, Anne, just his general whereabouts. And my people place him here.'

'Well, maybe Ted doesn't want to be bothered. It's not only we who have to adjust.'

Anne looked around but the street was empty. 'So, what do you suggest we do, short of throwing a brick through a window?'

Lethbridge-Stewart looked at Anne. 'Nothing so crude. Let's use the intelligence available. You go left, I'll go right.'

The penny finally dropped for her. Door-knocking. Simple as that. See if anyone in the street knew anything.

About twenty minutes later, Anne rejoined Lethbridge-Stewart outside Ted's residence. 'No one has seen him for ages.'

'That matches up with what I've been told as well. But where could he be?'

Anne had already thought beyond the immediate problem.

Ted appeared to be missing, yes. But they were also no closer to finding out what happened during the sleep experiments.

'A dead end on one front and a new mystery on the other,' Lethbridge-Stewart mused.

'I refuse to believe we can't uncover more than what's in that report.'

'So, what do you suggest, Anne?'

'The war only ended about twenty-five years ago. There are still plenty of people around who were involved.'

'Yes, but they weren't necessarily involved in this experiment.'

'But there may be *someone*, Brigadier.' Anne couldn't stand Lethbridge-Stewart's defeatist attitude at times. 'We should at least investigate that possibility.'

'It won't be easy,' Lethbridge-Stewart countered. 'Getting that report by General Dornan was hard enough. I've just about called in all my favours. Wouldn't be surprised if others were now contacting me to pull a few strings.'

'There had to be other men involved. Soldiers who oversaw what was going on. We need to find one of them.'

'Given the information was highly classified, they'd be bound by the Official Secrets—'

'Oh, Alistair!' Anne cut him off quick-smart, exasperated. 'Let's just try.'

'Yes, well, there's obviously something going on,' Lethbridge-Stewart acknowledged. 'Especially given what Bill and Samson have encountered.'

As they walked back to their vehicle, Lethbridge-Stewart ventured an opinion. 'I'm surprised you're not more worried about Ted's absence.'

'Worried? Like I said, whether I like it or not, he's still my father. Or, at least, the man my father once was. And that means often disappearing without a word to anybody.'

'Granted. But if there is a link between the experiments your father was involved in, and what's going on with all these missing students… Ted's own disappearance may be cause for concern.'

Ever the gentleman, Lethbridge-Stewart opened the car door for her. As Anne bundled herself in, she said, 'I do care. I care about a lot of things. It's just in this case, I'm not sure what I should care about the most.'

Lethbridge-Stewart, now in the driver's seat and buckling himself up, looked at Anne. 'Then let's find someone who was a witness to what happened during the war.'

*

Phone call after phone call followed. Lethbridge-Stewart was stonewalled in most instances – either people genuinely knew nothing about the experiment, or they were feigning ignorance. No matter what security clearance or codes were invoked, Lethbridge-Stewart was blocked at every turn.

He was used to some pushback when making inquiries, but it was rare that he didn't make any progress whatsoever. In the process, he had to be careful what *he* said, in case he accidentally gave away classified information. He longed for the simplicity of giving an order and someone dutifully carrying it out immediately.

Perplexed, Lethbridge-Stewart absent-mindedly flicked through another pile of papers in front of him. He wasn't sure why he stopped where he did but there was an application for compensation from someone during the war. But it had been rejected.

It all seemed fairly innocuous but the phrase 'compensation for exposure to experiment' made Lethbridge-Stewart's eyes light up. The specifics had been blacked-out – just like so many of the other documents before him – but if he held it up to the light, he could see a name underneath.

The applicant was a Captain Barnett, although he had been a private at the time of the incident.

Lethbridge-Stewart didn't want to get his hopes up… After all, the man might be deceased. But it was something that should be explored.

From one haystack to another, he thought.

He sighed and picked up the phone again.

CHAPTER EIGHT
Risky Business

PRIVATE ANDREW Christiner had to admit he wasn't pleased with the RSM's plan. He wasn't happy being assigned to any mission, if he was perfectly honest. He'd only signed up for the Army because he was sick of the unemployment queue, and this was at least a regular pay cheque. But he wasn't really cut out for the most basic tasks – he really didn't understand why he'd been transferred to the Home-Army Fifth Operational Corps (which he'd been told was the Scots Guards Special Support Group – so what was that about?).

Once in their ranks, he'd heard plenty of stories about various missions and always hoped he would just continue with the training exercises in Stirling, or maybe even be stationed at the oft-heard but never visited Dolerite Base (usually called the Madhouse – which was a little worrying).

He'd been trying to make the best of it with little success. He'd found an ally in Jack Miller, who had somehow drifted into the Fifth like him. They would be the first to admit they really didn't know what they were doing. So their strategy was to keep their heads down and try not to be noticed. But neither went as far as the C-word. Being called a coward was the ultimate humiliation.

Now it seemed Sergeant Major Ware (not sergeant, as Christiner had been forcefully reminded when he first made that mistake!) was calling on him and Jack to be the men of the hour. Christiner didn't have an explanation for what they saw at the warehouse, but why did they have to be involved? It seemed far too risky. But Ware insisted and Christiner had to follow orders.

This time, the sergeant major suggested going in as one of the patients. He believed that gave them a bigger chance of confronting whoever was behind the operation, given they seemed to come and go at the drop of a hat. Christiner wasn't even sure people were doing anything at the warehouse – he'd never seen anyone there, bar the screaming woman. So, he was doubtful the plan would even work. That was his theory and he'd certainly voiced it, but Ware had dismissed it. (And, apparently, the view of a private wasn't to be given freely, unless specifically asked for.)

So, as (bad) luck would have it, Christiner had drawn the short straw. He first called and booked an appointment (Gary had kept a flyer that had been luring students in, after seeing them on campus) and was then told to be at the warehouse at a certain time. Ware had told him to conceal his weapon as best he could – Christiner was trying to look casual in jeans and a plain, long-sleeve top. He glared when Jack smirked at his outfit.

Ware and Miller would be hidden somewhere outside, also in casual clothes, ready to make a move if necessary. It was all very well having cover, but Christiner was, for all intents and purposes, about to be experimented on like a lab rat. Needles usually made him faint, so what use would he be then?

Nothing about the plan thrilled him as he entered the same warehouse doors he had passed through earlier. But rather than the eerie quiet of before, there was a hive of activity. People went about, here and there, with conversations rolling into others and medical equipment being carried to and fro. The only indication it was the same building was the layout of the rooms and corridors.

It must be one slick operation to get in and out and barely leave a trace, Christiner thought.

After filling in various forms with complete lies – Ware had the forethought to advise him of this – Christiner was taken to a room. The same room where Jack had shot a man dead and both of them had to mop up the blood. As Christiner was told he should get on the bed, he noticed restraints for hands and feet. Blood drained from his face.

'Um, you know, I think I've changed my mind about this.' Christiner just managed to get the words out and started backing up towards the door.

What he assumed was some sort of nurse responded. 'Oh, there's nothing to be scared of. It's just nerves, dear. Happens to a lot of people.' She moved forward, trying to be tender in her manner.

'All the same, I don't think this is for me.' In his peripheral vision, Christiner could make out a large hypodermic needle. The mere thought of it being injected into his skin made him feel queasy. His head was spinning and his eyelids were beginning to droop. Get out now! a voice inside cried. But a second voice also spoke, albeit more quietly. This is your mission. A chance not to look like a bumbling fool for once. Don't succumb to the C-word.

Head swaying from side to side, instinct took over. Christiner was still aiming for the door. But as he stumbled backwards, a large hand grabbed his shoulder. A second one took a solid grasp on the other side. The nurse approached him with a smile.

'Now, now, don't be silly. Don't you want to be a part of science and be paid for it?' She raised a knowing eyebrow, directed at the people behind Christiner.

Two large men frog-marched the young private towards the bed. Even if he wasn't feeling so faint, Christiner wouldn't have been able to resist the men. Obviously, he wasn't the first person to change his mind after the initial sign-up.

He focused on trying not to faint. Once he was restrained, he knew he wouldn't have a chance to do anything, least of all make contact with the sergeant major and Jack. He threw all his efforts into pushing back and flailing while they tried to put him on the bed. The result was a massive backhander to his face and an agonising crack that was surely his cheekbone. But the momentum caused Christiner to break free of their grip as he went spiralling. The mix of confusion and tension was palpable, as nobody really knew what was happening during the next ten to fifteen seconds.

And then a shot was suddenly fired, with clarity and reality combining in an instant.

Outside, Samson's ears pricked up immediately. Miller had heard it, too. Both pulled out their weapons and emerged from their hiding places.

'Sounds like trouble.'

'Do you think so, Miller?' Samson couldn't help the jibe at his junior; the capacity for stating the obvious under the circumstances was remarkable, even for Miller. 'We better get in there.'

'Is that a good idea, sir? What if they shot him?'

'I thought he was your friend, Miller?'

'He is. But…'

Samson shook his head. He'd had to train some green soldiers during his time with the Fifth, the *best of the rest*, as the Brig called them. He really meant those that were left over after all the best went to noteworthy regiments. Miller and Christiner were a great example of what Samson would charitably call *the worst of the rest.*

Teeth gritted, he barked at Miller, 'Get in there!'

They burst through the doors, straight into the waiting room. Several heads turned, but those present were remarkably calm, given the sound of a gunshot just moments earlier.

'I am Sergeant Major Samson Ware of the Scots Guards Special Support Group! Stay where you are – this is now a military operation.' Samson waved his gun around. That's when he remembered he was in casual street clothes, as was Miller. No one was likely to believe him while dressed like this. For all they knew, he could be any nut off the street. Or a terrorist.

Miller fired a shot in the air – whether to emphasise they were military or simply add to the confusion, Samson didn't know. He glared at Miller for the unnecessary use of his weapon. Samson wasn't sure where the original gunshot had come from, so he stuck with what he knew. The room they had explored the day before.

Arriving at the door, Samson stopped before anyone could see him. Miller was trailing behind him and, for once, didn't slam into the person in front of him after coming to an abrupt halt. Two gunshots had been fired in the space of minutes and Samson didn't know who, if anyone, had been injured or what the resulting reactions would be. All he could hope for was some sort of chaos they could use to their advantage.

He peered around the doorframe. He first saw a pool of blood and its trail led to a corner where a typical heavy goon sat, going a whiter shade of pale each moment as he clutched his leg. Christiner was on the bed, now restrained, and another heavy and a woman with a giant needle loomed over him.

Given the gunshots, someone else was bound to join them soon. And it was fair to say they would most likely be armed. Samson considered his options in the space of seconds.

He strode through the door, gun at the ready and displayed his commanding presence. Miller followed suit, although couldn't quite pull off the same poise as a tall black man.

'Whatever's going on, it needs to stop immediately.' Samson pointed over at Christiner on the bed. 'That man is a member of Her Majesty's Army and any further assault will amount to treason, as you would be levying war against the sovereign.'

Samson was consistently surprised at what came out of his mouth at times. Especially bits of law he could stretch and make sound convincing.

The man and woman backed off and put their hands in the air. The injured goon stayed exactly as he was. Despite the soldiers' lack of military uniform, those present seemed to believe him.

'Miller, untie Christiner.' Samson noticed a weapon up against the wall. The first gunshot must have come from Christiner, protecting himself. The private certainly had a purple shiner down the side of his cheek for his troubles. Piecing together what happened, Samson concluded Christiner must have fought back and then shot one of his assailants before being overpowered and restrained. 'And give him his gun,' he said, nodding at its location.

'I suppose you're going to tell us you've got the place surrounded?' the woman scoffed.

Samson didn't respond straight away. If he called her bluff, it wouldn't be long before she discovered the truth. But no other thoughts sprang to mind… except another cliché.

'Take us to your leader.' Samson cringed as he said it. He chanced there was such a person and, while traversing the rabbit-mazed building, they might be able to escape.

Eventually, they reached a room deep within the warehouse. Surprisingly, they had encountered no one else on the way. That only served to make Samson more tense. *In for a penny, in for a pound.* He motioned for the two in front to go first, and quickly followed behind with Miller.

Samson wasn't exactly disappointed, but there was no resistance, no fighting and no yelling. No shock at all. A woman behind a desk just looked up at the new arrivals. She could easily have been a secretary, but there was something about her angular jaw that gave her a harsh appearance, matched with short hair and a severe fringe.

'I see someone has finally found us. Well done. We were thinking of running our own book on when we'd be discovered but we're just too busy for such inanities.' The woman remained behind her desk.

Miller had his gun trained on their two prisoners and looked at his sergeant major for some assurance. Samson opted to aim his weapon at the woman behind the desk to see if that changed

·her tune in any way.

'Who are you? Who do you work for?'

'Werwolf,' the woman said with an accent, making the 'w' sound like a 'v'.

'Werewolf? You don't look anything like one.' Samson shook his head, reminded of the tales Anne had told him about Fang Rock. 'Or do you need a full moon to change?'

'Werwolf.'

'I got that. Are you just going to repeat yourself?'

The woman didn't respond this time. She just looked at him blankly, as if she couldn't care less about what was going on. Samson exchanged a look with Miller. They were on shaky ground, even though they were armed.

'It would be in your interest to answer, otherwise you will be placed under military arrest.' Which, of course, he couldn't really do during peacetime, not without martial law being declared, but Samson was pretty sure this woman didn't know that.

'You're going to do that anyway, I imagine.'

This was going nowhere. 'Okay, get up. You're coming with us. You can join the other two.'

The 'Werwolf' woman's only reaction was to blink slightly. Frustrated, Samson moved around to the back of the woman's desk and attempted to pull her out of her chair.

While Miller was distracted by Samson's struggle, the guard under his watch smacked the gun out of the private's hands. Shocked by the sudden move, Miller then copped an elbow to the jaw from Werwolf woman. Samson turned on his heel to respond but was too late. Miller was now looking down the barrel of his own gun.

'Stalemate.' The angular-jawed female – the one who loved saying 'Werwolf' so much – almost smiled but it was more of a lip curl. 'What are the odds of you getting out of here now, do you think?'

'Do you know what your experiments are doing?' Samson decided to stall for time and maybe even get some information in the bargain. 'Surely you've seen your patients turn into rabid animals, tearing themselves apart?'

'All part of the process of discovery.'

As the stand-off continued, Samson heard thudded footsteps down the corridor. Werwolf woman smiled cruelly, knowing she now had the upper hand. Miller gazed up at Samson, and he could only look back apologetically. This wasn't his best planned operation. Christiner was probably either dead or a prisoner by now, too.

'Drop your weapons now!' a voice boomed. 'Sergeant Major! Miller! On the floor!'

They both dropped without question. There were a few shouts of surprise from their former female prisoner, Werwolf woman and the guard with the gun, but those were quickly followed by the sounds of people being subdued.

'You can get up now, sir! You too, Miller.'

Samson lifted himself up, and was just in time to see the captives being marched out of the room by troops from the Fifth.

'Thank you, Corporal…?' Samson began, not recognising the NCO before him. Which meant he was probably one of RSM Greenland's men.

'Corporal Northover. Fairly new to all of this, sir, I'm with Captain Younghusband's Company usually, stationed down at Imber. But we were called in to help.'

'Remind me to thank Younghusband the next time I see him. Who's in command here?' Samson rubbed his shoulder, retrieved his gun from the floor and nodded at Miller to do the same.

'Lieutenant Kenworthy,' Northover answered. 'Based on the intelligence you relayed back to the Madhouse, he thought it best to contain the building.'

'Good thing he did.'

Northover looked down at his boots, hesitant for the first time. 'There's something I need to tell you, sir.' Samson waited. 'I'm really sorry, but I had to shoot Captain Bishop. Private Christiner's okay, though.'

A concrete fist slammed into his stomach. The very thing Samson had been trying to avoid had happened. He shook his head, not wanting to believe it.

Looking at Samson's crestfallen face, Northover quickly explained. 'Oh no, not like that! He's still alive, sir. Gave him a bullet to the leg, that's all.'

'You just like to dribble these bits of information out, don't you, Corporal?'

Northover stood to attention. 'Yes, sir. I mean, no, sir.'

'Hmm. Carry on. What happened?'

'Captain Bishop was screaming and coming for us when we first arrived. Decided to hinder his movements so he'd be less of a threat. Obviously, he's a bit of a mess, what with the bullet and whatever else has happened to him. There are open wounds around his torso.'

That couldn't be good, since that's where his scar was. Anne would not be happy. Samson sighed inwardly. Nothing he could do about that now.

'What's Kenworthy's approach now?' he asked.

'Secure the building, secure all those *in* the building and interrogate them to find out as much as possible.'

'And Bishop?'

'We've secured him, too. Strapped down in one of the beds.'

Kenworthy and Northover had made a good start. This was definitely the epicentre of where things were happening. But Samson wanted to make sure the situation was fully under control. To have any hope of helping Bill, they were going to need more support – and fast.

'I think it's time we got the brigadier here. With backup.'

CHAPTER NINE
Casualty of War

IT WAS the worst cup of coffee he had ever tasted. Still, he didn't expect much from this roadside café. If they could manage a serve of eggs, beans and chips without a stray hair or two, you were one of the lucky ones.

Drizzle ambled its way down the window, adding to the overall gloom of the place. The only good thing was the prices; without that attraction, the café would have shut its doors years ago.

Captain Phillip Barnett (retired) looked down glumly as the clouds in his coffee dissipated and re-formed, over and over again. How had it come to this? Everything was miserable and he was sick of feeling this way. Just down all the time. Carol had left him years ago and his children were now adults themselves, barely making contact. He couldn't even remember the last time he'd heard from them. But that was kind of his fault, too, given he was rarely in a place long enough to lick a stamp.

Barnett pushed a chip around his plate to soak up some egg and the beans' tomato sauce, hardly registering as he put it in his mouth. At least his distracted thoughts took him away from the taste of the food.

He took a look around the café. Just the odd person here and there, same look on all their faces. Lost souls, all of them. Life had let them down in a big way and now they were just existing. Wondering why they bothered any more. Even the staff had similar expressions, as if to say, 'How did I end up here?' Some days, Barnett felt so overwhelmed he just wanted to break down and cry. But that's not something a man did. Especially not in public and especially not a retired army captain. He felt his eyes welling up, so he quickly gulped down a mouthful of weak coffee to help hold them back.

He was so focused on his task that he didn't notice two

strangers suddenly standing over him. A man with a moustache and an attractive young woman. The man had a military feel about him; he recognised it straightaway. Barnett didn't like being found or people knowing where he was. Not these days. He preferred to be off the grid, fading away.

'You're a hard man to find, Captain,' the man said.

'Not anymore,' Barnett grunted, hoping his dismissive attitude might make them go away.

'Sorry?' the woman asked, puzzled.

'It's been many years since I was a captain. No one calls me that. They haven't for a long time.' Barnett stared off into space, trying hard not to think about the past.

'Yes, well… I'm Brigadier Lethbridge-Stewart and this is Dr Anne Travers. Once a captain, always a captain in my book. May we sit down?' He gestured at the empty chairs on the other side of the table.

Barnett felt a desperate urge to run. Something the man said sent alarm bells going off in his head. But Barnett hadn't really been paying attention. He tried to tell himself he had done nothing wrong – not lately, anyway – and it was completely irrational to flee when he didn't even know what they wanted.

'Free country,' Barnett responded. 'Or so they say.'

Lethbridge-Stewart and the woman shuffled their way into their seats. There was an awkward silence before the woman finally broke the ice.

'It can't be easy.'

'What?' Barnett said through gritted teeth, unclear what she was talking about.

'Being of no fixed abode,' Lethbridge-Stewart said, waving away a waitress wanting to take any new orders. 'That's what I meant about you being difficult to find.'

Barnett shrugged. 'I usually find somewhere to doss down. No big deal. Been doing it for years.' He decided to keep eating, as way of a distraction. Plus, it was hard enough to eat the slop when it was warm, let alone cold. 'Hope you don't mind,' he said, pointing at the food with his fork. 'I spent what little money I had on this.'

'What do you do for money, if you don't mind me asking?' the woman asked, a touch of tenderness showing.

'Odd jobs here and there, when I can get them. No one wants an old wreck like me. That's why I move about so much.' Barnett thought about it for a minute. 'Yet you found me. A high-ranking soldier and a… Did you say *doctor*?'

'Yes,' the woman said, smiling. 'Dr Anne—'

'I guess you had me followed.' Barnett snorted, speaking as he chewed. 'Doesn't the Army have anything better to do these days? Or was it some form of punishment and training for a young private under your command?'

'Actually, that's what we wanted to talk to you about.' Lethbridge-Stewart met Barnett's stare. Definitely a no-nonsense man. 'Back to when you were a private. During the war.'

Barnett bowed his head. The war was something he had tried to put out of his thoughts. But it was there in its dark recesses, conjuring up horrific images when he slept. Or an occasional sight, sound or smell would suddenly trigger something in his mind. That's why he had hit the bottle so hard. Anything to destroy those memories or, at the very least, dull them so they were less frequent. He knew he wasn't the only veteran to suffer trauma, or shellshock, or whatever they called it nowadays. But that didn't make it any easier. And now two people, completely out of the blue, wanted him to remember and re-live a part of his life he desperately wanted to forget. A part of his life that had ruined the rest of his life.

'We understand it might be hard for you,' Anne said, soothingly. 'A lot of men came back changed. It was a difficult time for everyone.'

'Like you'd know.'

She would have only been a small child when the war started. She had no concept of what went on.

'I was in Korea, and I was breveted too. It takes a special kind of soldier to be breveted during war time, to move from the non-commissioned ranks to a commissioned officer.' Lethbridge-Stewart left the statement there for him to digest. Obviously to prove to Barnett he had some notion of what it was like.

'My father worked alongside the British military during the war,' Anne added. 'And that's why we wanted to find you. It was all under the cover of secrecy.'

'So why don't you ask him about it?'

Anne and Lethbridge-Stewart shifted uncomfortably. Touchy subject for them, apparently.

'My…' Anne hesitated. '…father seems to be missing.'

'We're dealing with it,' Lethbridge-Stewart said, quickly. 'That's why we've come to you, actually.'

Barnett's eyes shifted to the door. Then the doorway to the

kitchen. Lethbridge-Stewart followed his gaze.

'I don't think running will help. At this stage, we just want to ask you some questions.'

'At this stage? There's more than one stage?'

'Not at all,' Anne responded. 'It's just you might have some information that could help us.'

'Why should I help you?' Barnett just wanted to disappear. Not be hassled any more. Especially if it meant talking about the war. So, he tried a different tack. 'I mean, what's in it for me?'

'I'm sure we can find a permanent home for you somewhere,' Lethbridge-Stewart offered. 'Maybe even find you a regular job.'

Barnett wanted to scoff. Did they know how hard it had been for him? How could they succeed where he had failed? A voice in the back of his mind cried out: *Stay off the booze, maybe?* It was soon followed by another thought: *Maybe they really can help you?*

He sat there, pondering the offer, then looked from Anne to Lethbridge-Stewart, then down at the table. Another moment passed.

'So, what do you want to know?'

'Well, I want to know what my father did. I believe you met him.'

Barnett shrugged. 'Met a lot of people during the war. You said he worked alongside the military? What was his name?'

'Travers. Professor Edward Travers.'

Barnett almost choked on his food.

That was a name he hadn't heard in a very long time. And with it came memories, darker than even the worst battles during the war.

The miserable weather was showing no sign of abating. Barnett told of the experiment from all those years ago. How men had volunteered for the good of their country to become experimental subjects, all in an effort to create a better soldier. And how it had all gone terribly, terribly wrong.

'So, my father was sent to unravel the mess?' Anne was feeling slightly relieved that her father wasn't quite the monster she was beginning to imagine in her head.

'Seemed that way,' Barnett replied. 'Experiment was already well underway by the time the professor arrived. And out of hand.'

'You mean men were already succumbing to the effect *before* General Dornan had ordered Travers there?' Lethbridge-Stewart was aghast.

'It was all based on talk of what the Nazis had been doing in their attempts to make the ultimate soldier. Less sleep without any bad effects would mean they could go for longer. But it didn't work out that way. Hardly surprising.'

'What do you mean?' Anne asked.

'Any soldier worth their salt back then, even us young 'uns, had heard about the *vampires of the night*. But they only ever appeared on the battlefield, and it was only ever spoken about in whispers.'

Anne looked at Lethbridge-Stewart. He baulked slightly at the word *vampire*. She knew him well enough to know he was now questioning the credibility of their source. But they didn't have anywhere else to seek information at this point.

Barnett continued to tell them the most incredible tale of men gone mad, ripping themselves apart like wild animals and then doing so to other people who, in turn, similarly attacked themselves and others. And so the circle went on, unless they were killed, or died from severe injuries.

'We were under the orders of a Captain Gampfer, and he was a tyrant. He insisted the experiment continue at all costs. It wasn't until your father came along that someone tried to stop it.'

Anne managed a quarter-smile. That was more like the father she knew. But it did raise a question.

'So how *did* he stop it?'

'With the men too far gone, it was up to us soldier boys to go out and shoot them. But for the rest, who were still in the camp and hadn't started going wild, there was little that could be done.'

Lethbridge-Stewart spoke, already half-expecting the answer. 'They were shot?'

'I'm sure Gampfer wanted to do that. But Travers gave them something to alleviate the symptoms. Unfortunately, all he was able to do was put them in a permanent coma until a solution could be found.'

'And was it?' Anne's scientific curiosity had also been piqued.

'No idea. Travers left shortly after, and we closed down the base. The comatose soldiers were transferred somewhere else, but I don't know where.'

'Are you saying they may still be out there, in a coma somewhere?' Lethbridge-Stewart asked. 'Anne, is that physically possible?'

'People can be in comas all their lives, Alistair. Look at Owain; he's been in a coma for almost a year and showing no signs of improvement.'

Lethbridge-Stewart nodded, a cloud crossing his face at the mention of Owain. He cleared his throat.

'Is that all you need to know?' Barnett asked pointedly. Anne could see he was getting itchy feet. She was tiring of the same glum location, too. 'Didn't you say something about finding me a place to live?'

Anne turned her head to Lethbridge-Stewart.

'Yes, I'll have to make several phone calls to see what can be arranged.'

'Then why are we still sitting here? You've got some arranging to do and I need to find myself a pub.' Barnett started to leave but Anne stopped him.

'Please, come back with us. I know I have plenty more questions to ask and you'll have a roof over your head until the brigadier can sort something.'

Chuck Lynch didn't like what he saw. But as a private investigator, that was par for the course. Especially in a city like New York.

He'd been on the trail of a killer for six months now. Sure, the cops had dismissed his theories but when didn't they? No one on the force liked it when a PI showed them how to do their jobs. That's why he was always treated like something people scraped off the bottom of their shoes. This time around, Lynch was adamant he was right. People had been going missing for a while now and he was certain foul play was at work.

Rain swept down upon him as he turned up the collar on his trenchcoat and tried to pull the brim of his hat out further. Sludge formed in the gutters as Lynch trudged down West 81st Street. Turning into Columbus Avenue, he knew he needed a break in the case soon. A theory was all well and good but without something concrete to join the dots, his reputation as the gung-ho gumshoe with a knack for busting cases wide open would be severely diminished.

The small neon sign eventually came into view. Lynch made his way down the stairwell and pushed through the slightly ajar door, the only hint entry was possible at this time of day. There was little difference between the cloudy darkness outside and the innards of the venue. Bright lights weren't welcome here. Neither were nosy private investigators. But Lynch wasn't going to let that stop him.

Lynch wasn't familiar with Zed's Place, but he'd been in a dozen or more joints like it. Sticky, worn carpet, a couple of barflies by themselves and a bartender polishing his glasses with a dirty rag. Definitely a dive bar. Dank but not without its charm – to some people, anyway. He'd been told he could get some leads here but, even after slipping the guy a Jackson, he couldn't get much more out of his informant beyond cryptic clues.

'What can I get you.' It was more of a statement from the bartender which actually meant, 'You better buy a drink or get out'.

'Bourbon,' Lynch said, without missing a beat. 'On the rocks.'

'Fancy boy, eh? Can't get it down without the ice.'

'I'll take it as it comes.'

The bartender grunted and reached for a bottle of nondescript rough-gut.

After the transaction was complete, Lynch took his place at the bar. Not too close to the other barflies; a touch of subtlety was needed. He put his hat next to him and then took a swig. It was almost like paint-stripper, but he had to fit in. Besides, he told himself, he'd had worse. He forced himself to finish it.

'Same again, thanks.'

The bartender went through the same motions, not uttering a word. It was all part of Lynch's plan to ease himself into the setting. But he had to be careful about asking questions. If past experience was anything to go by, this was the type of place that would be suspicious of queries and unlikely to be forthcoming with answers, especially to a stranger. He wondered how many drinks he would need to gain the bar's overall acceptance.

The answer was six.

As time rolled on, Lynch managed to get some snatches of conversation with the bartender. Nothing major; just vague small talk. Even the barflies joined in occasionally. Was now the time to chance something bold? It was a calculated risk, as always. Lynch was packing heat, just in case, but it was a sure bet there would be at least one shotgun behind the bar.

Now on his seventh rough-gut, Lynch put it out there.

'So, what's out the back?'

As soon as he said it, the tension in the room became electric.

Both barflies suddenly raised their heads and turned to Lynch. The bartender froze for a moment, his back to the question. Time lingered indefinitely, although, in reality, it was barely a moment. Lynch was apprehensive, but knew he had to maintain a nonchalant presence. The bartender turned around, exchanging a look of mutual suspicion between the barflies.

'Who wants to know?' The tone in his voice was more aggressive than it had been.

'Rick Hughes.'

'Well, maybe *Rick Hughes* oughtta mind his own business.' The bartender now had his hands on his hips. 'Isn't that right, fellas?' His two regulars murmured their assent.

Lynch slapped down two Benjamins on the bar. The barflies' eyes widened. They'd probably never seen so much money at one time.

The bartender looked at the cash and sneered. 'And what do you think you'll get with that?'

'I didn't come in here for my health.' Lynch decided to match the resistance he was getting with a similar attitude. 'Or the company. Or your natural charm.'

'It's raining outside and you don't have an umbrella.' Despite appearances, the bartender was smart enough to notice little discrepancies.

'My trenchcoat and hat protect me enough.' Lynch wasn't going to let the man get the better of him. 'I'll cut to the chase. I'm here for the girls.' He hoped his informant had given him enough to go on. He'd been told to 'ask for the girls'.

'Looking for a good time? What kind of show do you think I'm running here?'

Lynch wondered if he was going down the wrong path. He tried to change tack.

'I meant the missing girls.'

The bartender moved under the bar with lightning speed and came up, shotgun at the ready.

'Sounds like you know a little more than you should about certain things. How about you spill the beans and tell me what you know? After all, I've let you drink in my bar all afternoon and I don't usually let strangers do that.'

Despite New York's size, it could still have a country town mentality. In reality, Lynch knew it had all sorts. It just depended on the circles you mixed in.

'Let's all just stay calm, shall we?' Lynch raised his hands.

'This *is* calm. You sure don't want to see me crazy.' The barman's stare pierced through Lynch. His trigger finger was steady. And ready. 'I just gotta know who you been talking to before I throw you out or shoot you dead.'

The barflies now had their heads turned, paying avid attention. Lynch was tense – the situation could go any number of ways – but he'd been in more difficult positions. He needed to decide on the best play with only seconds available to him.

'I want in on the action.' Lynch held his ground and returned an equal stare. 'I can get you more girls.' It was a gamble, but maybe this man's greed could be worked to his advantage. The bartender lowered his shotgun a little.

'Oh really? So why do you need my girls if you've got your own?'

It's a fair point, Lynch conceded, especially given he had no idea how these women were being used. Initially, he thought they were being exploited for cash, as was typical in the New York underbelly – but something told him he'd missed the mark completely.

'More money, for both me and you.' Lynch hoped this was all

about profit.

'Hey, fellas!' The bartender simultaneously laughed and sneered. 'This joker thinks this is about money. Well, well, well. Tell us what we might be missing out on.'

'I have access to a women's refuge.'

'Half your luck.'

'No one would notice if those women went missing.'

'And you think I'd be interested in them? Thanks for the tip. Will follow it up.'

Lynch had no time to react. Blood splattered out the back of his head as the gunshot echoed around the room. He fell to the floor, gone in an instant.

CHAPTER TEN
Wrong Time, Wrong Place

EDWARD TRAVERS knew he was in trouble. Aside from the fact he had been kidnapped and restrained against his will, his captor was under the assumption he was the Professor Travers who had died at the beginning of the previous year.

'So, are you going to help us?' The old man gave a curled smile. 'Like you did last time?'

Despite his age, he held a commanding presence. Edward suspected he was a former soldier and probably a high-ranking one, especially given his mass and unfailing posture. The man, who still refused to identify himself, could probably still hold his own in a fight.

Edward paused, as if he had a choice and was considering the offer.

'That was a long time ago… Um. Do you know, I can't seem to recall your name.'

The old man looked at him, and gave that same curled smile. 'Yes, I don't suppose we were ever on first name terms. The old boys from the war call me Charlie. You may as well do the same, I suppose.'

'Very good, that will make it a bit easier. Now, the point I was going to raise, Charlie, is that my research has gone down extremely different paths since then.'

'Such as becoming a robotics expert. I am aware. And, I can only assume, some miraculous cure to ageing.' Charlie waved it away. 'That does not matter right now, neither does it answer my question.'

'What I'm saying is that I'll need to refresh my memory and examine the patients in here, if that's what they are. Run a few tests, that sort of thing.' Edward had no idea if Charlie would play along. 'If you agree to it, of course.'

'So, we have an understanding.' It clearly wasn't a question.

'As before. You have everything in this room at your disposal.'

Edward desperately wanted Charlie to fill in the blanks. Edward had no idea who the patients were, or what had happened to them. And he certainly didn't know how Professor Travers had been involved.

Charlie went on, 'We want to see if we can bring these men out of their comas. Science has progressed rapidly since they were put in that state. See if you can unravel what you did during the war.'

If only Edward knew what *that* was…

'I'll need you to remove these restraints first,' he said. 'Then I can start looking into it for you.'

'Of course.' Charlie clapped his hands three times loudly. Two men came into the room and attended Edward. 'My guards will be watching you as you work. Just in case you had any notions of escape.' And with that, he left the room.

Edward was sure his two new supervisors had some form of weapons hidden on their person. As he stood up, rubbing the blood flow back into his wrists, he asked, 'Where do you want me to start?'

One of them pointed at the beds on the other side of the room. Obviously Edward was going to get little conversation from his guards. He made his way to the patients and busied himself checking temperatures, taking pulses and doing all the routine medical checks he suspected ought to be done.

At least the patients were alive. He understood people could stay in comas for years, but the patients were young men in their twenties. They would have been babies or toddlers during the war, which could only mean time had stood still for them, at least physically.

Edward briefly considered his own relative youth. The same could be said for him, at least from the point of view of people who had known Professor Travers in the past thirty-odd years. Maybe that's why Charlie didn't question his appearance; perhaps he thought Edward had just slept well in the past three decades?

Edward smiled to himself and dismissed the notion as folly.

He wanted to ask his guards if there were notes or files about the experiment he could look at. But to do that might give away the fact he didn't actually know anything. The only option was to start rummaging through things without looking like he was floundering too much. He couldn't exactly open every drawer and cupboard without arousing suspicion. But he also needed something to give him a clue. So, as he went back and forth from the patients, he opened a door here and compartment there, as subtly as he could.

In due course, Edward came across a desk stuffed with papers. He kept searching, until something caught his attention. He carried the files across to a bench near the patients. It looked as if someone had de-coded a Nazi message during the war. Or secret documents of some sort. But the methodology wasn't what had caught his eye; it was the content of the document. The ciphers used to translate the report were obviously flawed; Edward had trouble making the sentences flow. But he got the gist of it. The Nazis had been working on some sort of sleep experiment to make their soldiers gain greater endurance.

He looked up and surveyed the patients before him. Edward was only aware of World War Two history from what he'd managed to learn during the past few months, and he knew the Nazis had committed thousands of atrocities; it was a section of history no one could avoid, even if you hadn't lived it.

Edward considered the few details he had to work with.

The Nazis had conducted sleep experiments during the war to try to give their men more stamina. The experiments appeared to have involved keeping those men awake at any costs. Given the patients before him, it seemed the British had tried a similar experiment for the same reason. While he had no idea what happened as a result of the Nazi experiment, the British one looked like it had been an abject failure. Somehow, the men's lives had been saved – apparently by putting them in a coma from which they could not awake. And Professor Travers had been directly involved.

Wandering from patient to patient so the guards thought he was working, Edward didn't think his captors wanted his help for altruistic reasons. The very fact that he'd been kidnapped indicated there was some nefarious purpose behind it all.

Vertical lines ran up and down the black-and-white monitor. On it, Professor Travers could be seen going about the room examining the patients. The professor may have been under armed guard, but Charles knew his men were fallible, just like every other human. As such, a bulky camera had been hidden as much as possible in the roof to relay the images to the screen.

Charles inhaled from his cigar. He kept an eye on the surveillance system as much as he could, given there was no way to record and store the information without laborious magnetic tapes that needed to be changed manually. He'd considered getting one of the guards to do it, but it was a time-consuming, expensive and unreliable process. Besides, he took a perverse delight in watching Travers squirm as he was forced to work against his will. And the cigar made it all the more enjoyable.

Charles smirked to himself as Travers tried to pretend he wasn't looking for a way out, or a key, or something to use as a weapon while going through various cupboards and drawers. The professor even made it look like he was researching something by taking time to read the various bits of paper he had found.

Let the mouse run about in his cage, Charles thought. Taking another puff from his cigar, he almost purred with satisfaction, thinking about the game he was playing.

His plans were beginning to come together; wheels were turning and cogs were starting to fit neatly together. But there needed to be a breakthrough so it could become the well-oiled machine it needed to be. And once that happened… well, the world would change forever. Like it should have before.

Charles wished it had happened when he was younger but now, in his autumn years, he still revelled in the fact he could be part of something so glorious.

Travers was the key. Going back to the source was the best option to succeed where everyone else had failed. The professor would follow his will, either through gentle persuasion or brute force. He could delay as much as he wanted, but eventually he would yield and do what was necessary.

Hours had passed. Edward made copious notes about the patients. He hoped it was enough to convince his captors that he'd been doing *something*. He now had a vague idea of what the experiment had entailed, after taking blood samples, monitoring heart rates and doing physical checks as best he could. He was no medical doctor, but he knew enough. Even before he'd been sent on a mission through various alternative worlds, Edward had known it paid to diversify.

He didn't know how long he'd been working but he guessed twelve hours or so. It was hard to tell in this facility. There were no windows, and the lighting wasn't exactly effective. He hoped he would be offered food at some point. Unlike the comatose men, who had drips to feed them the necessary nutrients, Edward needed to ingest something so he wouldn't collapse. Obviously,

Charlie wanted to keep him alive.

Fortunately, there was a sink. He'd managed to drink water from a beaker a few times. The guards hadn't batted an eyelid. Which made him think that surely they needed to eat and drink too. They had been there just as long as he had. Fatigue was bound to kick in at some point.

Almost on cue, two guards came in and relieved the watch. And accompanying them was someone else; a rather dapper-looking gentleman with lustrous red hair and full beard to match.

The new arrival wasn't as icy as everyone else. In fact, he looked positively happy to be there.

'Well, hello, Professor Travers!' He grinned incessantly. 'Worked it all out yet?' He bounced over to the beds and looked at one of the patients from end to end before bounding over to another and doing the same.

It was almost too much exuberance. Edward didn't know what to make of him.

'Not exactly,' he admitted. 'Still considering all the factors. More information wouldn't go astray… And maybe some food?'

'But of course!' The ginger-haired fellow snapped his fingers and one of the guards left immediately. 'Need to make sure you can keep at it. But we need you to get results, too.'

Edward didn't comment on the implied threat. Instead, he asked, 'May I ask whom you might be?'

'Forgive me,' the man said, bowing elegantly. 'I am Dr Jarrod Buttery.' He clutched his lapels, extremely proud of this fact. It meant nothing to Edward, but he wasn't sure whether he *should* know this man and was just the wrong Travers, or if the man had an inflated view of his own self-importance.

'Right, Dr Butters…'

'Buttery.'

'Sorry, Dr Buttery. Why are you here? To help me? Keep an eye on me? Taunt me?'

Buttery was immediately taken aback. 'Taunt you? Oh, my dear fellow, how preposterous! Perish the thought.' He shook his head and then removed an invisible speck of dust from his jacket. 'I'm here to help you.'

Well, it would be the first sign of help Edward had seen so far. And if Buttery had information Edward didn't, then that could be useful.

'You passed the first test,' Buttery said. 'We needed to know you would comply of your own accord.'

Jeering in return, Edward couldn't believe the idiocy of the statement. 'I didn't have much choice, did I? First, I was kidnapped and then I was made to work against my will under armed guard. Kind of in my best interests to do as I was told.'

'Be that as it may, I'm sure you'd like these men to recover from their comas without incident. We have the same goal.'

'If philanthropy was the motive, then why not just ask me? I may have come willingly.'

The look Buttery gave him reminded Edward of the feeling he'd had since being brought to this place. Some sort of lingering evil hanging in the air. Ridiculous, of course, but he couldn't shake the feeling. He hated to think what had happened in the building previously. Sometimes places felt like they held onto their past and their influence continued to shape the present.

Resisting a shudder, Edward moved on from the thought and decided it was time for a few more questions.

'So, Dr Buttery, what are you going to help me with? I assume, as a bare minimum, you have a medical degree?'

'Oh, and one or three others. I'm here to learn from the man that started it all. To find out where the experiment went wrong.'

'I thought that's why I was dragged into this?'

'Oh indeed, Professor, indeed yes!' Dr Buttery clapped his hands together and almost had a twinkle in his eye. 'I want to *learn!*'

The way Buttery put the emphasis on, made him uneasy. *Learn what?* And then it hit him, plain as day.

Buttery didn't just want to learn how to undo the experiment – he wanted to learn how to replicate it. That's what this was all about. Not saving these men's lives at all.

Edward's eerie feeling had been right.

'Why do you want to replicate the initial experiment?'

'Well done, Professor Travers. Gold star for you.' Buttery continued to move about like an exceptionally annoying jack-in-a-box. 'Same reason as last time, my good sir. Surely you've figured that out by now?'

'The war ended years ago. Men don't need endurance beyond what's already normal for the human race.'

Buttery clapped his hands with glee. 'Oh, very good. You *are* getting it. I knew we acquired the right man for the job.' He looked over at the guard and then back to Edward. 'I can think of plenty of situations where it might be helpful in this day and age. Vietnam, maybe? What about rescue operations in the desert or frozen wastelands? Underground miners? Oh, the list goes on and on.'

As do you, Edward thought. He wasn't going to allow this Buttery fellow the satisfaction of knowing he was getting under his skin. He walked over to a bed containing another man. Alive, yet without the joys of life.

'This!' he thundered. 'This is why we don't need men of endurance. The experiment didn't work. It was a failure. Sometimes science simply goes up blind alleys and needs to be dismissed. You go back to basics and do a complete re-think. You wouldn't bash a man with a rock to cure a headache, like the cavemen did, would you? They thought it released the pain inside the head, not realising the extra pain and damage they were causing in the process.'

Buttery was silent for a moment. Then he broke out into his ridiculous bearded grin once again. 'Looks like I gave you more credit than you were due. You think this is the only operation? Yes, I want to learn from you to replicate the experiment and see if I can build on it. And then guess what? Can you? Can you really?' He leaned into Edward's face; his eyes maniacally opening wide. 'I'm going to tell everyone else around the world what to do. And they'll tell me anything that might help here.'

'Around the... world?' Edward was desperately trying to catch up. Not easy when you were bluffing your way along and your life depended on it.

'Abso-positively-lutely! The world, the globe, the thing we live on called Planet Earth. We're doing this experiment everywhere, across countries and continents. We're going to find a way. We're going to make it work.'

Edward stiffened. 'But you haven't yet. I'm guessing that's why you need me?'

'Yes, yes! Go back to where it all started, like I said. You're the key player – you're responsible for the men in here and your legacy is now taking place in hundreds of operations almost everywhere you can imagine. Now, don't you want to stop people suffering the same fate as these men? Or the other side-effect the experiment has?'

Edward didn't want to believe it. The other version of Professor Travers would not have been a party to such abhorrent experimentation – he *couldn't* be. At that point, in the early '40s, there had only been less than a decade between them; could Professor Travers' experiences have changed him so much from the man he'd been in 1935, when both Professor Travers and Edward were still the same person? Edward couldn't comprehend what had happened to change him so.

But then there was the war; a war he hadn't experienced himself. He'd been too young for most of the First World War, but he'd seen the way war had changed men. So, just how much could the Second World War change a man like Edward Travers?

Edward shook his head. *Focus on the present*, he told himself. If he got out of this, he would have to have a long chat with Anne about her father.

'So, I replicate the experiment and try to make it work for you, and Charlie, probably causing massive loss of life or, at least, thousands of comatose people just like this?'

'That's about the size of it. Although I don't know if we'd bother keeping them alive if it doesn't work.'

Their conversation suddenly came to an end. The guard had re-entered with a cloche and plonked it down near Edward. Despite the situation, he really hoped there was something edible underneath. He was hungry, but the idea of jellied eels really didn't take his fancy.

'Time for dinner and a rest, methinks,' Buttery said. 'Enjoy. We'll need you back working for the cause bright-eyed and bushy-tailed as soon as possible.' He turned to exit but stopped just before he left, with one last thing to say. 'Oh, and Professor...' He grinned. 'If you don't do as we ask...'

Edward was sure Buttery relished in drawing out the tension of his threat.

'...We can always acquire Anne, just as we did you, and force you to experiment on her.' The look on Buttery's face showed he was delighted by the thought. Travers looked at him stony-faced as he departed, waving goodbye. 'Toodle-pip!'

CHAPTER ELEVEN
Post-Mortem Analysis

NOT HAPPY with the idea of letting Captain Barnett know the location of the Madhouse (bad enough that Mr Merrin had been sent there by Samson), Lethbridge-Stewart had used his pull to requisition the use of the mortuary at the Western General Hospital (which, of course, caused no end of headaches for Dr Beauman, who looked upon this as yet another example of the Scots Guards Special Support Group's unwanted intrusion). Captain Lindsay accompanied them, to perform the actual post-mortem, while Anne assisted.

So now, while they went about their business, they had three observers. Lethbridge-Stewart, Barnett and Gary (as Mr Merrin insisted on being called). Far too many for Lethbridge-Stewart's liking, but since Anne had taken Barnett under her wing, there didn't seem to be much that Lethbridge-Stewart could do about it. But he did allow for the fact that Barnett could well provide some invaluable help still. As for Gary… Well, they'd see.

Gary looked on at Lindsay's work, fascinated. Barnett, on the other hand, was keeping his distance, trying to be stoic about the open body in front of them. He didn't know how they could stomach the stench.

'Cause of death was definitely several gunshot wounds,' Lindsay said, pointing at a kidney dish with four bullets. 'Without consulting medical records, I'd say he was a healthy young male up until recently.'

Lethbridge-Stewart noted his use of 'recently'. 'So, something happened before the poor fellow was shot?'

Gary shook his head in disbelief. 'Obviously.'

Lethbridge-Stewart raised an eyebrow. 'I beg your pardon?'

'Can't you see where the flesh and guts have been left hanging? Looks like something attacked him. Hate to think what.'

The man had a point, so Lethbridge-Stewart let his behaviour slide. For now.

'That's definitely something of note,' Anne said, as Lindsay continued with the scalpel. 'Those wounds don't have the clean-cut appearance you would get from a knife or any other sharp instrument.'

'What was it, then? An animal?' Lethbridge-Stewart asked, raising an eyebrow.

Barnett stepped forward with his head slightly bowed and face white as a sheet. 'I've seen this before.' His fingers started trembling. 'Not again! Can't you see what's going on? He did it himself. Just like in the war.' Barnett buried his head in his hands.

Anne put an arm around his shoulder, careful to roll up her bloody sleeve first. 'It's all right,' she said in a soothing tone. 'You can leave the room if you want.'

'No, I have to be a better man than that,' Barnett said, looking up at Anne, who gave him a reassuring smile. 'I need to be stronger. I've been running from this all my life. It's time to face my demons.' He gulped for breath. 'It just all came flooding back. Sorry, everyone.'

'Not at all, Captain,' Lethbridge-Stewart said, as if similar moments happened every day. 'But you're saying this man tore out his insides?'

'Brigadier, Captain Barnett is in shock. Maybe give him a moment. Or two.' Anne kept her arm around him. He managed a weak smile back, in recognition of her thoughtfulness.

'Actually, the screaming woman your men saw had similar injuries,' Gary said, reaching for the inside pocket of his denim jacket. 'They wanted me to show you the photos I took in Newcastle.' He laid them on a nearby bench and Anne, Lethbridge-Stewart and even Barnett gathered around. Lindsay, curious no doubt, placed the scalpel down and joined them. 'It was a shame I couldn't get close-ups of the wounds,' Gary said. 'I had to fire my camera off quickly before she lunged at me.'

Nobody said anything for a while as they looked more closely at the black-and-white prints. They were trying to get a better look at the woman's injuries. Unfortunately, some shots were blurred, due to her moving when the pictures were taken.

'Should have used a faster shutter speed,' Gary noted. 'But there wasn't really time to think about what would make the best photo, given she was attacking us.'

'Some shots are clearer than others,' Anne said, holding one closer to her face for a better look. 'From what I can see, the wounds appear to be consistent with what we have here.' She nodded back to the body on the table. 'And you say the woman in the photographs is still alive?'

'As far as we know,' Gary said. 'She was, before I left to come to your base.'

Barnett, now recovered from his previous shock, spoke up. 'It's only a matter of time. You better hope she doesn't infect anyone else before she pulls apart her body…'

'I think it's become fairly clear the experiment Captain Barnett witnessed during the war is being replicated now,' Lethbridge-Stewart said. 'Definitely here in the United Kingdom. My men have uncovered one major operation. There may be others. Our intelligence certainly points to that.' He let his statement sink in. 'And it appears there may be similar occurrences around the world.'

The enormity of what he was saying wasn't lost on those around him. Gary's face lit up. Anne's face was grim. And Barnett ran to the nearest sink to throw up. Lindsay gave no response at all, he simply returned to his work on the dead body.

'I'm sorry,' Lethbridge-Stewart said, 'but there is a pile of reports on my desk that tie in with what we've uncovered here in the UK to date.' He considered Barnett, now hunched over the sink. 'Captain Barnett, may I suggest a glass of water or sitting down? Oh, and Gary… don't even think about going to the press about this. I'll make it my business to stop you at every corner.'

The photographer was suitably humbled and shoved his hands in his pockets.

Anne managed to sit Barnett down and find him a glass of water, which he quietly sipped.

Gary pulled out more photos from inside his jacket. 'You'll probably want to take a look at these as well.' He placed them next to the other prints on the bench. 'Photos from inside the warehouse. Taken to see if Dr Travers here could see what they were using.'

'Anything useful?' Lethbridge-Stewart said to Anne, happy his ploy on the young photographer had worked.

'Give me a chance.' Thumbing through the photos, she looked up at Gary. 'Are these supposed to be in here? The old man?'

'He told me about the homeless people near him who were being taken and experimented on. It ties in with everything else that's been happening.'

'I don't know if it helps but I might have something.'

Lethbridge-Stewart hadn't been expecting anything from Barnett, given his state, but they all now turned their attention to him. 'There was a rumour floating about during the original experiment.' He took another sip of water.

'You told us about the vampires of the night at the café,' Anne said gently.

Barnett shook his head. 'I already told you. That was a battlefield tale. It led to the experiment here in Britain. This is something else. There were rumblings in the ranks when it was going on.'

Lethbridge-Stewart was more curious now. 'About what?'

Barnett looked him square in the eye. It was obvious the man didn't want to keeping thinking about the past. But it was vital to uncovering what was going on now.

'All right.' Barnett sighed. 'Let me try to remember.'

After a simple meal of stew and beans and managing some (albeit restless) sleep, Edward contemplated his options. He didn't want to be complicit in some horrific worldwide experiment but, then again, it was happening no matter what. And he hadn't forgotten Buttery's threat about Anne. She wasn't his daughter (he'd never returned home to have any children), but she was his blood. The offspring of his wife Margaret, conceived through a union with Professor Travers. His DNA ran through Anne; she (and Alun) was all that was left of Margaret. He didn't want to put her in danger.

His two guards were still present across the room, unflinching. Almost imperceptibly, one of them motioned his head as if to say 'get to work'. Edward shot them a look, picked up a clipboard and went over to one of the patients. There was nothing for it – he had to continue playing along until he could figure a way out or someone rescued him. He hated feeling so helpless but there was nothing else he could do.

Despite operating under duress, Edward wondered if he could at least help the men in front of him. He needed to see if he could bring them out of their comas and what would happen as a result. Definitely a risk, but every experiment, no matter how small, had an element of that. Except men's lives were at stake. And his captors could end up using whatever he discovered for their own horrible plans.

He went back to the bench, scratched his stubble, and went about searching for something that might bring one of the men round. Fortunately, the place had an incredible stock of medical supplies. Stolen, of course. Or bought on the black market. Now, if they could only increase the lighting…

Edward got to work, mixing this and that in test tubes, and checking items under the microscope. He finally settled on a combination of methylphenidate and zolpidem and hoped it would be enough to bring one of the men around. He also hoped his anthropology studies were enough. At the very least, there should be testing and clinical trials before even considering its use on humans. But he didn't have those resources, or the time.

After injecting the solution into the man's upper arm, he waited. A response wouldn't be instant, but should be fairly rapid. After waiting for what (he presumed) was half an hour, he realised it had been ineffective. That was the trouble with comas – no single treatment was ever effective. Back to the drawing board.

Edward quickly glanced at his guards, but they remained impassive.

He didn't want to dismiss the work he'd already done. Sometimes, scientists felt they were on the right path but just needed to tweak or modify their approach. Perhaps the addition of another nonbenzodiazepine would kickstart the awakening process?

It was tricky – too much of any one thing could cause an immediate overdose. He wiped his brow before proceeding a second time, flicking the end of the syringe to remove any air bubbles.

About ten minutes passed and Edward noticed the man's eyes starting to flicker. Ten minutes more and there was some twitching in the man's fingers.

Edward's initial excitement became more and more subdued when there were no further responses and the patient went back to his vegetative state.

It was frustrating but highly unrealistic to expect results so soon. But there had been *some* response, so Edward knew he was on the right track somehow.

'I've tried to put all this out of my mind for years,' Barnett said, obviously pained at having to dredge up the past. 'But, if I remember correctly, there was talk among the men about what happened to Corporal Grayden. At least one of them was witness to what unfolded and, of course, you know how stories can run rampant among soldiers. I was just a private then and some of those more senior to me liked to see how much they could scare those just out of training. As if there wasn't enough to scare young men during the war…'

Barnett had a captive audience. Lethbridge-Stewart, Anne, Captain Lindsay and Gary all gave him the space he needed to tell his tale.

'Apparently, Grayden had been happy to volunteer for the experiment. He wanted to do his duty for King and Country… Usual sort of grandiose stuff they brainwashed you with. The corporal hadn't seen any action with the Allies and had instead been posted to this base in the middle of nowhere, just like the rest of us.'

Taking a moment to breathe, Barnett eyed those around him. He was looking for a sign that he should continue but it was clear he didn't need one.

'The soldier who supposedly saw it all, watched as Grayden made his way to the makeshift medical area and rolled up his sleeve. Whoever was witness to all this was a little puzzled as to why Captain Gampfer was watching on but chose to think nothing more of it. The field medic had been busy mixing various items and then turned to Grayden with a syringe. The soldier, who had hidden himself to see what was going on, managed to catch a glimpse of what was being injected. It was darker than you would expect. Not the usual clear liquids for injections.'

Lethbridge-Stewart looked to Anne to see if this might be out of the ordinary. While she didn't say anything, her expression spoke volumes. For the moment, though, nothing was said so Barnett could finish his recollections.

'Once Grayden received the injection, he fainted. And then Gampfer laughed, calling him "England's latest prince" for some reason.'

Barnett was silent for a moment. 'No one knew what was injected into Grayden, or any of the soldiers, exactly. Other than it was a darker colour. But talk among the men was *blue blood*. I didn't really understand what they were on about, to be honest. Some saw more than others. There were always rumours during the war. At least half of them turned out to be false.'

'Or they were covered up,' Gary said, pointedly.

'Maybe it had something to do with the colour of whatever they were injected with?' Lethbridge-Stewart posited. 'Anne, Captain Lindsay…? Any ideas?'

'It's hard to know what it could mean without specifics,' Anne said. 'My first thought is that it's something to do with copper. Humans have haemoglobin but some animals have hemocyanins instead, used to carry oxygen.'

'But I don't see how that would apply to keeping someone awake,' Lindsay said.

'Me neither.' Anne shrugged.

'Blue blood,' Lethbridge-Stewart said, a thought coming to him. 'It couldn't be…'

Everybody looked at him.

'Well… Surely you've thought of it, too?' Silence.

'The floor is yours, sir,' Lindsay said.

'Where else have you heard the term *blue blood* before?'

'Royalty?' Gary put forward.

'Exactly,' Lethbridge-Stewart said.

'You think they injected the soldiers with blood from the royal family?' Anne asked. 'Surely you realise how preposterous that sounds? Somehow, they got the blood from Buckingham Palace in the first place – during war time, mind you – and then it turns people into some sort of rabid creature that tears itself apart?'

Lethbridge-Stewart knew how far-fetched it appeared. But he would have said that about a lot of things he had experienced in the past few years.

'They were trying anything and everything back then,' Barnett said. 'Nothing would surprise me.'

'Captain, did you ever see or hear of them injecting actual blood into the others?' Anne asked.

Barnett shook his head. 'Hate to disappoint you, but no. I reckon they were mixing things together to see what worked. From the Corporal Grayden story, that sounds like what they were doing. Y'know, to get the best result or reaction.' He looked at Lethbridge-Stewart. 'They would have injected them with dirt if they thought it might have worked.'

'Assuming there's some merit in your theory,' Anne said, looking at Lethbridge-Stewart, 'and I'm not saying there is, but whatever combination of drugs, solutions or even blood was used to keep the soldiers awake must have altered their biochemistry.'

'But to increase their metabolism to such incredible levels…' Lindsay added.

'Yes, Captain?' Lethbridge-Stewart didn't want to be left hanging.

'Well, it's unheard of. Not known in medical science.'

'Yet it happened, as Captain Barnett can attest.'

Barnett slowly stood, now recovered from his earlier spell. 'This theory about blue blood might work fine for Britain, but what about the rumours of similar experiments by the Nazis and the Red Army? Where would they have got royal blood from?'

It was a good point, and no one seemed to have an answer. Until Gary almost exploded with excitement.

'Hang on! If I remember my history from school, didn't many of Queen Victoria's children marry into royal families across Europe? Maybe that's how the experiments were done elsewhere?' Gary was evidently quite pleased with himself, then mildly deflated when no one cottoned on. 'You talked about blue blood, which has to come from royalty. There are royal families all across Europe who have ties back to Britain.'

Lethbridge-Stewart nodded. 'What do you think, Anne?'

She pondered it a moment. 'It's somewhere to start.'

'Good. A step forward is better than a step back.' Lethbridge-Stewart looked at the people assembled around him. 'Now, what's next?'

What seemed like hours passed. There were so many combinations and variables, and Edward was just one man. But he remained focused, trying one thing after another. The patients responded with more eye-flickering, more finger-twitching and even the occasional leg bounce. He kept going back, building on each concoction, hopefully creating a solution that would work.

He found the immense mental concentration extremely tiring. Even though he'd been recording his methodology, he was having trouble remembering what worked and what didn't. But he pushed himself to continue, forcing aside any resentment at being made to do the work.

He went through the process of injecting yet another syringe into a patient. By now, he was used to the eyes and hands moving, so didn't think any more of it when this man reacted in the same way. But then his head lolled slightly from side to side. His eyes opened and peered up into Edward's face. Dazed and confused, he looked around the room. At the other patients, the two guards, Edward's workspace and into the low-level lighting above him. He coughed and gagged, as if speaking was beyond him.

'Take it easy,' Edward said, trying a soothing tone. 'You've been asleep for quite a while. But there's nothing to be frightened of.'

Before Edward had time to react, the man leapt out of bed and went for his throat. At the same time, a horrible piercing scream shot out of the man's mouth.

Falling to the ground, Edward could see the man's face changing. In almost an instant, the youthful complexion changed to an old and haggard appearance. The man was falling and about to land on Edward. He quickly put his arm up in an effort to cushion himself, but the expected heavy landing never came.

Instead, the man fell apart into dust, completely desiccated.

Edward coughed as he inhaled the minute particles, wiping the dust away from his eyes and clothes.

I've just inhaled the remnants of a human.

He got up off the floor and noticed his guards had obviously felt the need to move closer and draw their weapons.

Edward ignored them and contemplated what had happened for a moment. Bringing the man round seemingly saw his age catch up with him and then go beyond it, into old age. No wonder they kept the men in their comas.

'Oh, tough luck!' Buttery had appeared from nowhere. 'Still, plenty more where he came from, eh?' He motioned towards the remaining patients.

Angered, Edward thundered back, 'Can't you see how dangerous this is? And you want to do all of this again?'

'Trial and error, Professor, trial and error.' Buttery grinned inanely back at him, his red beard making him look even more maniacal. 'As a scientist, you know that. And remember, you started all this.' He clapped his hands. 'Back to it, choppity-chop!'

Edward glared at him. A man was dead and he didn't appreciate Buttery's cavalier attitude one bit. In fact, Edward felt like strangling him.

'Come now, that attitude won't get you anywhere. Or do we really have to bring Anne here to join you?' Buttery turned on his heel and disappeared as quickly as he had arrived.

This time, the other guard nodded slightly at Edward, indicating he should get back to work.

Trung Sĩ Nhất (Sergeant First Class) Luu was ready. It was a fact of war. He had to be ready for anything. But even more so now since being a part of LựcLượng 66, otherwise known as the Tiger Scouts. He touched his Smith & Wesson Model 27, almost unaware, as if the subtle tactile sense gave him an unconscious reassurance that he was in control.

He eyed the captured enemy prisoners in front of him, stuck behind the fence. Luu had been part of the Việt Nam Cộng-sản once, before defecting. But now in the midst of the horrors and atrocities around him, there was a much bigger cause to consider. He was a small part, he knew, but his role could provide valuable information and tactical advantage to something on a global scale. Pity those around him focused on the north and south of his own country. Not even the Americans were thinking this big. They had no idea what he was really up to – and now he was doing it right under their noses.

Fortunately, Luu had rallied others to his cause, under the guise of efforts and practicalities for the current war. He called over Thượng Sĩ Nhất (Sergeant Major) Tran.

'Put them in the holes. Tie them down and get your men to inject them. Take whatever force is required.'

Tran nodded and turned about.

Luu didn't flinch when he heard the prisoners screaming. Neither did he react when he heard weapons being fired. Tran, or another under his command, evidently had to deal with a troublemaker or two. No matter. They had plenty of test subjects. And if they ran out, they could capture more prisoners. Failing that, he would get Tran to pick out any of his men showing signs of subordination. Luu allowed a little smile. It was all for the greater good. A better solution for the world. And he could do it under the cover of the current war.

Days and nights passed. The jungle humidity remained oppressive while thunder echoed across the sky. Men screamed from the holes. Luu didn't care. He wanted a report from Tran, who had appeared from the dense foliage of vines, fern and stiff bamboo.

'Injections have been continuing,' he said, his face dripping with perspiration. Tran's uniform was also soaked through, but he remained as disciplined as ever. 'Everything proceeding as ordered.'

'And none of the prisoners have slept since we began?'

'Correct.'

Good, thought Luu. If the experiment continued as planned, he could report back to his masters. Although getting a communication out of the country was difficult at present. Somehow, he would get the message to them, no matter how many lives had to be lost.

'Continue. Report any changes.'

Tran once again turned about and left the clearing to make his way back through the thick rainforest.

Useful soldier, mused Luu. *Must try to keep this one alive.*

Night came. A horrifying howl pierced through the air. The jungle was always hot, sultry and dangerous. And full of unidentified sounds that made even the most experienced soldier extremely wary. Luu reached for his Smith & Wesson, alert but not alarmed. He was sure this particular noise was something to do with the experiment. Tran would have the matter in hand. But he would do well to keep the prisoners quiet. Luu expected a shot to soon ring out to stop the howling. But it never came.

Instead, his tent flap was torn open and one of the prisoners lunged for him, wild-eyed and savage. A predator on the prowl.

Luu didn't even have time to consider how the man had escaped from his hole. He fired off bullets in rapid succession. The prisoner barely flinched as the first shot of lead entered him. But Luu's repeating shots did slow him down, eventually causing the man to fall.

Surely he is dead now? thought Luu.

Calling for Tran as he moved to the body, Luu finally ventured a look. He hadn't been able to see much in the dark. But now, with his flashlight casting an eerie illumination, the full horror of what had befallen the prisoner was clear.

He'd seen many atrocities during the war and some of the most horribly mutilated and decaying bodies. But this was unlike anything he'd ever seen. The red eyes gave away the man's internal angst and torment but, down the side of his body, it was as if an animal had attacked him. The wounds didn't look like they had come from a bear, tiger or water buffalo. On closer inspection, Luu was sure the man had attacked *himself*, pulling out his insides in the process.

Perhaps it was a result of the experiment. Either that, or madness, or maybe even a desperate attempt to escape somehow.

Before he could think about it further, Luu thought he saw

something move in the corner of his eye. A moment later, he was knocked to the ground and looking into the eyes of Tran.

The same red eyes his previous assailant had.

Tran let out an almighty shriek, rammed Luu downwards as hard as he could and then tightened his hands around his superior's throat...

CHAPTER TWELVE
At the Ready

THE QUIET street looked slightly ridiculous now that it was full of military vehicles and personnel. Partly because nothing much ever happened there. Captain Miles had been quick to lockdown the area, getting his men to evacuate people from their homes into a local community hall. There was some resistance from the more elderly residents, who hadn't been outside their humble abodes for years. But the Army presence took their minds back to the war and many widows were charmed by the handsome young men in the Fifth. They used a gas leak as a cover story – as they often did – and explained the military were needed in case of a potential explosion.

Meanwhile, Lethbridge-Stewart and his team came across a shocking scene when they arrived at the warehouse entrance. They were confronted with two dead bodies, their insides torn open and hanging out, just like the victim on the post-mortem table. Knowing looks were exchanged. Something had gone seriously awry since hearing from Samson.

It was only going to be worse inside, Lethbridge-Stewart knew it.

'Captain, maybe you should go back to the Land Rover and join Gary. I can't imagine this will be pleasant for you in any way, shape or form.' Barnett nodded his assent. 'Anne, you too. This place isn't safe.'

She moved to protest but relented. 'What about Bill? Is he in there?'

Lethbridge-Stewart looked at the men around him, waiting for a command. 'I'm sure Bishop, Samson, Kenworthy and all the rest are in there somewhere. Either that, or they have got away to safety.'

'I hope so,' Anne said, quietly. She left with Barnett to rejoin Gary.

Lethbridge-Stewart cleared his thoughts, put his gun at the ready and braced himself to go into the warehouse. The rest of the men were in similar positions.

'Only shoot if you have to,' he reminded them. 'Try to maim instead of kill. I'm still hopeful we can find a way of stopping this.' He indicated the two poor souls on the ground. It wasn't their fault this had happened to them. A terrible experiment had caused it. 'But don't become victims, either. From what RSM Ware said, the effect can be passed on if they attack or bite you. Use your best judgement and be prepared for anything.'

Lethbridge-Stewart hoped that was enough to ready them. He nodded his command. Corporal Sanford kicked the door open (should anyone be lurking behind it) and led the way into the main entrance. Soldier after soldier came after him, looking left and right for any sign of a possible threat. Several tripped over bodies on the ground, just like the ones outside. Others were stunned into paralysis as men and women dragged themselves along the floor, screaming and hollering, with all manner of organs and insides trailing behind them. Some of Lethbridge-Stewart's men didn't have the intestinal fortitude for what they saw, and several breakfasts were brought up, adding to the overall bloody mess and horror. It was like someone who didn't know what they were doing had been let loose in an abattoir.

Lethbridge-Stewart spotted the military uniforms on some of the victims. Some of Kenworthy's men had not been so lucky. The effect had been passed on to them and they had torn themselves apart, too. But there was no time to mourn, no time to be shocked and certainly no time to be violently ill.

'Stay alert! People could still be alive and unaffected. And we could still come under attack!'

The men started branching off down various corridors and through different doors. Screeches echoed through the building, but it was impossible to pinpoint their source.

Coming to a room full of medical equipment, Lethbridge-Stewart and Sergeant Langdon were greeted by a body strewn halfway through the door into the corridor.

Private Christiner.

Another one of his own. Lethbridge-Stewart bent down gently and closed the man's eyes, giving him a slight dignity in his death. How many more was he going to find? Two young privates had been tailing him and Langdon, and it was obvious they had known the young chap. They'd probably been through training together. The two didn't say anything; the look in their eyes was enough.

'Let's try to stop any more of this happening, eh, lads?' Langdon said. 'Come on, let's keep going and look for the living. That's the best thing you can do to honour his life right now.'

Lethbridge-Stewart decided to stay where he was, leaving the privates to the command of their sergeant. He spotted a body in one of the beds and decided to check if the person was alive or dead. As he got closer, the blood drained from his face.

It was Bishop.

Forcing himself to take a closer look, Lethbridge-Stewart could see the man was restrained and in extremely bad shape. The blood-soaked sheets were a mere precursor to his injuries. A bullet wound to his leg and a large portion of his left torso exposed, leaving a gaping wound.

An image of finding Bill's bloodied body in Vaar's operating room rushed to his mind. Lethbridge-Stewart shook it away, focusing on the now. But he still couldn't help but think, *This can't help but aggravate his old wound.*

At least Bishop was alive. He was asleep and breathing, not howling like the others. But it looked like an extremely restless sleep. Lethbridge-Stewart had to get Bishop to Captain Lindsay as soon as possible; he'd be able to repair any damage done.

'Brigadier, get down!' a voice cried.

Instinctively, Lethbridge-Stewart dived to the floor.

Gunfire rang out, the sound so close he knew bullets were whizzing past his head. He chanced a glance upwards and saw a haggard old man lurching forward. A hideous piercing cry suddenly emerged from the man's throat. More shots were fired. It took some effort, but the man finally fell.

Dusting himself off, Lethbridge-Stewart was about to say thank you to the men who had warned him – but there wasn't time. He barely managed to scramble for his gun as two more victims came around the corner. They were in military uniform but not as affected as some of the others.

Lethbridge-Stewart and his men readied themselves to fire again. And that's when he spotted it.

They were from Lethbridge-Stewart's own team.

Anne knew she was in the Land Rover for her own safety but that didn't cure her feelings of wanting to do something practical. Barnett was looking absently out over the door. Gary was peering over her shoulder, looking at the photos she was thumbing through. She'd already gone over them, so she didn't really know why she was looking at them again.

'Do you know what any of the equipment is?' Gary asked eagerly.

'Mainly standard medical devices to measure heart rates and so on, to check the body is in working order. This EEG is a bit advanced.' She noted Gary's puzzled look and Barnett looking over. 'An electroencephalogram, which measures brain waves of sleep and wakefulness. Not sure what this device is...' Anne pointed to equipment in another photo. 'Maybe it's for magnetoencephalography? The University of Illinois was experimenting with that a few years back.'

'More brain stuff?' Barnett offered, apparently more interested now.

'It's a technique for mapping brain activity by recording magnetic fields produced by electrical currents occurring naturally in the brain, using very sensitive magnetometers.'

'Gone over my head. For all I know, you just swore at me.'

Anne gave a little smirk, happy Barnett wasn't always doom and gloom.

'Did you hear that?' Gary quickly turned his head to the warehouse. It was a redundant question. They all had. The sound of gunfire. Repeatedly. 'That can't be good.'

'They're probably just containing the situation,' Barnett explained, looking at Anne. 'Standard military tactic.'

'Thank you, Captain, but this isn't my first raid.'

Not to say she wasn't concerned about Bill, of course, but she trusted Lethbridge-Stewart.

She looked away from the photographs, back to the warehouse and stopped short. A rifle was pointing right at them.

Lethbridge-Stewart didn't want to shoot his own men. Not unless he had to, anyway. While some of Miles' team had succumbed and had to be killed, this lot didn't appear to be too far gone. And the fact Bill was still alive, despite being in much worse condition, gave him hope it might be reversible – if his body could just hold on long enough.

On that basis, Lethbridge-Stewart called for his colleagues to quickly retreat and hoped the infected would leave Bishop alone, given he was already affected.

Lethbridge-Stewart and the few men with him needed backup.

He could see why they were nicknamed vampires back in Barnett's day. They weren't vampires in the traditional sense, but they certainly had the capability to prey on people and pass on their repulsive traits. But whereas vampires supposedly lived forever, these humans ultimately killed themselves by tearing out their insides. Some sort of insanity was at work behind all this.

'Brigadier, we need back up!'

Lethbridge-Stewart was making his way back to the building's entrance. He turned around to see Kenworthy panting.

'Yes, I know, Lieutenant. Where do you think I'm heading?'

Kenworthy caught up with him as he reached the door. 'No, you don't understand, sir. The ringleader here. She escaped.'

'How did she…?' Lethbridge-Stewart shook his head. Now wasn't the time.

'She said something about werewolves, sir. That's what RSM Ware and the others told me.'

Lethbridge-Stewart hesitated for a moment. Vampires, and now werewolves? Was it Halloween and somebody had forgot to tell him? Kenworthy could see the look on Lethbridge-Stewart's face.

'That's all she would say. The word werewolf over and over again. Maybe it's a code word or something?'

'Let's hope so. I know only one person who's encountered a werewolf before, and that didn't end well for a lot of people.' Lethbridge-Stewart nodded abruptly.

Outside, ten men, armed to the teeth, were waiting for them. In the middle, a woman was holding Anne, bound and gagged, a gun to her cheek.

Instinctively Lethbridge-Stewart aimed his weapon at the woman. But the look of horror in Anne's eyes was enough to convince him otherwise. He lowered his gun and indicated Kenworthy should do the same.

CHAPTER THIRTEEN
The Road Less Travelled

THE TRUCK had rumbled along, going to goodness knows where, for over an hour before stopping. At first Lethbridge-Stewart thought they'd reached their destination, but it soon became clear it was a brief respite in the journey. At least for their captors. Their guards jumped out of the back, and Lethbridge-Stewart and the others listened to the sound of movement outside.

'What do you think, sir?' Kenworthy asked. 'An opportune moment?'

'Let's not be hasty, Lieutenant.'

Although Lethbridge-Stewart agreed they should try to escape, part of him wanted to find out who was behind the disappearance and experiments, and he suspected that playing the role of prisoner would lead to the answer. But at the same time, he didn't wish to have Gary in any further danger. Anne could handle herself – she'd proved herself many times in the past couple of years. Barnett, despite his obvious emotional issues, was still a trained soldier. But Gary was a civilian. Taking him on the raid was bad enough… And that was entirely on Lethbridge-Stewart's shoulders.

Since he was closest to the flap in the tarpaulin, Lethbridge-Stewart shuffled along the bench, made difficult by the bindings that limited his movements. He managed to get his nose to move the flap enough to take a glimpse outside.

And for his troubles a rifle was aimed directly at him.

'Ah, just getting a whiff of fresh air, old chap,' he said, before hastily shuffling back up the bench to where the rest of the captives sat.

'Did you learn anything?' Anne asked, not bothering to hide her mirth, despite the seriousness of the situation.

'A surprising amount actually.'

Everybody looked at him expectantly.

'They're more trained than I thought, for one. I didn't recognise the man with the rifle, which means they've probably changed the guards. Presumably not everybody is cleared for wherever we're going.'

'Wherever that is,' Gary said.

'Well, I have a beat on that, too. I saw a signpost a short way up the road. Maidens Port, four miles.' Lethbridge-Stewart stopped and looked at each of them, stopping on Anne. 'Mean anything?'

Anne thought about it. Shrugged. 'Obviously it does to you.'

'It was in a file I read a while ago, shortly before you joined the Fifth actually, when I was looking up the outfit that preceded ours.'

'Research on the—'

'Precisely.' *On the Doctor.* Although Lethbridge-Stewart didn't want anybody else in the truck knowing about him, especially not a wannabe journalist. 'Anyway, Maidens Port started out as a much smaller place called Maidens Bay, before becoming Maidens Point in the late '30s. What's most interesting, is that it is supposedly the place where Dracula came ashore in Stoker's novel.'

'Wouldn't have thought that would be your kind of book, Alistair.'

'It pays to diversify, Anne,' he returned. 'Which means we're near Whitby. Ironic, or perhaps intentional, bearing in mind that the results of the experiments are sometimes called *vampires.*'

'There must be more to it than that, sir,' Kenworthy said. 'It can't be just for irony.'

'No. But there is an old naval base there. Disused, no doubt.'

'Or not,' Barnett said. 'As the case probably is now.'

'Quite.'

Silence for a moment.

'What good does that do us?' Gary asked.

'Right now, nothing,' Lethbridge-Stewart said. 'But it may come in useful later, if one of us is able to escape.'

Gary nodded, then shuddered. 'What do you think they'll do with us?'

'Interrogation, then they'll force the experiment on us I imagine,' Kenworthy said. Noticing Lethbridge-Stewart's scowl, he immediately stopped talking.

'What about Bill?' Anne asked, clearly making the most of the sudden pause in the conversation. 'Did anybody see him in the warehouse?'

'Um, yes,' Lethbridge-Stewart said, turning to look at her. 'He was unconscious. Wounded, but essentially okay. I was going to bring him out, but…'

'You all got attacked.'

'Yes.'

Anne nodded, taking it in.

'There's nothing we can do for him now,' Lethbridge-Stewart told her. 'We'll just have to hope that some of our men survived. If not, then Captain Miles and his men will turn up at the warehouse when we don't report in.'

Anne closed her eyes. 'Let's hope they're in time.'

He looked at the men, all of them now uncomfortable by Anne's obvious pain. It was time to change the topic, give Anne something else to focus on.

'What do you make of this werewolf business?' he said, looking directly at Kenworthy. 'You said that's the only thing the woman in charge would reveal?'

'Werewolves?' Anne opened her eyes.

'That's what she said, miss,' Kenworthy said. 'I don't think it's literal, though.'

'Good. Once was enough.'

Lethbridge-Stewart explained. 'Miss Travers here was the person I was referring to, Lieutenant.'

'You met a werewolf?' Kenworthy's eyes widened in awe.

'Yes, before your time,' Lethbridge-Stewart said.

'Before all our times, actually. Before any of us were even born,' Anne added. 'In 1823.'

Gary and Barnett were both about to say something, but Lethbridge-Stewart silenced them with a look.

'Never mind that. I think Kenworthy is right; it might be a code word or some such.'

Barnett flexed his shoulders as best he could with his hands bound behind his back. 'It could be the name of an organisation. In fact, it probably is.'

The others looked at him, curiously.

'Go on, Captain,' Lethbridge-Stewart said.

'Most put it down to Nazi propaganda. But right near the end of the war, there was talk of an outfit called Werwolf. Without the second e. German spelling, probably. Supposedly set up to be a secondary guerrilla operation in case the main Nazi force fell. It was in response to the Allies' success at Normandy.

There was even a Radio Werwolf. I remember reading about it in the paper years ago.'

'What did the articles say?' Gary asked.

'Just that the radio broadcasts were telling every German to stand their ground and die against the Allies. The motto was *conquer or die.* It was said they recruited from the SS and Hitler Youth.'

'But the Nazis did fall,' Anne pointed out.

'I know. The idea was for Werwolf to carry on the Nazi ideals but remain in secret. As far as anyone knew, Werwolf ended pretty much the same time as the war did. There were a few scattered terrorist attacks before the Nazis surrendered, but the Yanks ultimately made some arrests right at the end. Officially, that was the end of Werwolf.'

'You think differently, Captain?' Lethbridge-Stewart didn't like where this was heading. But it did start to make certain things add up.

'I'm sure the history books put this down to Goebbels' propaganda. But I've spoken to more than one person over the years – in a pub, admittedly – who claim Werwolf attacks continued for months or even years after the war. A United States police operation was blown up in Bremen a month after Germany surrendered and a Soviet commander was assassinated. And there were plenty of other terrorist attacks for a few years after. No one really reported on them, so they were kind of forgotten about.'

'Yes, but those could have been isolated incidents,' Kenworthy said. 'Is there any real evidence that Werwolf was behind them? You don't know all those things were connected in any way.'

'But that's not to say they *might* have been,' Anne pointed out.

'It is possible,' Lethbridge-Stewart asked, 'that Werwolf is in operation, even after all this time?'

Barnett looked at the floor of the truck and shrugged. 'I'm just telling you what I've heard over the years. They could just be tales from old drunks, like myself. But after seeing the experiment Anne's father was involved in, I tend to think anything's possible.'

Anne looked at him apologetically.

Gary had been listening closely, evidently fascinated by the possibilities that could stem from Barnett's story. 'But why would they go quiet and disappear, only to re-appear again now?'

'A lack of means, I expect.' Lethbridge-Stewart had enough trouble with his own resources and his was a funded organisation. 'Everything usually comes down to money. Plus, look at the state of the Nazis when the war ended. It would take years, even decades, to build up their forces. Then imagine having to do it in secret with the world continually on watch for something like that ever happening again.'

Kenworthy digested everything that had been said. 'So why pipe up now?'

'If all this is true, that's the scary part,' Anne said. 'For Werwolf to be this active, I'd say they're just about ready to start their main plan of action.'

It took a moment for Anne's words to sink in.

Gary looked around at all of them. 'You mean here in England?'

'No, Gary.' Barnett gritted his teeth. 'She means across the world.'

The photographer's eyes widened at the thought. Lethbridge-Stewart looked knowingly at Anne and Kenworthy.

Guards climbed into the back, and the conversation ended there, leaving each of them with their own thoughts. Speculating on what it could all mean.

The truck resumed on its way to Maidens Port.

They were all bundled out of the back of the truck, prodded with rifles in their backs, and quickly marched into a building. There wasn't much time to take in the surroundings but, as Lethbridge-Stewart had worked out, they were definitely on the coast. Maidens Port, near Whitby.

Lethbridge-Stewart, Barnett, Kenworthy and Gary were all marched in a different direction, much to Anne's dismay. She was now on her own with a lone guard behind her, taking her through the building. Her mind raced furiously, trying to dismiss each imagined scenario as she conjured them up. They obviously had something else in mind for her.

Eventually, they reached a dimly lit room. She could see beds on the other side and what appeared to be patients lying in them, hooked up to medical apparatus. Anne had a feeling this was the sleep experiment in action; more students and homeless people who had fallen victim to Werwolf's scam. Blood rushed to her cheeks in anger.

This was it. And she'd heard of the result. Turning people into rampaging monsters, deprived of sleep and reason.

From what she could see, these patients weren't moving. If anything, they were the complete antithesis of what she'd heard about the experiments. She was suddenly prodded and pushed forward by her guard, further into the room.

Out of seemingly nowhere, a ginger man with a ginger beard was in front of her, smiling. His red follicles were really quite astonishing. Anne admonished herself for such a nonsensical thought while being in danger. Humans really did have the strangest reactions in times of stress.

'Ah, Dr Anne Travers,' he said, an evil glint in his eye. 'I must say this is an absolute pleasure! Welcome!'

'I can't see getting caught, being manhandled and marched around with a gun in my back is in any way pleasurable,' Anne returned acidly.

The man bowed a little. 'My apologies, our methods can be a little unorthodox at times. But you're here now and that's the important thing.'

'Not by choice.'

'Be that as it may, you are needed. By us, and… Drumroll, please!' He looked around as if the imaginary staccato beats were playing, waiting for a special guest to walk out. 'Professor Edward Travers!'

Ted Travers was pushed out by two guards, causing him to almost trip over his own feet. A wave of mixed emotions surged through Anne as she took in the man before her. She hadn't seen him for a while, and she was still not used to this man who looked like the father she had known when she was a child. Anne wasn't sure how to respond. Surely they must have known he wasn't the real Professor Travers – or at least not the man who had built up his eclectic career for the past thirty-odd years? But then she remembered the way he – Ted! – had been passing himself off as her father.

Those chickens have come home to roost, she thought and, with a sigh, decided she'd better play along. For now.

'Father!' she said, forcing down the pain she felt at calling him that. 'What are you doing here?' She went to run to him but her guard stopped her.

Ted looked back with curious surprise in his eyes. 'I see you've met this buttered-toast fellow, or whatever he calls himself.'

'Dr Jarrod Buttery,' the man said with a sniff, clearly irritated at the insult.

Ted glowered at him. In that respect he was like her father. Neither suffered fools gladly. 'There was no need to bring Anne into this.'

'Oh, but there was, Professor Travers,' Buttery said with glee. 'You're not getting anywhere with your work on the patients, so we brought along *Dr* Travers as an added incentive.'

Anne looked across at the patients in their beds and tried putting two and two together. 'Are they forcing you to do those terrible sleep experiments here, Father?'

Before Ted could answer, Buttery was at it again. 'Of course, you would have been about five at the time, wouldn't you? And I guess he never told you some of the things he got up to during the war. Well, Anne, today's your lucky day!' He made a grand gesture towards the patients. 'These men are the result of what your father did. They responded extremely badly to the experiment he was involved in. And he didn't know what to do with them, beyond this.'

Thinking back to the classified report she had read, Anne remembered there was no mention of what ultimately happened to the volunteers. Only what Captain Barnett had relayed to her and Lethbridge-Stewart. Even the captain was at a loss as to their whereabouts after her father's involvement.

Buttery motioned for the guards to lead their prisoners closer to the beds. 'They've been like this ever since the war.' He grinned maniacally at both of them, looking rather pleased with himself, as if he had a secret another child didn't.

'But they all look like they're in their twenties.' Anne hadn't wanted to say anything but even she was surprised.

'Don't they just?' Buttery came up and smiled right into her face. 'Seems Daddy caused an interesting side effect. And, one wonders, if somehow he didn't perfect something similar on himself?'

It was a pointed question, one Ted simply turned his nose up at.

So, that's it, Anne thought. *They think he's somehow slowed down his ageing through some sleep experiment.* Anne shook her head at the idea of it. If Buttery believed that, then he was further gone than she'd first thought.

'And you want to harness that in some way?' Anne asked, choosing to ignore Buttery's question too.

He walked away, dismissing her with a flick of his hand. 'Not in the slightest. We want him to make the original experiment work. If he can unravel what he did before, that might help us with the other experiments we're replicating.'

Anne took in what Buttery was saying. Ted was in trouble. He hadn't performed any such experiment. He'd skipped the entire war – indeed, the past three decades – through the wonders of time travel. No wonder he was having no success here. Ted was as much in the dark as Anne was – more so, probably.

'The experiment was a failure then and it will be a failure now,' Ted said defiantly.

'But you have so much more technology and research at your disposal now, Professor.' Buttery leered, a hint of malevolence now present. 'Despite that, we thought you could use a little help.' He beamed his ginger-bearded grin once again. 'Guards, make sure Travers does what he's told.'

Anne looked at Buttery, confused.

'You're going to be such a big help,' Buttery said, as the guards pulled Anne over to a chair, forcing her down and quickly putting restraints on her. 'Professor Travers, we thought you could use another experimental subject. And if you fail this time, well, it's your daughter who will suffer the consequences. What a wonderful incentive, eh?'

CHAPTER FOURTEEN
Captive Thoughts

IT ALL happened so fast.

Samson pumped bullets into the screaming woman they'd encountered only days before. She lunged over him, shrieking like all the others. He didn't know how she was still alive; her insides were now fully torn open, and she even had an eyeball hanging from her face. There was a river of blood wherever she went. Samson couldn't see how there would be any hope for her, even if the process could somehow be reversed eventually. Her quality of life, once she was stitched up and recovered (and who knew how long that would take), would be next to zero. Samson told himself he was putting her out of her misery. Her misery now, and in years to come. It didn't make the task any easier. She had fallen victim to an experiment; a procedure done without her consent. But there was nothing he could do. He had to protect himself and others around him from both her and the infection, because it *was* infectious… They'd learned that much at least.

Other thoughts plagued Samson's mind. Ones he could simply not allow himself to think about. Bill, laid up in the bed in the warehouse, succumbing to the infection. Even if Bill could hang on, what was the likelihood of a cure?

One thing at a time, Samson told himself. Backup was needed urgently. He had to contact Captain Miles for reinforcements.

Samson found a room to hide in, while he considered his options, after picking his way through a room laden with fallen soldiers and experiment victims. The amount of blood was enough to make even the sturdiest man turn; the horror of mangled bodies and their innards as bad as the worst slaughter on a battlefield.

He flinched as he felt the nub of a gun in his back.

'Drop your weapon.' The voice was female.

Samson did as he was told and raised his hands. He then

turned around, slowly and cautiously. He recognised her instantly – it was the ringleader of few words. She would have been an attractive woman if she hadn't let bitterness take over her face. There was a harshness to it; definitely cold and calculating.

'How are you? Miss… Werewolf, wasn't it?' Samson knew he probably shouldn't antagonise her, given a gun was pointing at him, but he couldn't help himself.

'Don't be an idiot,' she spat back. 'Werwolf is what you're up against.'

Samson considered his options. He could still hear gunshots and screaming ringing around the building as the battle continued. He didn't have long, he could tell, and this could well be his only chance to learn vital details about what was going on.

'And what is Werwolf, exactly?'

The woman sneered at him, her finger poised on the trigger of her gun. 'As if I'm going to tell you.'

It wasn't the first time Samson had been defenceless at the end of a loaded weapon. He stood his ground and tried a different tack. 'Where have you taken Brigadier Lethbridge-Stewart?'

'Refer to my last comment.'

She wasn't going to budge. He was at a disadvantage and had no bargaining chip. But he needed *something* out of her.

'Don't move.' A male voice cut in on the conversation.

Samson had been so wrapped up in trying to save the day himself that he'd forgotten there were other good, solid soldiers going about their mission. But the last person he expected it to be was Miller, fire in his eyes and ready to pounce.

Samson felt a little bit of pride.

Miller's firearm was trained squarely at the woman. Samson saw the flicker of annoyance wash over her face.

'Thank you, Private,' Samson said, his hands still in the air. 'Now we're at a stalemate, perhaps you could be a bit more talkative?' he said to the woman. 'We could start with where Lethbridge-Stewart has been taken, maybe?'

The woman remained silent.

'How long before another of my side comes in? Where will you be then?'

'You face the same dilemma.'

'And if one of your out-of-control experiments ends up in here, it could go either way.'

Before the woman responded, two shots were fired. One came from Miller's gun, into the woman's leg. The other was from her gun as she collapsed, missing Samson completely. He took the opportunity and, without missing a beat, kicked the gun out of the prostrate woman's hand. Miller ran forward and pointed his weapon directly at her head.

'Where's Lethbridge-Stewart?' he screamed.

Samson had never seen such rage in the man. And he'd been smart enough not to kill the woman outright, so they still might get information from her.

The woman was gasping, in shock at what had happened. She glared at both of them with pure venom. 'You're going to kill me anyway, so why should I tell you?'

Samson looked nervously at the door. There was so much going on in the warehouse, the sounds were likely just part of the overall sound of the other gunfire. But one of those screaming travesties was likely to descend upon them soon.

Miller reached down, pulled the woman's hair back and put his face into hers. 'Perhaps some extended torture would do the trick?'

Samson hoped the private was bluffing. They were still soldiers after all and when (if?) this was all over, he didn't want to have to report him. But there was an evil relish to Miller's voice that unsettled Samson.

Fortunately, it didn't go any further. Miller's threat had been enough.

'Maidens Port,' the woman blurted and then lapsed into unconsciousness.

'Come on, Miller, we've got to get out of here.'

'No.'

Samson looked at the young man, puzzled. 'What do you mean, *no*? That's an order, Private!'

Miller looked back at his commanding officer, determination etched across his face. 'Only one of us needs to get out. I can stay and fight.'

'Are you serious? You're fighting a losing battle until I can get reinforcements here.'

'You're going to need someone to give you cover to help you get out.'

Samson couldn't fault the private's reasoning.

'Private Miller, you…' Then it dawned on him. 'Christiner. Private, this is not the way to honour him.'

'This is more than about honour, sir,' Miller said. 'Andrew and I… We were friends. Sir. Like you and Captain Bishop.'

Samson understood. He thought of the lengths he would go to for both Bill and Alistair. Samson nodded and picked up the woman's gun.

'You've become a fine soldier, Miller.'

Lethbridge-Stewart looked at the others.

Like him, Kenworthy, Barnett, and Gary still had their hands tied behind their back and were sitting on the floor. They had been unceremoniously thrown into a room by their captors and were now squashed up against each other. It obviously wasn't designed for four people but worked fine as a holding cell. There were no windows; only a door – and it was firmly locked. Lethbridge-Stewart had tried ramming his shoulder into it and giving it a kick as soon as he had the chance. There were probably armed guards on the other side, anyway.

Not that Lethbridge-Stewart hadn't been in this position before.

'So, what are we going to do?' Gary asked hopefully, albeit not confidently. The young man didn't have the experience of the others and was fishing for some type of reassurance.

'Not much we can do,' Lethbridge-Stewart replied. 'I'm sure you can see we're at an extreme disadvantage here.'

'But you military types always have something tucked away, right?' Gary nudged Kenworthy as he spoke, looking for any signs of possible hope.

Kenworthy shook his head. 'They confiscated everything when we were captured. We had the full rubdown. Anything concealed was found pretty quickly.'

Barnett chose not to say anything, but shook his head and muttered quietly to himself. 'No hope then,' he said, finally.

Lethbridge-Stewart was trying to maintain a steady hand. The last thing they needed was someone having a breakdown. 'You're forgetting about Captain Miles and his men.'

'But they don't know where we've been taken.'

Lethbridge-Stewart didn't know how to respond to Barnett's comment, so he left it.

'Surely we can try to escape?' Now Gary was trying to rally everybody. 'I mean, people have got out of tighter situations before, haven't they?'

Kenworthy shot him down in flames. 'I enjoy Steve McQueen movies as much as anyone, but reality is somewhat different to the silver screen.'

Lethbridge-Stewart managed a weak smile. 'I admire your spirit, Gary, but I already tried the door. Unless you have a suggestion? One that won't get us all killed?'

The young photographer rolled his eyes. 'Come on, can't we at least untie each other? I want to check my inside pockets.'

'Guards won't be too pleased if they come in and find we're loose,' Barnett said, ever the pessimist.

'I doubt they'd care very much one way or another,' Lethbridge-Stewart retorted. 'They're armed and we're not.'

'That's assuming they're guarding the door,' Gary said pointedly. 'Come on, let's get these ropes or whatever they are off us.'

Much to-ing and fro-ing followed, as they shuffled around as best they could, and were soon back to back. The room was cramped enough as it was, and their new positions didn't help the matter. Everyone muttered under their breath as they fumbled to untie each other, losing and re-gaining their grip, falling awkwardly from sitting positions and then having to start again. After numerous attempts and much grunting and sweating, they were all loose.

While the others were catching their breath, Gary started poking around inside his denim jacket. He, too, had been frisked by the guards but it looked like they had missed something.

'I don't know if any of this is useful in any way,' he said, ferreting through his inside pockets and hidden flaps of material that had cushioned anything hidden. 'But I thought I'd show it to you all the same.' He placed several items in the middle of the group and they all craned awkwardly to see.

'Miniature lightbulbs?' Kenworthy looked at Lethbridge-Stewart, who responded with a humour-him expression in his eyes.

'Flashbulbs!' Gary said, excitedly. 'I use them with my camera.'

Now that Lethbridge-Stewart was looking more closely, he could see that was indeed what they were. He recognised them from various press photographers he'd encountered over the years. They were getting smaller and smaller as the years went by. A few other bits and pieces were strewn about on the floor. *Other camera parts,* he decided. *But how can these flashbulbs help with an escape?*

'There are no windows, Gary,' Lethbridge-Stewart said, with a sigh. 'Even if we could get them to flash, there's no way anyone could see a signal from in here.'

'Unless you hoped to dazzle the guards with the light?' Barnett's attempt at humour fell flat. If anything, it made them all feel more miserable about their predicament.

Absent-mindedly, Kenworthy picked one up and rolled it around in his palm. He looked at it a few times and then had a eureka moment.

'Maybe there *is* something we can do with these,' he said, holding it up to everyone. 'Have a look at the filament inside.'

Lethbridge-Stewart looked to the door. 'Maybe you better quiet down first,' he said softly. 'If you've come up with a brilliant plan, let's not let the whole world know about it, Lieutenant.'

Sheepishly, Kenworthy crouched his head and then spoke at a more appropriate volume. 'Gary, what are these filaments made from?'

'From what I've read, it varies. It can be aluminium, magnesium or zedco… zirtan… something starting with z anyway.'

'Zirconium?'

Gary looked at Kenworthy in surprise, then nodded. 'Yes!'

'Why would that be of interest, Lieutenant?' Lethbridge-Stewart asked.

'I'm hoping at least one of the flashbulbs, if not most of them, has a filament made of magnesium.' Kenworthy was met with blank looks. 'Come on, don't any of you remember any of your comp science or chemistry classes?'

'That was quite a while ago for me.' Barnett stared blankly at the ground. 'And I imagine a lot has changed, too.'

'Magnesium burns very intensely,' Kenworthy said, in an excited whisper. 'It glows a tremendous white and can be ignited with water or fire. It's extremely reactive. That's why they use it in flares and sparklers.'

Lethbridge-Stewart took in the information with interest. He wished Anne had been locked up with them so she could help. Wherever she was, he hoped she was safe.

'Assuming the flashbulbs contain the metal we need, how are we going to light it?' he asked. 'There's no water in here and no flame, either.'

'I can help with that,' Barnett said, reaching into his clothing and producing a lighter. 'Given my clothes are often threadbare, I tend to lose these. So, I learned to keep them very close to me. That's why it wasn't confiscated – they never found it because I tucked it down deep.'

Lethbridge-Stewart didn't want to think about where Barnett may have been keeping the lighter, but things were starting to look a bit more hopeful. 'Any thoughts on what we can do with all this?' he asked, indicating everything on the floor before them.

Gary, eager as ever, was quick to chime in. 'Why don't we kind of shove the flashbulb filaments under the door and set them off? We could burn the door down.'

'I think we'd all die of smoke inhalation before it burned enough for us to break through.' Lethbridge-Stewart looked around the room for the umpteenth time. 'There's just no ventilation in here.'

'That might be true,' Barnett said. 'But if there *are* guards on the other side and they see smoke puffing up from the bottom of the door, I'd say they'd open it very quickly to see what's going on.'

'And probably let loose with four bullets very quickly,' Kenworthy said. He let out a deep sigh. 'Sorry, everyone, thought we were on to something for a minute.'

Lethbridge-Stewart gave a half-smirk. 'We might still be. Combining all these ideas could have some merit. But it involves some risk.' The others didn't appear particularly worried at the thought. They would likely grasp any opportunity to escape. 'Right then, here's what we'll do...'

While Gary and Kenworthy set about crushing some of the flashbulbs as quietly as possible to extract their filaments, Lethbridge-Stewart kept an anxious eye on the door. The thin metal strips were placed carefully in the gap between door and floor, and Barnett's lighter soon set them off. All but two were made of magnesium.

As they became bright lights of white intensity, the wood started to smoke and catch alight.

'Cover your mouths, men!' barked Lethbridge-Stewart, as best he could in a loud whisper.

The next few minutes went by achingly slowly. All they could do was watch as the small blaze started to take hold of the door. It was almost as if they were transfixed by the hauntingly beautiful flames of a campfire, just for a moment – but it was already getting uncomfortable in the cramped room and the heat was radiating back towards them. Gary started to cough as the wisps of smoke became denser. The base of the door had become engulfed and was continuing to flare.

Finally, the door flung open. Two guards were trying to swat out the flames while trying to see what was going on inside. Everyone pounced as soon as the door moved. As with any plan, not everything ran smoothly. The unknown factor always lay in how the other side reacted.

Kenworthy tripped up a guard with some rope.

Barnett lunged at the legs of the other, causing him to buckle and fall.

A shot was fired.

Gary tried smashing a flashbulb, but it bounced off the floor.

The door continued to burn.

Plenty of yelling ensued.

Lethbridge-Stewart swooped down and grabbed a fallen gun. Despite the smoke haze, he could see there was one casualty already. The target of the earlier gunshot had been Kenworthy. Absolutely nothing could be done; the bullet had struck him at point blank range. Blood ran from his temple and his eyes remained wide open. There was no dignity in the death, but time didn't allow Lethbridge-Stewart to think about it. The situation was as urgent as it could be, and they had to get out of there.

Gary had already bolted ahead but Barnett was on the ground, wrestling the guard he had taken down. Despite his age, the old captain was putting up a good fight – but it wouldn't take long before he was overpowered.

Lethbridge-Stewart broke him free and pulled him up, pushing him on ahead. Lethbridge-Stewart stomped on the guard's stomach, severely winding him, and carried on after the others.

Samson just about managed to escape.

It had been close, but Miller had provided the cover he needed. As soon as Samson was clear of the warehouse and safely on his way, Miller went straight back into the thick of things, where he would attempt to hold out until reinforcements came. Bishop and other infected Fifth troops needed protection.

Before, the sight of so many dead men would have made Miller recoil in horror. And the blood and entrails everywhere about the place would have made his legs and stomach turn to jelly. But not now. In many ways, it made him stronger. More determined.

Miller knew it was because of Andrew… The loss of his friend was the thing that had finally made him stand tall to embrace whatever challenge presented itself. Part of it was bravado; part of it was the pure shock. He just couldn't deal with the emotion, with the feeling of loss, and didn't really care what happened now.

That wasn't to say he was deliberately running into the path of the enemy's bullets or throwing himself into the arms of the experiments gone wrong. Miller was thriving on adrenaline and wanted more than anything to be on the winning side.

He made his moves through the warehouse, hiding when necessary and firing whenever under threat. Screams, gunfire and other sounds had become white noise – Miller was vaguely aware of it at some level, but it simply didn't have the same impact as before.

Eventually, he found the room he was looking for. Captain Bishop, lying in agony, holding on for dear life and trying not to succumb to the wild creature-like way of the others. Miller was glad nothing more had happened to the captain. No matter what occurred from this point on, no matter who challenged him, he intended to keep it that way.

Samson would be forever thankful for Miller's help in getting out of the warehouse. He just hoped the young lad kept a reasonably level head. It was all well and good to throw yourself into the action, but an overly cavalier attitude could also be dangerous.

But there was little time to dwell on the private's well-being.

Samson had managed to get clear of the warehouse and the battle that had spread outside. There were plenty of vehicles from the Fifth in the streets, but just as many of the enemy firing madly, ready to take out anyone trying to drive off. Instead, Samson had cautiously gone from property to property and wall to wall, hiding where he could, before gradually moving on to his next place of cover. Eventually, after what had seemed like an excruciating amount of time where he might have been discovered at any point, Samson made it to the end of the road and bolted around the corner and up the next street.

If he'd been able to access one of the vehicles, he could have radioed back to the Madhouse. But that was something he just couldn't chance. Samson thought about knocking on the door of a local resident and asking to use their phone, but thought better of it. He was a coloured man in a bedraggled army uniform, covered in patches of blood. He didn't want to scare the life out of some old dear.

The only option left to him was to use a payphone and, without any money on him, reverse the charges. Fortunately, a couple of streets away, he found one.

Samson realised he was gabbling as soon as he reached Sergeant Maddox. He forced himself to regulate his breathing before stating the situation and what was required.

'Take a breath, Sam,' Maddox said. 'I read you loud and clear. I shall get word to Captain Miles immediately.'

'Thanks, Jean.' Samson followed her advice, and breathed in deeply. 'We also need a strong force out at Maidens Port.'

'Say again, Sergeant Major. Maidens Port?'

'We have two situations, Jean. We have heavy casualties in Newcastle. Men are dying and even more will die if that isn't contained, but we also have a second problem. The Brig and several others, including Anne, have been captured and taken somewhere in Maidens Port.'

'But why…?'

Samson listened as Jean muffled the phone and spoke to one of her girls. 'Samson,' she said, 'there's an old naval base in Maidens Port. That would seem a likely destination.'

Samson took that in. 'Right. I'm going to try to get there first, and if there's any change, I'll find a way to report in.'

'Understood. Captain Miles has been alerted about the situation in Newcastle. Sam…'

'Yes, Jean?'

'Be careful.'

Samson smiled, knowing she'd hear it in his voice. 'You know me, Jean. Always careful.'

Olekeia wasn't sure where he was. He'd been lost before but had always been able to find his way back to his people. Even when he was a boy. Getting lost was to be expected when they moved around the land so much. But it was a land he knew, and he liked to think he knew it well. So, he was troubled at being disoriented. If he could find his way to one of the Great Lakes, that could help him set his course. When one of the lakes was in his sight, he could usually work out how to get where he needed to be – it helped to show him where others were and which path he should take.

Being lost wasn't the only thing troubling Olekeia. He didn't know he'd come to be suddenly out in the open, wandering the plains among the cattle. *At least there is cattle about*, he thought. That meant meat, milk and blood were available, no matter how lost he became or what path he chose. His stomach rumbled; when was the last time he had eaten something? Usually there was morning feed or evening meal, but he could remember neither. It seemed liked days ago, but he knew that couldn't be right.

As the intensity of the sun grew by the minute, Olekeia looked to the heavens. What had he done to upset Engai Na-nyokie? A proud Maasai man would only try to please his god and he couldn't see what he might have done wrong. Which made him think something very bad had happened. Had he been cast out from his people? Or worse still, had there been a massacre? If so, why had he survived?

Marching on, Olekeia tried to remember what had occurred. Was it poachers from Nairobi? Fragments of memory – or were they dreams? – floated through his mind. There were men but they weren't interested in animals. No, it was him and others from his tribe they were after. Many of them had shown great courage and strength in the great lion hunts but, despite their fearlessness and skills as warriors, the poachers had used cowardly nets and darts to capture them all. Olekeia had felt a sting when one of the darts hit his leg and, he was ashamed to say, fell asleep. In this way, he could see how he might have dishonoured Engai Na-nyokie.

Olekeia bowed his head, trying to get past the feelings of dishonour, as he kept walking. True men would have fought each other and he with the greatest strength would be the victor. These poacher men were nothing but cowards. It wasn't his fault he fell asleep; it was the strange poison on the darts! That must have been what caused it. But he had never come across a poison like it himself.

As the heat grew, Olekeia ignored its effect. He needed to show his god he was capable of endurance, at the very least.

Alone with his thoughts, more recollections started to surface.

He had been in a hut, tied down with strange vines. There had been men and women in white coverings, both on their bodies and half their faces. There were smaller darts this time. But they didn't make him fall asleep. In fact, they did just the opposite – they made Olekeia very awake. It was after many of these darts that everything was more dream-like. But not really dreams… It was as if Olekeia wasn't there anymore. Yet he knew he was. It was all very confusing.

He wondered if he had died. But there was screaming and yelling, as if hyenas were in the hut. Others like him had been tied down and they were becoming wild beasts. Like him. Something took control of Olekeia; some inner power. He knew he didn't want to be there. With sheer brute force, he broke free of the strange vines and–

Olekeia couldn't remember what happened next. Maybe he didn't want to remember. Now, he was no longer walking; he was running free. Howling at the sky. *Is this what it's like to be a beast?* There was an anger inside; some latent desire that made him want to attack anything and everything.

He chased a lazy cow and somehow managed to bring it down. With only his hands at his disposal, Olekeia was unable to get through the tough hide. He found himself reaching down to his own torso, scrabbling and tearing at the skin.

Had the heat made him go mad? He had heard of it happening to men in other tribes. They had been cast out; ostracised for their silly ways. But he had a desperate craving to do what he was doing; a thirst for raw flesh. Olekeia's scratching back and forth drew blood as he went faster and faster. Deeper and deeper. Until he could put his fingers into the cavernous scratches, up to their knuckles.

A cry went up into the sky. The cow shifted itself along, now recovered from its fright. Olekeia knew he was descending into a whirlpool of madness, a fury of his own making. But he couldn't stop himself. He just had to get under his own skin.

Blood was now running down his leg, flowing copiously from his wounds. If he kept going, he would be seriously injured. Olekeia howled in agony as he pushed deeper into his own flesh.

He now knew how all the cattle they slaughtered over the years had felt.

This time, he called for Engai Narok. The god of benevolence.

As more blood seeped away from his body, it appeared no one was listening.

CHAPTER FIFTEEN
Two Heads Are Better Than One

LETHBRIDGE-STEWART, BARNETT and Gary eventually found themselves clear of the smoke and far enough away from the guards to stop and gather themselves for a second. Lethbridge-Stewart was taking in his surroundings, trying to figure out the next best course of action.

They were in an abandoned room.

'Where's Kenworthy?' Gary asked.

'Didn't you hear the gunshot?' Barnett said, shaking his head in dismay as if he didn't quite believe the reality of it himself. 'I'd say he didn't make it.'

'True, I'm afraid.' Lethbridge-Stewart didn't have time to mourn a fallen soldier; there would be time for that later. 'We have to find Anne. Usually, I would suggest splitting up, but I've got the only weapon,' he said, holding up the gun he had retrieved. 'There might be strength in numbers. Probably better if we stick together on this occasion.'

'That certainly works for me.' A new voice emanated from the other side of the room.

The three escapees turned to see an old man, a once proud and strong fighting soldier, flanked by armed guards on either side of him.

So much for our escape, thought Lethbridge-Stewart.

Despite the man's elderly nature – he surely had to be in his mid-eighties – there was a presence in his voice that couldn't be denied. A man that had kept on going, refusing to let the old man in. It would almost be admirable, if the man wasn't the enemy and quite clearly the ringleader of everything that was going on.

'Brigadier Lethbridge-Stewart,' he said. 'Been making quite a name for yourself, haven't you?'

A raised eyebrow was all he decided to offer in return. The place clearly had some sort of internal surveillance, however rudimentary. Depending on Werwolf's intelligence and communication networks, it wouldn't have taken long to figure out who they had captured.

'Nothing to say, Brigadier? How very stoic and English of you.'

Gary, itching to know more, blurted out what was on everyone's minds. 'Who are you?'

The man smiled malevolently. 'You can call me Charles.'

'Charles?' Lethbridge-Stewart asked. 'And what was your rank?'

Charles smiled. 'Ah, the old soldier in me is still present, eh, Brigadier?'

Lethbridge-Stewart did not smile back. 'Something like that.'

'I reached the esteemed rank of general back in the day.'

Lethbridge-Stewart quickly thought. There was only one general connected with the experiments back in the '40s. 'Of course… General Charles Dornan.'

Dornan bowed slightly. 'The very same.'

Barnett's face went white, and he buckled at the knees. Lethbridge-Stewart immediately went to grab him, but he righted himself quickly. The former captain was seething, fists clenched.

'Steady on, Captain.' Lethbridge-Stewart couldn't allow an ill-timed fit of rage to bring them all down now.

'But he's the one responsible!' Barnett yelled, as Gary and Lethbridge-Stewart held him back. 'He started all those horrible experiments during the war! Think about all the lives he ruined!'

Dornan didn't flinch. He simply looked bemused. 'Started? Well, yes, I gave the orders. And I'm happy to say I'm quite pleased we've managed to pick up where we left off, despite the passage of time.' Barnett glared at him. 'But, on this occasion, we're operating on a much grander scale.'

Miller looked at Captain Bishop, anxiously. The man was in no condition to be moved but, given they were essentially in the middle of a battlefield, the likelihood of both of them surviving an attack was slim. Miller had barricaded the door to the room as best he could, but he also knew it wouldn't hold for long, given the brute force exuded by everyone who had succumbed to the horrible experiment in some capacity.

Glancing at the captain, Miller tried not to look at his horrific wounds or whatever the horrible infection was doing to him. As the muffled sounds of screaming and bullets managed to permeate the door, he realised he could soon find himself in something of a predicament. Miller understood the risk of holding the position and trying to defend it – but should Bishop's condition worsen, he could soon be under attack from the very type of creature he was trying to keep out.

The horrific thought was soon put out of his mind. Intense pounding of what he presumed were fists started hammering against the door. Miller couldn't tell if there was just one person or several contributing to the noise. It became relentless – thud, thud, thud – with the screeching evidently much closer than before. He'd already put a bench and chairs against the door but they only went so high, leaving weak spots towards the top of the doorframe.

If he couldn't barricade it anymore, could he protect Bishop some other way? Miller desperately looked around for anything he could use to shield the captain. But no matter what he considered, he felt he would only injure his superior further – or any attacker would use it against them both.

He shook his head at the sheer idiocy of some of his thoughts, such as putting the spare bed over him… But Miller was desperate and fast running out of options.

Thud, thud, thud. The noises were definitely getting louder. And more frequent.

Looking towards the top of the door, Miller could see the wood beginning to splinter. He only hoped it was solid wood, rather than the hollow-core type. That would at least give him just a little more time.

Wishful thinking… A bloodied fist crashed through the wood, then pulled back and kept going for more strikes. Other bloodied hands scrabbled at the small hole, desperate to make the aperture bigger. The incessant screaming could now be heard at almost full volume, piercing his ears.

Only one thing for it, Miller decided.

He aimed at whatever was trying to come through the small wooden hole and fired. Howls and shrieks intensified – Miller must have hit a hand or two.

There was a brief respite where the door-pounding stopped. Miller couldn't quite believe what he'd done. It would have been unthinkable just a day or so ago. But that was before they had lost Andrew. It was true what they said, it seemed.

You never know how strong you are until being strong is the only choice you have.

And then it started again. Thud, thud, thud.

Even if Miller had wounded some of them, it appeared there were others just as ready to take their place. If they kept it up, they would eventually break through. Of that, Miller was certain.

How long could he hold them off?

Edward tried to give Anne a reassuring look. Buttery had left them, but the guards were ever-present, ready to take action should he not comply with their demands. There was little chance to exchange words with Anne, and he didn't wish to risk their captors overhearing them sharing information.

Anne looked sideways at him as he went to the bench. Edward got to work, readying himself by mixing test tubes, looking at things under the microscope and generally making it appear he was busy. They were all things he had done before while examining and testing the other patients. He was hoping by going through the same motions, the guards – or anyone else watching, perhaps – wouldn't be suspicious of his actions.

Ultimately, he was going to have to make it look like he was doing something to Anne.

Going over to one of the beds, Edward knew he had only one chance to play his card. He hated what he was about to do, but there was no other option. He looked at the comatose soldier before him. The man might technically be alive, but he hadn't had a life since the war. Perhaps there was a solution for these poor souls somewhere, but it was just as likely the men would live out their days unconscious until their bodies finally gave in. Given their youthful appearance, that wasn't likely. But at some point, someone wouldn't care about keeping them alive anymore. Eventually someone would take away the drips feeding them or simply kill them outright. Edward gave a quick glance towards the guards, but neither was looking particularly at what he was doing; just standing and staring towards his side of the room. Unflinching and unnerving at the same time. But ready to pounce at any sign of defiance, he was sure of that.

It was now or never.

Edward did his best to mask what he was doing. To any watcher, it would look like he was using a syringe to take a sample from the man. But he was actually making an injection. Edward moved over to Anne with another syringe and whispered, 'Get ready.'

Anne's eyes widened at the needle, but Edward shook his head slightly, trying to reassure her it was nothing to worry about. As he faked an injection, he managed to manoeuvre himself so he could loosen Anne's bonds.

Anne had played along perfectly, hollering 'No! Don't!' and struggling as Edward went about his business.

He looked over his shoulder to the bed and there it was. Groaning and coughing, the soldier awoke from his sustained slumber. Just like the previous time. The guards showed a flicker of interest now there was more movement on the other side of the room. The man, groggy as he was, got out of bed and staggered forward a few steps.

'Quick, over here! This one's woken up!' Edward called. 'Don't shoot, we need him for the experiment.'

The guards raced over, unsure what to do next. The man started screaming an ear-splitting screech and lunged for Edward, his eyes flashing wildly. 'Restrain him as best you can, near the bed! I have to give Anne a second injection.'

He raced over to Anne, another syringe at the ready for his façade. The guards struggled to hold the crazed man as he squealed with banshee-like intensity, his strength a force to be reckoned with. Their attention distracted, Anne slipped out of the ropes that held her.

Edward waited for the moment.

The screaming soldier's face started to change.

Edward nodded at Anne.

Both were already running as they heard the sound of a strange puff in the air and the guards choking and spluttering. The sound of a bullet being fired soon followed.

A couple of steps in front of him, Anne found a door. It was around the corner from the sleeping soldiers and confused guards. They burst through it, ready to continue their escape.

The alarm would definitely have been raised by now.

'We have to find Alistair and the others!' Anne said, panting.

Edward was surprised to learn there were others with her. He thought she had been captured alone. He had planned on just escaping, but if there were others…

He didn't care for the risks involved. But he knew Anne; she was so much like her mother. She wouldn't just leave Lethbridge-Stewart and the others.

'Then we have to make sure we give them the slip,' Edward said, hurrying to the end of the corridor, which turned out to be a junction with three doors. He opened the first on his left and, once Anne was through, they both set about barricading it with chairs and whatever else they could find in the room.

Finally, they were allowed a moment to catch their breath.

'Ted,' Anne said. 'Believe me when I say thank you.'

It seems genuine, Edward thought, allowing himself a small smile. They were a long way off her accepting him, but he'd take any small advancement.

'We're not out of the woods yet,' he said. 'But let's make the most of this small respite and compare notes.'

Anne hurriedly told Travers about the missing students, the experiments at the warehouse, her post-mortem and how they had been captured. In turn, he relayed the events of his kidnap and how he was forced to work on the comatose patients.

'It's a global operation,' Anne said. 'Based on what we've learned.'

'That certainly ties in with what I discovered. And, the other me was involved.'

'I know,' Anne said. 'I read the reports. But Father was forced into the situation against his will, to try and fix what was going on at the time.'

'Yes. I have to confess at some horror when I first learned that I was involved in this...'

'You?'

Edward nodded. 'Quite so, my dear. Think about it, not even a decade after I was split in two, a version of me became involved in this. Now, I can't pretend to have lived through anything like World War Two, but... Well.' He smiled sadly. 'None of us know what we're capable of until we're tested, but I would have hoped that if I was presented with such a situation I would have been, at the very least, reticent to take part. But, it seems, that was not the case.'

Anne shook her head. 'But you're not my father.'

'I am not, but I could have been. Indeed, had I returned to 1935, I would have been. I would have made all the choices the man who became your father made.'

Anne was silent for a moment, while she let that settle in. 'I never... I don't think I truly thought of it that way.'

'I'm sorry,' Edward said, 'that I remind you of such a great loss, and I'm sorry you see me as a shadow of your father, but...'

'You're still the same man?'

'Yes,' Edward said, unable to hide the sadness in his voice. 'I am the same man who returned to 1935, albeit with a few months' worth of different experiences… What I'm saying is, if I had returned to 1935 a few months ago, I would have lived those years and ended up making the same decisions as your father. *I would have been the man who helped with these experiments.*'

'But… Father's role was a reaction, rather than playing an active part in it all.' Anne looked towards the door.

Edward followed her gaze; he was worried, too. 'I hope we haven't made ourselves sitting ducks,' he said, trying to inject a bit of humour into their situation.

'Charming thought,' Anne said. She looked over at the electronic equipment in the corner of the room. It was an array of wires, screens, microphones, speakers, copper foil circuit boards and more. A couple of logos caught her eye: Magpie Electricals on some components; International Electromatics on others. 'Someone here is certainly keen on communication. This looks like an operations room.'

Edward joined her and rifled through various components, picking up items here and there, eyeing them with a fascinated curiosity. 'Quite an extensive set-up.'

'Mix of old and new equipment here. Some newer than I've seen.' Anne smiled. 'Now there's an idea. This is so they can keep track of experiments happening around the world, which means someone would be able to hear the broadcasts.'

Edward twiddled a few knobs, just to get a better sense of what was before him. At the moment, everything looked to be powered off so it was unlikely his fiddling would alert anyone to their presence.

Anne sighed, and straightened up. 'I don't like the feel of this place. I know it's unscientific, but there's an underlying sense that something horrible happened here. Or maybe that's because something horrible *is* happening here now.'

'The experiments weren't exactly ethical. And for them to be occurring around the world…' Edward trailed off. He didn't need to speak what they were both thinking. That there was probably an active Nazi force at work here, some kind of underground network that had linked up across the four corners of the globe. Edward sat down. 'Soldiers with everlasting stamina…' he said, more to himself, while staring thoughtfully back at Anne.

'Maybe we're looking at this the wrong way?' he finally said, and tapped his fingers on the back of his hand. It helped him think. That's what he told himself, anyway.

'What do you mean?'

'Our thoughts have turned to stopping whoever's behind this, which is something of an insurmountable task at present. Perhaps we should be looking at how to stop the experiment working?'

'But isn't that what you were doing with those poor comatose soldiers back there?'

'I was trying to bring them back around. Reversing the experiment, if you will. But I'm talking about *interrupting* the process somehow, so whatever they're doing doesn't take hold. Or neutralising the effect of whatever's being injected into people.'

'But there's no way you can inject people around the world all at the same time with some counter-agent. Or use force to stop the initial injections.' Anne looked back at him apologetically, as if she wanted to support him but couldn't.

Edward stood, making a sweeping gesture with his hand. 'Look at all this equipment around us. We're living in a technological age, Anne. It's going to become the essence of our lives. Think big!' He could see she was struggling to make a connection.

'Something to do with brainwaves?' she offered. 'There were photos of an EEG in the warehouse where they were doing the experiments. I thought it was just to monitor neural activity when the patients were stimulated to stay awake.'

'It probably was. But that's a clue, surely? The brain is a hive of electrical activity. Neurons firing here and there, one after the other. It's a complete, complex network. Yet everyone's been focusing on biology for this experiment. Getting the body to react with this injection and that solution; always concentrating on the physiological aspect.'

Anne was similarly now deep in thought. 'Are you saying we need to give these poor patients some sort of electric shock treatment?'

'You're on the right track now.' Edward was pleased to see his other self had taught Anne well. 'Maybe the solution is electrical. What if we transmit delta waves into their consciousness? It might correct what's gone wrong. Like giving the brain a jump-start to correct itself. Or a boost of more power to cope and repair everything?'

Looking around the room, Anne was doubtful. 'And you plan to do it with this equipment? These are just communications devices. Sound waves only.'

Edward shook his head, indignant. 'I know that! This room just helped me think of the idea. It won't be easy. It's something that needs to be done on a global scale. Worldwide cooperation is essential.'

'Easier said than done,' Anne noted. 'We're going to need to find Lethbridge-Stewart before we can do any of that.'

'And therein lies the risk,' Edward said. 'But it doesn't mean we can't get a head start, does it? We're trapped in here for a while, let's make the most of it.'

Anne nodded. 'Yes. And maybe we can even get a signal out to Captain Miles.' She grinned. 'If I know Alistair, he'll be busy extricating himself. He won't need our help. And he'll find us. He's good like that.'

Edward rubbed his hands together. 'Then let's make a start, shall we?'

And together they set to it.

Edward felt a warm glow inside. Anne wasn't his daughter, and he wasn't her father, but right then, it felt like maybe, just maybe, they could mean something to each other after all.

CHAPTER SIXTEEN
Dancing with the Devil

TWO JAMAICAN undergraduates in a Ford Escort took pity on Samson and offered a ride. Even though they weren't actually headed for Maidens Port, they said they were up for a day trip and happily took Samson to his coastal destination. Upon parting, Samson gave the students a warning not to take part in any experiments if they were looking to make a few quid. He hoped they heeded his advice.

Now on foot, Samson welcomed the opportunity to stretch his legs after two hours. His first priority was to find the old naval base. It was clear Maidens Port had grown from a village into a town with its own fishing industry, while also becoming a quaint tourist spot in the process. For every bait-and-tackle shop, there was another gift shop offering cheap bric-a-brac. But the village roots remained. Samson noted a nearby cemetery and a church by the name of St Jude's, which looked like it had a long history.

He decided the local post office might be a good source of information, given the variety of people that would use it daily. Samson quickly found it on the main street and went up to the counter to the postmaster.

'Hello there!' A jolly, middle-aged man greeted him. 'What can I do for you today? Posting a letter, perhaps?' The postmaster – Reg Bamford according to the A-frame nameplate on the counter – looked Samson up and down, noticing the blood on his clothes. 'Been in a spot of bother?'

Samson was pleasantly surprised the man wasn't focusing on his colour. 'Sort of… Look, I'm in a bit of a hurry.'

'Fair enough, then.' Reg wasn't quite as jovial now; he seemed mildly offended his friendly customer service had been rejected.

"I'm looking for the naval base. I'm told there's one in the area.'

'That's right, near the beach,' Reg said. 'Been quiet for years, up until recently. Nowadays, all these people are coming and going from there, doing goodness knows what.'

'Does anyone know what's going on?'

'There's a lot of vehicles down that way. More people than you'd expect in a place like this, too. Bit of a palaver going on by the looks of it.' Reg looked out the window at a couple of passers-by. 'Locals tend to keep away from it all. So do the tourists. Once they see the big keep out signs, they tend to stay away. No one really gets involved. They stick to their own business.'

'Can you give me directions?'

'Something going on, you think?' Reg pointed out the best path to the old base. 'We all just presumed it was military operations and top secret. You know, because of the keep out signs.'

'Thanks for your help.' Samson made for the door to exit but had a thought on his way out. He turned back to Reg. 'Have people been going missing around here at all?'

'Not as such.' Reg shrugged. 'But we get plenty of tourists through the area, so it's hard to keep track of everyone.'

Samson thanked the postmaster a second time and made a beeline for the beach.

The conversation only reinforced what Samson already knew. He followed the directions he'd been given and, despite it being slightly off the beaten track, he found the base soon enough. The keep out signs were big and bold, telling people in no uncertain terms to stay away. If that wasn't enough of a clue, the barbed wire around the perimeter certainly was.

Hiding himself as best he could in the seaside vegetation, Samson kept a close eye on the surroundings. A pair of binoculars would have helped, but he was near enough to see what was going on. Sure enough, people in handcuffs were being unloaded from vehicles and marched in under armed guard. Various pieces of equipment were being offloaded, too. There was definitely plenty of activity.

But Samson now found himself in a precarious position. He was just one man. There was no way he could infiltrate the place by himself; not with so many armed guards around. He desperately needed that backup Maddox had promised; he was sure Miles would send some men over once they'd secured the warehouse.

Which meant, for Samson, it would be a bit of a waiting game. He settled himself down, keeping his eyes on the activity in the base.

Meanwhile, Miller was engaged in his own waiting game. His screaming attackers continued their quest to break through the door and had succeeded in making the hole bigger. It was only a matter of time before they could squeeze through and wreak untold havoc.

I have to protect the captain, Miller reminded himself. *At all costs.* Easier said than done, though.

He came to the conclusion that firing at anything trying to come through the door hole would only be a temporary measure. Sure, it held the attackers at bay for a little while, but at some point he was going to run out of ammunition. His mind flashed back to a short story he was forced to read at school during English lessons. *Leiningen Versus the Ants.* The owner of a plantation in a Brazilian rainforest finds his estate under attack by soldier ants and, no matter what he does to stop them, they keep finding ways to break through. And no matter how many he kills, there are always thousands more ants to replace those lost.

Strange what you think about when your life's on the line, Miller mused. He was sure there was a lesson in the story somewhere, but he had never been the best student and wasn't sure how he could apply it to his current situation.

As another almighty crack echoed around the room, Miller looked up to see a large splinter of wood fall down from the door. By now, he knew to fire to keep the scrabbling hands at bay. But he needed something else.

Keeping an eye on the door while the banshee-screaming outside continued, he started desperately opening every cabinet door in the room. He was in a warehouse that was used for medical experiments. Miller eyed the cleaning products but questioned whether Ajax, Domestos or Vapona fly killer would do the trick.

Thud, crack, thud. They were back at it.

Looking at the door, Miller could see fists and arms pushing through, more wood splintering as the attack continued. Bloodied hands dripped scarlet onto the freshly-broken wood, creating dark mahogany patches as it soaked into the timber.

Rifling through the next cupboard, Miller finally had a

moment of triumph – acid! Bottles of it.

He lugged them out and moved closer to the door. It was going to be tricky, he knew, but at least he had another line of defence. Or so he hoped. Time was of the essence but he also knew he had to take care, so he didn't injure himself in the process. But with the constant pounding, screaming and splintering, it was hard to concentrate.

Whack! Another part of the door broke off, making the hole sizable enough for more than a hand or arm to come through. A face appeared, eyes slightly detached, shrieking horribly as blood drooled from the person's mouth. There was nothing for it.

Miller unscrewed the lid from the bottle of sulphuric acid in his hand and then squeezed, aiming the projectile right at the face coming through.

Acid flew across the room, hitting the intended target, who immediately backed away from the door, howling more intensely while scrabbling at the pain on his face. The acid landed on other hands trying to come through, too. And it landed on some of the barricade, eating through whatever it came in contact with. That included the back of Miller's hand, which was now in agonising pain.

But the bottles of acid had and would give him another line of defence. He would just have to grin and bear any damage he did to himself.

And look at the state Captain Bishop is in, Miller reminded himself.

Lethbridge-Stewart, Barnett and Gary had all been handcuffed and were now under armed guard. Dornan had led them to some sort of surveillance room, sat down in an armchair and lit himself a cigar. The trio stood in front of him. He didn't say anything; just puffed away. Like he was toying with them. To show that, in no uncertain terms, he was in control. Lethbridge-Stewart knew better than to say anything for the moment, unless Dornan did. He hoped the others would do the same.

After methodically getting through his cigar – and taking his time about it – Dornan finally chose to speak.

'You there, in the middle,' he said, pointing at Barnett. 'Captain, wasn't it? You seemed to know about the sleep experiments during the war. Only a few people have first-hand knowledge and you look about the right age to have served at that time...' Dornan deliberated. 'So, you must have encountered

Professor Travers back then.'

Lethbridge-Stewart's ears pricked up at the mention of Travers. 'Where's Anne?' he demanded.

'The daughter? She's here.' Dornan smiled, cruel delight evident on his face. 'With her father.'

Lethbridge-Stewart wasn't surprised. It made sense that he'd be tied up in all this, especially after what they knew of his role in things during the war. Even if, technically, that had been a different man. No doubt Dornan didn't know that bit, so Lethbridge-Stewart decided he would keep it to himself. As long as Dornan thought Ted was Professor Travers, the man would be useful.

Lethbridge-Stewart chanced another question. 'Doing what?'

'Helping us refine the experiment, of course.'

'But what's it all for?' Gary asked.

Dornan smirked. 'Inquisitive fellow, aren't you?' He absently fiddled with some of the controls in the room, took his time as he pressed the odd button here and there, and then looked back at Gary. 'Part of the greater plan. The final solution, you might say.'

Barnett lunged forward, pure hatred in his eyes. He was quickly pulled back into place and the end of a gun was pressed against his cheek. 'Traitor!' he spat. 'You're Nazi scum.'

Lethbridge-Stewart winced internally as the captain's head was smacked from side to side by the guards.

'Always was.' Dornan was revelling in the reactions. He remained seated, exuding calm. 'And through Werwolf, we shall rise again.'

Lethbridge-Stewart appreciated Barnett's anger. The man who commanded the Fourth Operational Corps, his predecessor in a manner of speaking, had just admitted to being a Nazi. Lethbridge-Stewart couldn't think of a bigger betrayal.

And with that simple admittance, Dornan had confirmed Barnett's theory.

There had been a secondary Nazi network set up to continue after the first one failed. It made sense in a way, as repugnant as the thought was – it was always prudent to have a backup plan.

Lethbridge-Stewart knew his history well enough. Occasionally there was a pocket of Nazi ideology that sprang up here and there, but it was usually quickly extinguished. Like the ODESSA ratlines to Argentina. Not to mention the World Union of National Socialists. Lethbridge-Stewart was just surprised something like Werwolf had bided its time over the years and grown into a worldwide network while remaining secret. The strategy had worked, making the organisation very dangerous indeed.

'Nothing to say now?' Dornan surveyed his three prisoners. 'Come on, I wasn't the only Nazi spy working within the British Forces during the war. It can't be that much of a shock, surely?' For the first time, the general revealed the slightest bit of surprise on his face.

'So, the experiments on the British soldiers were really done for the Nazis?' Barnett said, fury barely simmering under his voice, although he had the sense not to lash out this time.

Lethbridge-Stewart felt for the man. Not only was Barnett's life destroyed by his revulsion at the experiments, but he now had to come to terms with the fact it was all done for the enemy. He couldn't even console himself with it being part of Britain's 'great war effort' anymore.

Dornan's response was simply one of bemusement. 'The experiments will help our cause once again. But it's a much more consolidated effort this time. With so many Werwolf operatives around the world, we will ultimately find a way of creating the supreme soldier.'

'But at what cost?' Barnett cried.

'Thousands of lives, probably. A small price to pay to ensure we establish the Thousand-Year Reich correctly this time.'

'What makes you so sure this experiment will work when it didn't before?' Gary asked.

'Werwolf was set up before the end of the war. We've been gathering data and modifying our approach ever since then, whenever and wherever we can. Our network reaches into countries everywhere; anywhere test subjects can be found. The poor, the weak and the stupid.' Dornan folded his arms and leaned back in his chair. 'That's the beauty of having a global network. Each location has its own unique circumstance that allows us to scoop up different aspects of society. Sometimes it's under the cover of war; sometimes it's famine. Here in Britain, it's those who need money. Sooner or later, as medical science keeps on advancing, we will make the experiment work.'

Lethbridge-Stewart had heard it all before. Despotism at its worst. Unfortunately, these sorts of people and organisations were also the most dangerous.

'Can't be going too well if you've had to kidnap Professor

Travers.'

'Merely another avenue of investigation,' Dornan retorted, looking Lethbridge-Stewart squarely in the eye. 'Just to see if the process might be able to be reversed and whether that unearths anything useful for the new experiments. Besides, he followed my orders easily enough during the war.'

'I daresay that would have been different had he known you were the enemy.'

Dornan smiled. 'We'll never know, Brigadier. I was good at my job; nobody knew. Not Travers, not Tobias Kinsella, not even Churchill. And the Fourth was his pet project.'

'The war ended years ago,' Barnett almost growled. 'Can't you see the world would never let something like the Nazis ever happen again?'

'There's a flaw in your argument,' Dornan said coolly. 'The Nazis never went away. Werwolf was specifically designed to carry on that legacy. Slowly re-building until the time was right. We've planted seeds all over the world and they've grown into a global force.' He smiled, pleased with himself and what had been achieved. 'We have learned from our past mistakes. Rather than start from one country and then invade others one by one, we've planted ourselves where we need to be and have quietly built up our strength until we are ready.'

Lethbridge-Stewart was happy to hear the man almost brimming with pride. He hadn't achieved his goal just yet – and that kind of belligerent confidence often led to a downfall.

Gary took umbrage again. 'But what about China? The United States? Even the Soviets? You think you can stand up against the might of those nations?'

'Werwolf is active everywhere around the world. The experiments are being conducted under the cover of a convenient war here, a tragic ghetto there… Anywhere the body count matters little.'

Dornan's callous, offhand manner was to get a rise out of one or all of them. Lethbridge-Stewart had a feeling what was about to come next. Dornan stood, ready to leave.

'All this is rather tiresome.' He nodded slightly at the guards. 'You know what to do. Three perfect experimental subjects.'

Gary struggled but was soon pulled back into place by Dornan's men. Barnett tried elbowing one of them and was quickly met with a blow to the head. Lethbridge-Stewart knew any sort of reaction was fruitless.

At least, right now. He'd survived worse than a few hired thugs. An opportunity would present itself...

CHAPTER SEVENTEEN
Ready to Ware

CAPTAIN MILES knew he would be engaging in battle. And that was messy at the best of times. But even he was taken aback at the sheer chaos waiting for him in Newcastle. Nothing from Maddox's brief would have prepared him for this.

Bodies were strewn about in front of the warehouse – not just the opposition but also members of the Fifth and the unfortunate experimental subjects caught up in it all. Miles had seen dead men in battle before, but this wasn't quite the same. The sheer amount of blood leaking from the bodies… Miles had read the reports about people ripping themselves open and doing the same to others, but to actually witness it first-hand made it more real. And absolutely horrifying.

Numerous military vehicles now lined the street. Miles had managed to recruit enough men for a small platoon but, even so, he still wasn't sure whether that would be enough. He could hear occasional gunfire from inside the warehouse… A soldier – one of the Fifth – catapulted from the front door, firing back into the building. He awkwardly ran and jumped over the bodies and made his way to Miles' vehicle, where the captain was standing and surveying the scene.

'Sir!' he said, offering a quick salute. 'Struggling to contain the enemy.'

Miles was already motioning for his troops to come forward – it wouldn't be long before the enemy spilled into the street to engage. Not unless they went in first.

'Name, Private?'

'Underwood.'

'How many of ours are left?'

'Hard to tell. Rabbit warren in there, sir. Blood and guts everywhere. Sheer hell, if you don't mind me saying so, sir.'

Miles looked over to the warehouse entrance. How could it

be worse than what he was seeing?

'Sir!' Underwood evidently had more to say. 'We're under attack on two fronts. The enemy and…' It was clear the private didn't quite have the words he needed.

'Human experiments gone wrong?' Underwood nodded at Miles. 'I've been briefed, Private. Are you up to going back inside?'

Underwood looked unsure for a moment but then nodded.

'Righto, flank me as we go in. You have some idea of the layout.'

At that moment, static crackled on Miles' radio. He reached into the vehicle to grab the handset.

'Mayhem Four. Over.'

'Madhouse reporting, good news. Over.'

'That'll make a nice change. Report. Over.'

'Mayhem Three has found the location where Mayhem Leader and Dr Moreau are being held. Over.'

'Acknowledged. Once we've cleared this mess up, I'll send reinforcements over. Please advise Mayhem Three if he reports in again. Over and out.' Miles put the radio mic back in its cradle.

By now, some of the battle had erupted at the front of the warehouse.

Miles mustered the troops to join him and Underwood.

'On my command…' Miles tempered, as a screaming, ravaged patient emerged, ready to pounce. 'Attack!'

The Fifth was a well-oiled machine when it came to military operations and Miles couldn't have asked for a better start. He swatted away the patient with the butt of his rifle as he raged through the door; Underwood was at his side, ready to lead the way where he could.

Bullets bounced, ricocheted and penetrated. More bodies were on the floor. But it was the horrible, continuous screeching that made it more than a battle. It was as if the sounds of tortured animals were baying for blood while shrieking for help at the same time.

'This way, sir!' Underwood pointed up a corridor.

Miles and his men followed.

Adding to the confusion were the not-quite-dead Fifth soldiers. Some of them were turning into horrible beasts and the captain struggled at the thought of shooting them outright. But as a former private, entrails exposed, loomed over him and bawled his agonised cry, Miles had little choice.

No sooner had Miles put the private out of his misery, than

a bullet flew past him. One of the enemy guards had rounded the corner and fired blindly. The bullet had missed Miles, but Underwood copped it in the shoulder, knocking him backwards. The captain could only push forward and gun down the guard who had fired.

He wanted to find Bishop, but that couldn't take precedence over the primary assignment: containing the facility. Underwood had been right. There were corridors everywhere; all painted and lit the same, so it was hard to know whether he'd been the same way before. Gunfire continued to rattle off in different parts of the building. Miles thought about entering some of the rooms, but he learned his lesson very quickly when trying to go through a doorway. A patient cried out and shot up from the floor, knocking him backwards. He managed to fight him off, but the sight of organs hanging loose from his attacker's torso was not something he would easily forget.

Covered in blood, Miles forced himself up. Other members of the Fifth had battled their way through similar circumstances and were now at his side.

Venturing into a room was a potential deathtrap but, somehow, he knew that was going to be the only way to find Bishop. With troops at his side again, he felt he'd have a chance – however slight it might be.

This was going to be a long, bloody mess. Miles just knew it.

Anne looked at the array of wires and panels before them. Ted was doing his best but, unlike the father she knew, this version hadn't veered from anthropological studies to electronics over the past thirty years. But the same raw talent was there, she was sure – Ted just didn't have the benefit of experience in the field. Anne wasn't without skill herself but the complexity of the array before them was somewhat daunting. Touch the wrong wire or component and who knows what might happen.

It was all well and good wanting to send a message. The key was not getting caught. Anne was sure the equipment in the room had to be monitored in some capacity, and a rogue signal could easily lead to them being found. She didn't imagine either of them would be treated particularly well if re-captured, given what they had already endured.

'Blast!' Ted pulled his arm back and sucked his finger. The soldering iron clattered to the side. He scowled and shook his head, his irritation at his incompetence showing.

'Are you all right?' Anne withheld a smirk, trying to show concern instead. It was something she had done on several occasions herself.

'Yes, yes, yes,' Ted muttered. 'Just annoyed at myself.' He pointed to an input at the back of one of the control panels. 'What do you think? If I take that jack and pass it through there…' He indicated a relay switch. '…and make sure I create a bypass switch with what I'm working on now?'

Anne tried to follow the logic. 'What are you bypassing, exactly?'

'The main output. So if we send a signal it won't be noticed through the usual monitoring systems. Like using a back door.' Ted surveyed the room. He didn't exactly sound sure of himself.

Anne wasn't too sure, either. Surely equipment this advanced was set-up to detect any form of interference or sabotage? But, given their predicament, what other choice did they have? Besides, they had already started tampering with the set-up and no one had discovered them. Yet.

Ted noticed Anne's furrowed brow. 'Trust me, I have my doubts, too.' He busied himself with the soldering iron again, taking slightly more care in his movements this time.

Anne followed the wiring from component to component so they could be clear on their pathways and function. She didn't want to miss anything. As she went about her work, she suddenly had a thought.

'I know we've mentioned sending a signal, but what does that mean, exactly? If we just radio for help, anyone can hear us if they happen on the right frequency, no matter what we bypass here.'

Rubbing his chin thoughtfully, Ted considered this. 'They would have to be on the right frequency in the first instance. We'd have the same problem with Morse code, too – anyone could intercept it.'

'Can we mask the transmission at all?' Anne thought there must be a way, although she wasn't sure how to go about it.

'Hmm.' Ted went over to the RF receiver and switched it on. A burst of static spewed forth. He quickly turned it off, in case the noise drew attention to them. 'That might be the answer.'

'Would you care to tell me, then? I can't help if you keep your thoughts to yourself.'

'All RF receivers are plagued by noise. I'd say it's possible to generate an RF signal that resembles noise but is actually a signal. In essence, we'd be burying a message in the static. Anyone listening by chance wouldn't know what they're hearing, but someone with the right knowhow would.'

Anne shook her head. 'It sounds like a very long shot. Not only do we have to bypass the system here, we also have to bury the signal and then hope the right person unscrambles it.' She let out a heavy sigh. 'More chance of a female prime minister.'

'Your friends at the Fifth seem a resourceful bunch.' Ted was trying not to look disheartened.

Anne smiled, sympathetically. 'Jean would work it out.'

Smiling, Ted nodded. He motioned for her to go over to the RF transceiver. 'When I wiggle this bypassed wire – let's call it a switch – I want you to press down on the transceiver as if to talk. At the same time, I want you to also turn on the receiver and then use Morse to send the message. If this Jean is listening carefully, she'll hear there's an actual signal of static against the background static.'

'Good job the transceiver and receiver are separate to each other.' Anne took her place. 'But I don't know Morse code off the top of my head. Sorry.'

Silently, Ted pointed to the wall and chuckled slightly. Anne kicked herself. There was a Morse chart on the wall right in front of her, but somehow she hadn't noticed. That wasn't like her at all. Must be the stress of the situation, she decided.

'Are we ready, then?'

'Hang on.' Ted poked about with his soldering iron for a few more moments. 'There, that should do it.' He gave the wires a chance to cool down.

Anne and Ted got themselves into position, hands in place and ready for what needed to be done. Coordination was necessary to make the plan work, so they kept an eye on each other with their peripheral vision to get the timing right.

'Now!' Ted whispered, firmly.

Nothing happened for a second. Then a flash of sparks erupted from Ted's confused mixture of wires and a puff of smoke engulfed the room. Anne did her best to suppress a cough. Ted stood there, stunned.

Both of them stared at the blackened mess before them. Ted looked sheepishly at Anne.

'Well, that didn't work.'

*

Lethbridge-Stewart surveyed the room around him. It was a medical room, of sorts, and given Dornan's last order, this was obviously where the experiments were done. It seemed inevitable that all three of them would be subject to the same process others were experiencing across the world.

At least there was a bench to sit on. It was the smallest consolation, but Lethbridge-Stewart was doing his best to find a positive thought somewhere. The idea of descending from a man into some horrible primal beast was bad enough, but the fact he could pass on those attributes in such a vile and disgusting way was abhorrent.

He looked at his fellow prisoners. Barnett, given his age and world-weary attitude, seemed resigned to his fate. Gary was a picture of worry, which wasn't surprising, bearing in mind his youth.

Lethbridge-Stewart could see the guards were obviously the surly, silent type. So, as long as they weren't provoked, the guards would probably leave them alone. But would they allow them to talk among themselves? Lethbridge-Stewart knew morale was important, even though the situation seemed hopeless. He felt he should try to make his fellow prisoners feel more at ease. Particularly Gary. He was a young lad with no military training whatsoever and absolutely no experience with these types of matters. The important thing was to keep the chat general and not give away anything that could be used against them.

'I wouldn't say all is lost yet, Gary.' One of the guards turned his head and frowned – but just as quickly moved back into his static position. Lethbridge-Stewart noticed that, despite appearances, he was making sure to keep an ear on the conversation. He wouldn't have been surprised if the man was ex-military or police, at the very least.

Gary looked up, curious. 'What makes you say that?'

Barnett also turned his attention to Lethbridge-Stewart.

'There has to be a reason to keep on going.' Lethbridge-Stewart gave what he hoped was a genial smile. 'Otherwise, what's the point?'

'There is no point!' Barnett spat. 'Not that I've seen anyway.'

'Aside from photography, there must be other passions in your life?' Lethbridge-Stewart was focusing on Gary for two reasons. He hadn't built a wall of cynicism around him like Barnett, and he also needed his spirits lifted the most.

The photographer thought about it for a moment. He looked

at the guards and Lethbridge-Stewart gave him a gentle nod, indicating it was fine for him to speak.

'Music, I guess. I do spend a fair bit of my time at concerts.'

'That wasn't quite what I was getting at. Got a girl, maybe?'

Barnett snorted

'Oh right!' Gary said, finally realising. 'Not as such, no. Do you?'

'I have a fiancée.' Images of Fiona flashed through Lethbridge-Stewart's mind. If anything, she was the reason he had to get out of there. He didn't want her to suffer the torment of his death. He always tried to bury those thoughts, putting it down to the life of a soldier, but they came to him more often than he liked to admit. He turned his focus back to Gary. 'Must have someone you're keen on, though?'

'I did. Once,' Barnett said.

Lethbridge-Stewart and Gary turned to him, taken aback by the response.

'Did you, Captain?' This was a side of Barnett that Lethbridge-Stewart hadn't seen before. Was there something more underneath this tortured, vengeful soul? 'What was her name?'

'Phoebe. We met not long after the war. Dark chestnut hair, deep soulful eyes to match.' Barnett looked at his feet, obviously reflecting on a memory he had pushed aside long ago. 'This was before I met my wife Carol, which is another story all together. But Phoebe… Well, I guess she's the real one that got away.'

'What happened?'

Lethbridge-Stewart shot Gary a look. Trust someone so young to be so tactless. Barnett was unlikely to say any more now. But the captain decided to respond.

'All this,' Barnett said, motioning his hands around him. 'These experiments. Everything I saw. I couldn't tell her, and I couldn't deal with it.' He bit his lip. 'I turned to the bottle and the more I turned to that, the more she turned away from me. We eventually drifted apart, and she went on with her life without me.'

The three remained silent for a little while.

'Have you ever thought of trying to find her again?' Lethbridge-Stewart asked.

'She could be dead by now, for all I know.' Barnett crossed his arms, as if that was the end of the matter.

Lethbridge-Stewart didn't want to push too hard, but he

wanted to give him a reason that would make escape seem worthwhile.

It was Gary who countered Barnett's thought, though. 'You don't know that.'

'Maybe we could help you,' Lethbridge-Stewart said. 'We have plenty of resources that could track her down.'

Barnett looked at the guards and then back at Lethbridge-Stewart. He raised his eyebrows as if to say: *Really? We'd have to get out of here first.*

'What would she want with an old dosser like me anyway? I'm hardly a prize catch. Look at how things turned out with my wife. I messed that up completely. Anyway, Phoebe's never bothered to get in touch with me again over the years.'

'You're not exactly an easy man to track down, as Anne and I both found out. Remember?' Barnett considered the comment and gave a sideways nod. Lethbridge-Stewart continued. 'You don't know what's happened in her life, either. That's why it's worth trying to re-connect. I'm not saying magic will happen twice, but wouldn't you like to know more about what happened to Phoebe over the years?'

'I guess so.'

'There is someone, actually,' Gary said, no doubt spurred on by Barnett's openness.

'Is there?' Lethbridge-Stewart asked.

'Her name's Trish. Works for Rod Stewart's record company. Gets me upfront at the gigs so I can take pictures.'

One of the guards finally turned around. 'Enough talking!' he demanded.

Lethbridge-Stewart gave the others a knowing look and they all knew it was time for silence. At least his two fellow captives had a little hope now.

Miller was continuing to tough it out but, by now, exhaustion was beginning to set in. The initial adrenaline had worn off and he now found himself in a dangerous game of throwing acid at the door every time an attacker made an advance through the hole.

The effect was three-fold. It gave him a brief respite as they tore themselves away in agony (and Miller hated to think of the extra pain he was causing, but he didn't have any other option). But the acid was making the hole even bigger each time, making it easier for those outside trying to force their way in. And the fumes were now affecting Miller, to the point where he was having trouble thinking straight.

If he passed out, all hope would be lost. But hope was already fading fast. Most of the acid was now gone. Miller was again reminded of Leiningen, when he ran out of the petrol he had used to incinerate the waves of attacking ants.

How much time did he have? A sickening crack gave him the answer.

The top half of the door had finally been hollowed out enough for his attackers to push themselves through. Miller grabbed the last of the acid and threw it. The first through the hole screeched back in pain but, sure enough, another started to come through, with others trying to claw inside at the same time.

The fumes from his latest attack overwhelmed Miller, so much so that he crashed to the floor. He looked toward Captain Bishop…

Had he failed again? He had doomed them both, it seemed. Miller's eyes were becoming heavy… But he could see his gun on the floor, next to the empty acid bottles. Maybe he could just reach it? Perhaps there was a bullet left…

That was Miller's last thought as he lapsed into unconsciousness.

Dornan was amused and irritated. Amused that Lethbridge-Stewart was his prisoner again, and mildly irritated at the actions of the Fifth Operational Corps. Word had got to him about events in Newcastle. Werwolf was managing to hold its own, but it was touch and go. The incident would also bring about unnecessary attention which would be… unfortunate. *That particular operation might have to quickly disappear,* he mused. *Or whatever remains moved to a new or existing location.*

At least Newcastle had scored him the prize of Lethbridge-Stewart and Anne Travers. They were bonuses Dornan hadn't been expecting.

Werwolf had suffered losses, but his guards were expendable. They had committed to the cause and were expected to put their lives on the line to ensure victory could be achieved. As he looked around at the surveillance equipment before him, Dornan knew that playing the long game was paying off. Victory was getting closer, day by day. He could feel it.

Reports from other Werwolf operations were generally positive, in terms of test subjects and analysis. But no one had yet solved the problem of the experiment. Another irritation.

With Professor Travers at his disposal, he was determined to make Werwolf's plans come to fruition. He knew there was merit behind it – just looking at the ageless comatose patients from the war, not to mention Travers himself, proved there was definitely something that could be harnessed. Solutions could always be found one way or another. It just took time. Being ruthless also helped.

Dornan considered retiring to his quarters. But that would make him want to nap, like an old person. Dornan refused to accept his age and used his drive and passion for Werwolf to keep him going. Both were inextricably entwined, one fuelling the other.

He was interrupted from his thoughts by a sharp rap on the door.

One of his nameless underlings entered.

'Details?' Dornan didn't need pleasantries with his men. It was a sign of inefficiency.

'Newcastle is under heavy attack.'

'I am aware.' The response was flat, without emotion.

The guard stood there, unsure what to say next.

'Was there something else?' Dornan didn't look up. He remained focused on a monitor in front of him, not expecting a response. 'Good.'

'For the cause!' The man turned on his heel and promptly exited.

Dornan thought the guard lucky. He'd got him on a good day. Of course, Dornan knew what was going on. Everything he needed was in the room, whether it was surveillance or connections to networks that could keep him up-to-date with Werwolf operations around the globe.

It was time to visit his new pets. Maybe taunt them a little before they were experimented on. But Dornan was going to take his time. Something to eat and a whisky first. Better than having a nap, all things considered.

Dr Jarrod Buttery was delighted with the way Werwolf's plans were going. General Dornan would be ever-so-pleased. Not only had they bagged Professor Travers' daughter, but they had also caught Brigadier Lethbridge-Stewart, commander of the Fifth Operational Corps. Who would have thought it?

Sure, there had been some collateral damage at the warehouse in Newcastle but, really, that was to be expected. They were losing people, anyway, through their experiments, so a few more really wasn't worth worrying about. Besides, Werwolf would have taken back control of the warehouse by now. A mere hiccough. They happened all the time. Especially when you were part of a global network. Not everything would pan out exactly as you planned it, although it was always nice when it did. And when things did go wrong, you could end up with bonuses like Lethbridge-Stewart.

Buttery admired his reflection in the small mirror he had on his desk. He couldn't help but give himself a knowing, bearded smirk. There was something quite devilish about his facial follicles, he decided. And that suited him to a tee.

He relished the way things were rolling along. He'd been holed up in his little office for hours, plotting this and that, as per the general's instructions. Naturally enough, he was making sure it all aligned with Werwolf's core purpose. Buttery had to stop himself doing a little jig each time a phone call set certain wheels in motion, or whenever he'd cooked up a little plan that would bring in more experimental 'volunteers'. *It is a good thing,* he thought, *that no one is really following the money trail or why certain purchases are being made from particular accounts on regular occasions.* Sometimes the pursuit of physical evidence made people overlook what was right before them. If only they'd join the dots. It was only the occasional pesky journalist that sniffed out such things – and Buttery didn't think the young denim-clad photographer they had captured was at that level of his career.

The work was now done, and more ideas had been turned into action. It had been a while since he had ventured outside his office door, Buttery realised. Shacking up in an old military base didn't really give him the class and grandeur he felt befitted him, but that would soon change. He wasn't after his own Eagle's Nest, but some wood panelling, polished floorboards and a banker's lamp would be nice. Time for a change of pace.

Should he taunt the Travers team again? Or maybe make himself known to Lethbridge-Stewart and his fellow captors? He could start with a quick walk by the seaside to take in some of the fresh salty air. He'd definitely been cooped up too long; the room was almost soundproof, and it was as if he was completely cut off from the rest of the world. Unless he was disturbed by a momentous noise…

…which suddenly there was.

His door splintered and cracked apart and two men –

obviously military – hurled their might through the aperture and aimed their guns at him.

'Oh, I say! Who are you, big fella?' Buttery took in the man's height, dark tones and his ruggedly handsome square-set jaw.

'Sergeant Major Samson Ware of the Scot's Guards Special Support Group. We're shutting you down.'

Buttery raised his hands in the air and offered the biggest grin he could muster. 'How dramatic!'

'Anyone attempting to escape will be shot on sight,' Sergeant Major Ware said, and nodded at the soldier next to him.

He was an older chap – probably in his late forties – with a sergeant's stripe on his arm. He stepped forward, and motioned with his rifle for Buttery to leave the room. With a grin, Buttery raised his hands in the air and followed Ware out, with the sergeant right behind him.

Buttery's effervescent mood did not last for long.

There were soldiers everywhere. And they didn't belong to Werwolf.

Dornan had told him many stories of the Home-Army Fourth Operational Corps and what they had to do during the war, and now it seemed their successor was just as efficient.

For the first time in a long time, Buttery's brow furrowed. Why hadn't someone thought to call him? If anything, it would have been a chance to hear his chirpy, cheerful voice.

Shots were fired. Miller was roused but, in his haze of confusion, he wondered how he had managed to fire his own gun. More shots. And then he noticed.

The screaming and the endless banging had stopped. Near him, anyway. There were still muffled sounds of shrieking elsewhere in the warehouse.

A man's torso tentatively came through the broken door, careful not to touch any of the fuming wood (a result of acid burn) or the blood that had been left behind.

'Private! Are you with us? Land of the living?'

Miller nodded and crawled across to the door, pulling away what was left of his barricade. It was then he noticed the man was one of his own. One of the Fifth. And seemingly unaffected by whatever had been desperate to get in.

'Captain… Miles?' Miller was only just now able to bring some coherent thoughts together.

'Goodness! Miller? *Private* Miller?' The look of shock on

Miles' face would have been comical, if the situation hadn't been serious. Of course, he didn't know what had transpired since he had last seen the young soldier.

Eventually, Miller was in a position to open the door.

'All clear out here, Private. We've contained this section.' Miles looked around. 'Same can't be said for other parts of the warehouse. Yet.' He came in and surveyed the room. 'Made a bit of a mess in here, I see. What's that stench?'

Miller pointed at the acid bottles and Miles nodded.

'Explains some of the deformed faces on the ones we shot.' It was then the captain noticed the bed. 'Hang on… Who's that in the bed? Not another one of the experiments?' he asked, slightly horrified.

'No, sir. It's Captain Bishop. Had to protect him.' Miller gulped for air. 'He's not in a good way, sir.'

'But he's still alive,' Miles said. 'That's got to be a good thing, in anyone's books.'

'Ward, keep him under guard,' Samson said.

Sergeant Tracy Ward nodded. 'Yes, sir.' He prodded his prissy prisoner in the back. 'This way.'

'Yes, yes,' the ginger-haired man said. 'I can walk without being prodded, thank you.'

'You're lucky that's all you're getting.'

Ward glanced at Samson as the sergeant major ran off to join the crossfire nearby. Ward would have preferred to join in, rather than guard this ferret-looking man, but orders were orders, and in truth he was just glad to be back out in the field properly. Although harrowing, helping to clear the warehouse in Newcastle had been fun, and he was glad when Captain Miles assigned him to lead the reinforcements to Maidens Port. The clean-up in Newcastle wasn't over, but it was far enough along that Miles could spare the men.

Ward had spent far too long tied down to administration work in Imber in the past six months, but with his new promotion, and his clean bill of health, it was good to be back out in the field.

Bullets strafed the ground beneath Samson as he broke into a sprint. A stray Werwolf operative had spotted him out in the open and saw him as an easy target.

Ward went to move his rifle, to fire and save Samson, but men from the Fifth spotted Samson's danger and fired back. The

Werwolf operative went down. Ward smiled. Good; he liked Samson.

Ward blinked, and looked up. A strange beam of blue light was shooting out of the sky.

'What the hell is that?' he shouted.

His prisoner looked, too. 'Oh, I say! Nothing to do with us. At least... Well, Dornan does have his secrets, so I suppose it might be ours.'

Whoever owned it seemed to matter less in the seconds that followed.

The beam hit the ground just before Samson and, his momentum working against him, Samson ran straight into it.

'Oh, shit!'

It was all Ward could think of to say.

As soon as Samson hit the beam, his body seemed to explode. Moments later the beam vanished, and on the ground where Samson had once been, was nothing more than ashes.

'Well,' said Ward's prisoner, 'if that was a Dornan surprise, I'd say that's one point to Werwolf.'

Angered, Ward didn't say a word. He simply struck the man on the back of the head with the butt of his rifle, knocking him out cold.

Ward stood there, the sound of gunfire receding into the distance, his mind turning numb at the thought. The sergeant major had always been there, had always been supportive of Ward after he'd been prematurely aged by the dream eggs. Ward couldn't imagine the Fifth without him, and yet...

Samson...

He was dead.

CHAPTER EIGHTEEN
A Battle Won

THE DOOR handle finally completed its turn. Anne looked at Ted, who looked down and shook his head apologetically. Anne instinctively reached out and held his hand.

She was somewhat surprised when the door opened and two soldiers from the Fifth were standing in front of her. She was about to ask if they'd received her signal… Only it hadn't been sent. Unless she and Ted were wrong.

'Dr Travers,' said one, who Anne was sure was Private Carbis. 'We're here to rescue you.'

Anne smiled at the young private. 'And I'm glad of the rescue. This is…' She paused, unsure how to introduce Ted.

'Ted Travers,' he said.

Carbis frowned a moment, then nodded sharply. 'This way, Dr Travers and… erm, Mr Travers?'

'Professor, actually.'

Carbis' frown deepened, no doubt trying to put the pieces together. There weren't many in the Fifth who didn't know of Anne's father, and the fact that he had died almost a year and a half ago.

'Never mind that,' Anne said. 'Lead the way, Private.'

'Of course.'

The two soldiers, rifles at the ready, led the way through the corridor.

'Is the brigadier safe?' Anne wanted to know.

'Unknown at the moment, Doctor. We've just stormed the place and there are skirmishes happening everywhere. We need to get you outside and to safety.'

'No arguments here,' Anne said, hoping she'd be able to have a word with Lethbridge-Stewart soon. They still had much to do.

*

Lethbridge-Stewart could hear footsteps coming closer. Looking up from the bench, he tried to see past the guards in front of them but couldn't quite discern who was approaching. Gary was also craning his neck for a look. Barnett remained staring at the ground, seemingly resigned to his fate. But the smell permeating the air gave Lethbridge-Stewart a good idea of who it was. Stale cigar smoke was unlikely to be exuding from anyone else in the facility.

'Gentleman!' a voice boomed. 'I trust you're excited to be part of the advancement of science?' By now, Dornan had moved past the guards and was standing in front of the three prisoners sitting on the bench.

Barnett glared at him in disgust. Gary looked away. Lethbridge-Stewart wanted to ignore him and treat him with the contempt he deserved, but he knew Dornan was the type of person who would become more and more aggressive until he triggered some sort of reaction. Just like a schoolyard bully. Better play the game for now, to avoid unnecessary angst from their captor. But, deep down, Lethbridge-Stewart knew they were only delaying the inevitable.

'I wouldn't say "excited" is the right word.'

'Come now, Brigadier. Surely you can see we're trying to make a better world?'

Barnett shook his head. 'If Werwolf is anything like the Nazi regime, I can't see how another seventy-five million dead is a good thing,' he spat, also clenching his fists to keep his anger under control.

Dornan tilted his head back and quietly laughed. 'Nazi Germany was a highly efficient society. Most effective system of government ever devised. Werwolf seeks the same efficacy.'

'And the same horrors experienced by millions during the war, it would seem,' Lethbridge-Stewart said. He maintained a measured, flat tone. He could tell that Dornan wanted to get a rise out of them and he was determined to not give him the satisfaction. 'Describe it however you want, but what you're saying is the typical propaganda the Nazis used to justify their methods. Inhumane and brutal, all of them.'

'Purely a different way of thinking. People have a way of coming around to your ideas in the end. You just need to find the right way to convince them.' Dornan smirked, obviously relishing the hidden threat in his comment.

Lethbridge-Stewart looked at the old man, wondering how

someone could have become so caught up in their own delusions. Then he thought about Barnett next to him and realised war could have different effects, depending on the person. But there was no way he could find any sympathy or even rationalise Dornan's plans. The man appeared to be without a moral compass.

'Ready to be a part of history?' Dornan was obviously taking immeasurable pleasure in making them uncomfortable. 'Once you're part of the experiment, you become royalty, in a manner of speaking. That's if you survive, of course.'

'What do you mean?' Gary said, finally looking at Dornan. The young photographer had been listening, becoming more depressed the more he heard.

'We needed a starting point. And what better place than with Edward and his wife Wallis? Charlie Coburg was a great help, too.'

Dornan was teasing them with information. Lethbridge-Stewart knew the tactic all too well. Playing with the prey. To make them as uncomfortable as possible with the facts before they met their demise. But the information was a nagging thought in the back of Lethbridge-Stewart's mind. The royal connection to what was going on. It was something they had discussed as a possibility.

'So you're blaming the royal family for this now? More rumours and allegations.'

'Not blaming. Thanking them.' Dornan clasped his hands together, pleased he could see their minds ticking over. 'They were so kind to make a donation during the war. As have so many royal relations since. Right around the world.'

'Grubby money, no doubt.'

'No, Gary,' Lethbridge-Stewart said. 'He's talking about blood donations.'

Dornan stepped forward and looked at him more closely. 'Well done, Brigadier. The blue blood of nobility. Say what you like about Nazi scientists, but they were certainly ahead of their time when it came to advancing medical techniques. And they found something slightly different in royal blood when compared to standard human blood.'

'Something that turned humans into rabid animals?' Barnett shot Dornan another disgusted look.

'Not on its own. But it was certainly a starting point for the original experiment. Since then, it's become a game of mix and match with various elements on our journey of discovery.'

Just as Dornan finished speaking, out of nowhere, someone shouted.

'Get down!'

Lethbridge-Stewart instinctively reacted to the command, pulling Gary and Barnett to the ground with him.

Barnett put his hands over the top of his head and, seeing Lethbridge-Stewart had also done the same, Gary followed suit. It was a matter of bracing themselves and waiting for whatever happened above them to play out – and hopefully not get caught up in it.

Warning shots went off. The three Werwolf guards turned around, ready for combat. Instead of surrendering, they opened fire. Lethbridge-Stewart glanced up. A soldier from the Fifth was struck down. At the same time, a volley of bullets was returned, quickly ending any resistance from the guards. Lethbridge-Stewart seized the moment and leaped up, then charged like a bull at Dornan. While he was thrown off-balance, Dornan didn't fall. Instead, he steadied himself and went to lunge back at Lethbridge-Stewart. Bracing himself for the impact, Lethbridge-Stewart was surprised when it didn't come.

Instead, Barnett had picked himself up and channelled his raging torrent of emotions into toppling Dornan. Disoriented from Lethbridge-Stewart's original charge, the general finally fell. Barnett jumped on top and started choking him with every bit of pent-up anger and frustration fuelling the pressure of his fingertips.

'Gary, help me with him!'

Gary looked around, no doubt wondering why Lethbridge-Stewart hadn't ordered his own men to help, and seeing they were busy making sure the room was secure, he joined Lethbridge-Stewart in pulling Barnett off Dornan.

'Enough, Captain, enough!' Lethbridge-Stewart barked. 'We'll see that he gets his just deserts. But not like this.'

The angry fire in Barnett's eyes glared back at him. Lethbridge-Stewart understood the man's resentment and even pitied him.

'Secure that man,' Lethbridge-Stewart ordered his men. 'He's a top priority prisoner.'

Two of the soldiers complied.

'Corporal Sanford,' Lethbridge-Stewart said, calling over the third. 'What's the situation?'

He listened to the report. Samson had worked it out, and

Captain Miles had sent men after securing the warehouse in Newcastle.

'Right,' Lethbridge-Stewart said, once the report was concluded. 'Time we were on the move. Still a lot of mess to tidy up, I imagine. You two, watch him,' he told the two privates, ignoring Dornan's glare as he attempted to rub his throat better. 'Do whatever it takes to keep him secure. He must not escape.'

'Yes, sir!' they said in unison, and forced Dornan to march out.

Lethbridge-Stewart watched them a moment. Dornan didn't look defeated at all.

Letting out a hmm, Lethbridge-Stewart picked up a rifle from the floor. He checked it over, and silently thanked the fallen Werwolf operatives. The weapons left behind would prove useful.

'Corporal, lead the way,' he ordered, and looked at Barnett and Gary. 'I would advise you to arm yourself – even though we've got their leader, I imagine not everyone from Werwolf has been caught.'

Barnett didn't hesitate, and retrieved one of the abandoned rifles. He followed Corporal Sanford out.

'A problem, Gary?' Lethbridge-Stewart asked.

Gary looked down at the remaining rifle. 'I… I haven't fired a gun in my life.'

'Very well, too late to be trained now. Stick by me. Just in case.'

Emerging from the base, their exit had been uneventful. When they'd heard gunfire, they stopped and waited and then continued on after ensuring silence for several minutes. They quickly ran to the safety of a nearby vehicle, as soldiers from the Fifth gave them covering fire. Lethbridge-Stewart was relieved to see Anne safe, and Professor Travers – well, Ted – with her as well.

Anne rushed up to Lethbridge-Stewart. 'Any word on Bill?'

'Steady on, Anne. I've only just escaped myself. I need time to be fully briefed and get up to speed with things.'

Lethbridge-Stewart turned to Corporal Sanford, and the men still covering Dornan. A little distance away several other Werwolf operatives, including a chap with the most remarkable red hair Lethbridge-Stewart had ever seen, were kneeling in the mud, hands on heads, rifles trained on them.

'Put him over there with them. We'll deal with them all later.'

'Yes, sir!' The corporal turned to the men and gave them their orders.

Lethbridge-Stewart looked around the naval base. The Fifth may have liberated the base and caught the main offenders, but occasional gunfire was a reminder that things weren't quite over.

'We need to move out,' he decided sharply. 'We have a lot to do.'

'More than you imagine,' Anne said. 'But aren't you forgetting something? What about the patients? There are some here. They're the ones originally experimented on.'

'From the '40s?' Lethbridge-Stewart looked at Barnett.

'They're alive?' Barnett asked.

'Yes, alive and still in a coma,' Ted told them.

'Very well,' Lethbridge-Stewart said. 'Is there anything you can do for them?'

'Not at the moment, but—'

Lethbridge-Stewart cut Ted off. 'In that case, I'll leave some men to monitor the situation. Werwolf isn't defeated yet, so others may well turn up here. I also need to be fully briefed on Newcastle – and Bill,' he added, looking at Anne, before continuing. 'We need to get word out about Werwolf around the world.'

'How are you going to manage that?' Gary asked, inquisitive as ever.

'Talk to my higher-ups, and use every contact I have. Maybe even involve the United Nations. Whatever it takes, because there's a global Nazi threat and it needs stopping.'

Ted cleared his throat. 'Actually, Brigadier, Anne and I came across some equipment in there that gave us an idea.'

'Excellent. Corporal Sanford!' Lethbridge-Stewart called. Sanford looked over from where he was talking to the men guarding the prisoners and quickly jogged over. He saluted and stood to attention. 'Who's running this operation?' Lethbridge-Stewart asked.

'Sergeant Ward, sir.'

'Good. Go and find him, bring him to me.'

'Sir!' Sanford saluted and rushed off.

Lethbridge-Stewart looked at Ted. 'This idea of yours, Professor, what is it?'

He listened carefully as Ted explained his theory about halting and even reversing the process. Lethbridge-Stewart only stopped him once when the scientific jargon started to become indecipherable. With a smile, Anne broke it down for him.

'I confess,' Ted added, 'we don't know if it will work, but...'

'It's the best you've got?' Lethbridge-Stewart smiled grimly. 'Frankly, Professor, if you're even half the man I once knew, I'd trust your efforts on even your worst day. Especially if you have Anne assisting you. And... Ah!'

Sergeant Ward came jogging around the corner of the nearest building. He stopped in front of them and offered a salute.

'Sir, reporting as ordered.'

'At ease, Sergeant.' Ward relaxed and Lethbridge-Stewart continued. 'I'm leaving you with a platoon of men here. Liaise with Sergeant Major Ware. We need to maintain control of this base. There are still patients here, Sergeant, men who have been in a coma since World War Two. Protect them.'

'Yes, sir.'

'Contact the local authorities, so that these men can be placed under arrest,' Lethbridge-Stewart said, indicating the prisoners. 'They will stand trial and be punished accordingly.'

'Very good, sir.'

Lethbridge-Stewart nodded. 'Right, now that's settled, Professor, Anne, Ga—'

'Sorry to interrupt, sir,' Ward said, now looking very uncomfortable. 'I regret to inform you, sir, that Sergeant Major Ware is dead.'

'I beg your pardon?' Lethbridge-Stewart ignored the gasp that came from Anne. 'What happened?'

'Hard to explain, sir. A beam of light shot out of the sky and...' Ward looked at a loss. He shrugged. 'Disintegrated him, sir.'

This was troubling. The loss of Samson was... difficult to process, and Lethbridge-Stewart had to force himself to put his grief and anger aside. He still had a job to do, and the threat to the world was bigger than the loss of one man. As for the news of a new weapon...

Lethbridge-Stewart quickly marched over to the prisoners. Ward kept by his side.

'You,' Lethbridge-Stewart said, pointing at Dornan. 'Explain this new weapon.'

Dornan looked up at him. 'And what weapon would that be?'

'A satellite of some kind, one assumes. Capable of firing some kind of laser, with enough power to disintegrate people. Ring a bell?'

'I'm afraid I don't know what you're talking about, Brigadier.'

Lethbridge-Stewart stared at Dornan. The man took such pleasure in what he did, it seemed unlikely he would not take pride in such a weapon. On the other hand, Dornan and this base was but one part of Werwolf's larger plan. It was possible he did not know everything.

Lethbridge-Stewart looked at Sergeant Ward. 'You have your orders, Sergeant.'

'Yes, sir!' Ward saluted and Lethbridge-Stewart returned to his own little team.

He paused. Anne looked at him, clearly only just holding back tears.

'Alistair, is it true? Samson can't be…'

Lethbridge-Stewart glanced at the men watching. None of them knew Samson (although Gary had, of course, spent some time with him recently), and they were clearly at a loss over what to do with Anne's naked emotions. Even Ted stood there, uncertain. Proof, if any more was needed, that he really wasn't Anne's father.

Lethbridge-Stewart placed a comforting hand on Anne's shoulder. 'Ward wouldn't lie about that.'

'No, of course not,' Anne said, looking over at the sergeant. 'But…'

'Anne, we'll have to process this later. Right now, we have a world to protect.'

Anne swallowed and nodded. 'You're right.'

Lethbridge-Stewart turned back to the men. 'Right then, Pro—'

'Actually, I think I should stay here with the patients,' Ted said. 'They haven't survived any attempts at being woken up.'

'No, this is your plan. I need you at the centre of things. Sergeant Ward will keep them safe.'

'I'd like to volunteer for that role, sir.' Barnett hadn't said much since their escape, but now stepped forward. 'Think about it. Assuming these brainwave things work, and they wake up, maybe someone who was at the same base with them could help? Will be a bit of a shock to find the war's over and all this time has passed.'

Lethbridge-Stewart considered the offer. 'Permission granted, Captain. Report to Sergeant Ward, let him know.'

It was… unusual… for a captain to report to a sergeant, but Barnett didn't seem to have any problem with it.

'What about me?'

Lethbridge-Stewart looked at Gary. 'What about you? You're coming back to the Madhouse where I can keep an eye on you.'

'Well, um…' Gary looked around, watching Barnett walk over to Ward. 'Can't I backup Barnett? I'm sure I can be of more use here.'

That was unexpected, but Lethbridge-Stewart nodded. 'Very well. Can't think of two people better suited. But, remember, no photographs.'

It took what seemed like a hundred phone calls. Explaining, requesting, demanding… almost begging. Lethbridge-Stewart maintained his dignity throughout the proceedings, although sometimes his annoyance at bureaucracy filtered through. Never mind there was an organisation determined to start another world war – no! The proper procedures just *had* to be followed.

Fortunately, when it came to the scientific side of things, Anne and Ted pulled it all together, frantically calling in whatever favours they could.

Lethbridge-Stewart had made the almost-grovelling-but-not-enough-to-give-him-satisfaction call to Peyton Bryden. The industrialist was the financial backer behind the Fifth Operational Corps. Lethbridge-Stewart and Bryden had a rather fractious relationship at the best of times but, after Lethbridge-Stewart rattled off the list of what was required from Bryden Industries, Bryden sounded almost bemused. Manpower was duly allocated to collect and deliver all necessary equipment to Anne and Ted at Nuffield.

Which was where Lethbridge-Stewart found himself now. Nuffield Radio Astronomy Laboratories, previously known as the Jodrell Bank Experimental Station. He didn't know why people had to keep changing the name of things. It just confused everyone.

He looked at the setup around him. Cabinets of flashing lights, hundreds of switches and tapes spooling forward and back, surrounded him. Added to this was Ted's own array with hundreds of components, wires and cables hooked up in numerous different ways. Lethbridge-Stewart wasn't going to pretend he understood it all. To him, it looked like the insides of transistor radios had been thrown haphazardly across the room.

Anne and Ted were working with Nuffield's top two boffins, Drs Birch and Jones, who were, in a roundabout sort of fashion, under the direction of Lethbridge-Stewart. The Fifth Operational

Corps hadn't exactly commandeered Nuffield, but the staff had been told to adhere to the Fifth's requests. Feathers were ruffled; things were said. Ted had regurgitated his explanation of what he was planning for the umpteenth time. The impossibility of the scale of the task had been mentioned on myriad occasions.

Similar conversations had taken place across the world via phone, telegram and telex. Objections had been raised, concerns dealt with and, finally, there was (often begrudging) acceptance of what needed to be done.

Peering out the window, Lethbridge-Stewart found the height of the control room made him a little giddy. He looked back at the assembled team. They had been working around the clock to get everything ready. As had everyone involved right across the world. But a doubt still lingered in his mind.

'I'm sure you all know what you're doing,' he conceded. 'But is creating a global network really such a good idea?'

Anne frowned. 'Impeccable timing, Brigadier. Do you really want us to abandon all this work now?'

'Obviously not, but the last thing we want is anything to go wrong. Professor Travers here has stated from the outset he's not sure it will work.'

Birch looked up through his horn-rimmed glasses, concerned. Jones kept ferreting away with a soldering iron, occasionally flinching as she accidentally burned herself. They had been reluctantly pulled away from their research work on quasars, pulsars and gravitational lenses to work on this special project.

'I was just thinking of the Post Office Tower incident, that's all.' Lethbridge-Stewart didn't want to give away too much in front of the Nuffield boffins.

'Brigadier, that involved a massive computer network and an artificial intelligence,' Anne said. 'There may have been radio transmissions involved, but we're in control of what's being sent out this time around, not some deranged computer.'

Ted was listening intently, as were Birch and Jones. Lethbridge-Stewart glared at Anne. She shouldn't have been talking so openly about classified information – but he'd been the one to bring it up.

'Very well, then. Proceed.'

Lethbridge-Stewart hoped that would close the matter. Fortunately, there were no follow-up questions from the others. He decided to check on their progress instead.

'How close are we? We've got Whitehall, MI5 and MI6 all

breathing down our necks,' he said. 'And that's just in this country. If it wasn't for an emergency United Nations ratification–'

'Yes, we understand, Brigadier!' Anne was clearly frazzled. 'But we don't have a magic wand. It will take as long as it takes. I'm sure every other scientist at every other telescope around the world will be saying the same thing. You want it done yesterday, but you don't want it to go wrong. Well, you can't have both.'

Lethbridge-Stewart looked at his feet. She was right, of course. But he was the one who would ultimately be held to account for everything. 'How are you going to get this delta brainwave to transmit?' he asked.

Ted decided to answer. 'It's something we replicate quite simply. Delta waves are normal brainwaves in the encephalogram of a person in deep, dreamless sleep, occurring with high voltage and low frequency. About one to four Hertz. We've just built a circuit that can do this.'

'And that will do the trick, will it?'

'It's a type of cranial electrotherapy stimulation that has been known to cure insomnia in the past. But only at an individual level. It's never been tried on this scale before.'

Dr Birch added, 'When it's hooked up to the radio telescope, it becomes a giant neuro-transmitter.'

'We're hoping it will fix or reset the brains of those who have been experimented on,' Anne explained. 'At its most basic, they have been deprived of sleep. Delta waves are associated with the deepest levels of relaxation and restorative, healing sleep.'

Lethbridge-Stewart thought he understood. 'So, the wave goes from this telescope to the next one and so on?'

Jones sniggered and shook her head. 'No, that's not quite how it works. Each telescope needs to connect to a circuit that will replicate the delta wave.' She rubbed her tired brow. 'The tricky bit is the coordination – they all need to come on at the same time. That way, the world will be surrounded by them. It's kind of like clouds coming together and forming one big cloud, although in this case it's all invisible.'

'Thank you for bringing your knowledge down to my level,' Lethbridge-Stewart said. 'Excuse my ignorance once again, but won't it also have an effect on others, putting them to sleep? Could be very dangerous for people driving cars or even flying aeroplanes.'

Ted grimaced, then considered the question. 'Unlikely. Our

working theory is that it will only have an impact on those who have been severely deprived of sleep. The people injected with the blue blood concoction.' He paused as other possible scenarios played out in his mind. 'I suppose there's potential for it to affect those with severe cases of insomnia. I'm not talking about new mothers or students worrying about exams, but those rare instances of people suffering badly with it for years. Those people know their limits, so I doubt they'd be operating any sort of vehicle or machinery. Admittedly, it's a risk we're going to have to take.' He stopped again, thoughtfully. 'This may even help them.'

Lethbridge-Stewart thought it best to leave that to the boffins around him. 'Let me know as soon as you're ready to go. Authorities around the world are ready to storm known or suspected Werwolf operations. But they're under orders not to do anything until the delta wave transmission starts.'

CHAPTER NINETEEN
Calling Out Around the World

ANNE LOOKED at Ted, then to Birch and Jones. They had run tests, they had burned out circuits, replaced them and started again. They'd argued – in a scientific manner, of course – on the best way to go about things. If they weren't under so much pressure, Anne would have enjoyed the insightfulness of the others. They completed yet another check of the equipment and Lethbridge-Stewart had been notified. Everything was prepared. They had been getting responses from other radio telescopes all day, declaring they were ready for the main order. Scientists were sitting in similar control rooms around the world, going through similar motions, waiting for one word.

'Who would like to do the honours?'

Anne didn't want to be presumptuous and just do it herself, especially given she was a guest at Nuffield. But Drs Birch and Jones shook their heads.

Ted just smiled and replied, 'Go ahead.'

Nothing like a bit of pressure, Anne thought, as she surveyed the controls. *Especially when the whole world is involved.*

Taking a deep breath, she flicked the necessary switches and adjusted several dials. Her hand hovered over the last switch as she leaned into the microphone before her, making sure it was also ready at the same time. She hesitated for the briefest of pauses and then…

'Activate.'

In a sheep paddock outside the little town of Parkes in New South Wales, stood the pride and joy of Australian astronomy: a radio telescope. It wasn't the only one in the country, but it had played an integral part in the moon landing just a few years before. Not that a lot of people knew about it, but those involved certainly felt an honour about the achievement. The local mayor had tried to drum up interest in a film about it, to no avail. But the locals remained chuffed all the same.

The imperturbable Cliff, the scientist in charge, puffed on his pipe in the control room and looked to his colleagues: softly-spoken maths whiz Glenn, and Mitch, who prided himself on keeping the equipment humming along. With the moon landing experience under their belt – with NASA, they had engineered a space-to-Earth interface to carry video and telemetry signals from the Lunar Lander – they felt they could handle pretty much anything.

But the request that had come to them, via ASIO, to help the Brits was quite unlike anything they had been asked to do before. Their director insisted it had to be done and no questions, beyond the scientific, were to be asked. It was even more heavy-handed than when the Yanks were in town. True, there were no men-in-black secret service types this time, but the veil of secrecy they had to operate under had been dictated to them in no uncertain terms. Cliff was unsure how well such a secret could be maintained, given radio telescopes around the world were all being asked to do the same thing. Honeysuckle Creek, Tidbinbilla and Carnarvon were all in on it – and that was just Australia.

Whatever was happening, Cliff knew they had a job to do and they were going to do it to the best of their ability. It would be another feather in their cap. Glenn and Mitch had wired everything as instructed. Some of it was a bit of an ask, but Mitch had managed to bodge certain things together when they didn't have the right component. The barbed wire, tin lids and empty jam jars looked rather incongruous among the more technical equipment, yet somehow it all worked. The tricky part was not tripping over everything and accidentally snagging yourself on the wire. Mitch was typically in a pair of shorts and thongs, so had to be extra careful, lest he pierce his skin and need a tetanus shot. There was no time for that.

Finally, they had run all the required tests and everything pointed to success with this mission.

The only hurdle, Cliff knew, might be the town's occasionally erratic power supply. The last thing they needed was the mayor's pie warmer to go on the blink at a crucial moment and short out the entire town. There had been a few touch-and-go moments in the past.

'How long d'ya think before we can get this show on the road?' Mitch was a trooper, through and through, but now they had set everything up and were ready, he was keen to get on with it.

The often-quiet Glenn spoke. 'You can't ride roughshod into something like this. Precision is key. You need to do all the checks and balances.'

Cliff liked it when the young man spoke up; his confidence was improving.

'Mate, I know that,' Mitch said, impatiently. 'We've been through this before. Neil and Buzz – we helped the world see them. But we knew what was happening then. A little spaceship would land on the moon; they'd go for a stroll and then take off again. This time, all we know is that we have to transmit this delta wave thing.' Mitch motioned to the specialised circuit among the jumble of wires, transistors, conductors and resistors. 'We don't know what the end goal is here. It's like playing a game of footy without knowing you should kick the ball between the goalposts to win.'

'Which is why I think we need to take extra care,' Glenn said, quietly. 'If we don't know the full extent of what we're doing.'

Cliff plucked a thread from his cardigan and inhaled from his pipe again. 'We've had other assignments where we've not been told the whole picture. I'm sure the CIA keeps a close eye on NASA and what they share. And let's not even go into what British Rocket Group might be up to.'

Glenn and Mitch exchanged glances. There had been rumours which had even reached Australia. Sometimes the director gave them orders to position the telescope a certain way at a specified time, and the Parkes trio was usually left out of the loop as to why. Supposedly it was to monitor satellites and ensure they had achieved their required orbit but Glenn, in particular, had found some of the coordinates weren't in keeping with an Earth trajectory. He did as he was told but, occasionally after far too many beers at the town's only pub and with no one else around, they got to speculating as to where the telescope was actually pointing on those occasions – and what that could possibly mean.

'The important thing is we're ready,' Cliff said, keeping his cool. 'I've already sent word to the Brits that all they need to do is give us the command.'

Mitch screwed up his face, slightly annoyed. 'When d'ja do that?'

'When you were rabbiting on just before. Best we all get into position now.'

As they all got into place, being careful not to step on anything strewn across the floor, they were interrupted by a female voice coming through the speaker. Cliff nodded at Mitch, now sitting down, who quickly but methodically went through the rehearsed procedure, then pressed the final switch.

Similar stories played out across the world... From Puerto Rico's Arecibo Observatory to Itapetinga in São Paolo through to Peach Mountain, Haystack, Leuschner and Greenbank in the United States and the Dominion in Canada. One by one, they activated their delta wave.

As did France's Nançay and Bordeaux Observatories, Germany's Effelsberg and Stockert, Dwingeloo in the Netherlands, and Medicina in Italy, then the Ooty Radio Telescope in south India. Amazingly, the Soviet Union had also agreed to cooperate with RATAN-600, Pluton in Crimea and the recently completed Ukrainian T-shaped radio telescope. Werwolf had been active everywhere and no one was taking any chances.

Even not-yet-complete telescopes joined the network. New Mexico's Very Large Array and Finland's Metsähovi Radio Observatory had enough infrastructure in place to allow delta waves to be transmitted from them, even though they were not operating at full capacity.

Every bit helped.

Closer to home, the University of Hertfordshire chipped in with the Bayfordbury Observatory and Cambridge joined with its One Mile Telescope.

For once, the world put their differences aside, coming together for one purpose. No one wanted another world war. Not like the last one, anyway.

And it all led back to the Scots Guards Special Support Group in the United Kingdom and one man's theory on how to solve the problem. A man who, in reality, was an impostor.

Edward was keeping a close eye on Nuffield's output of the delta wave, as Anne liaised with the other radio telescopes around the world. Birch and Jones monitored the equipment, their hands dancing over the switches and lights to ensure everything was doing what it was supposed to be doing.

The enormity of it all wasn't lost on him. He wondered if the other Professor Travers would have come to the same solution as him. It was useless speculating, he knew that. But he did hope that Anne might see him in a more positive light now.

He was also getting ahead of himself. There was no way of knowing if the delta wave plan had been a success until someone monitoring the experimental subjects reported back to Lethbridge-Stewart. Edward had horrible visions of thousands of people exploding and crumbling into dust like those two poor soldiers back at Maidens Port. He shuddered just thinking about it.

'Everyone has come online now,' Anne said, bringing him back. 'Delta wave transmissions have been activated and are continuing.' There was a low hum in the room as waves oscillated on display panels, increasing to a pulsating throb.

'How long do we need to transmit for?' Jones asked.

All eyes turned to Edward. 'That's a good question,' he pondered, almost to himself. 'Until we get a report of success somewhere, I suppose.' More thoughts went through his mind. 'Or until part of the network gives way. Remember, while each telescope may have its own delta wave transmitter, the world needs to be engulfed by the waves to be entirely effective.' He rubbed his stubble as he spoke. 'It's a bit like when you tug a stray thread on your jumper. One wrong move and you could end up unravelling the whole thing.'

'Let's hope we remain tight-knit, then,' Anne said, her eye on a flickering needle moving closer to its red zone.

At Metsähovi, it had all started out smoothly enough. Everyone had understood the risks, and they were confident enough the new radio observatory was up to the task. Väinö and Juhani had followed the instructions from the United Kingdom to the letter. Finnish efficiency had ensured that. There were some misgivings about whether there was enough power for the task, but their officials had told them it wouldn't be a problem. The two had no reason to doubt them. It was just that... Metsähovi hadn't been tested before. The majority of it had been put together and, hypothetically, would work. But the big Finnish scientists hadn't yet gone through the arduous rounds of trials that were needed to ensure everything was working, fixing any glitches in the process. That was the usual method before declaring any major project open for business and taking on any assignments.

Despite this, Väinö and Juhani were extremely proud of what they had done with a looming deadline breathing down their necks. In fact, Väinö had turned down a dinner of poronkaristys, sugared lingonberries, mashed potatoes and cucumber pickles with his wife on more than one occasion while he worked frantically to achieve what was necessary (Juhani had no such offers and was happy getting by with rice pies and salmiakki). Neither had dared say it to each other, but the whole experience had been particularly straining.

They received the command to activate, and their delta wave started transmitting. Several minutes passed. Väinö allowed himself a drink of water and left Juhani to keep an eye on things. But the moment his back was turned, there was a terrible groaning sound. The background hum rapidly grew in volume. Lights started to flicker.

'We're losing power!' Juhani said.

'Evidently!' Väinö leapt back to the control panel and scanned it as quickly as he could. 'Can you compensate?'

'I don't know,' Juhani admitted, the pitch in his voice making it clear his panic was rising. 'The power supply is phasing in and out!'

That isn't good, Väinö knew. Too much disruption and it could cause a component to blow or, worse still, the whole system would shut down as a safety precaution. That was assuming the safety precautions were built into the system and hadn't been overlooked in the rush to get everything ready. *Surely the powers-that-be can't have been that stupid?* Väinö's mind was leaping ahead and playing out possibilities that hadn't yet happened. If the system didn't shut down when it was supposed to, that would mean…

Every single light in the control room lit up and a massive spray of sparks exploded from half the panel, singeing Juhani, causing him to cry out. He grabbed his hand in a mixture of shock and pain.

'*Jumalauta!*' Väinö couldn't help but curse as he reached for the fire extinguisher.

Juhani staggered backwards in somewhat of a daze. It was now that Väinö wished he'd paid more attention during the fire drills – but they had been so boring compared to the excitement of creating the Metsähovi telescope. Now he found himself trying to read the instructions written in fine print while smoke was lingering around the room. The warning siren that had also gone off wasn't helping matters.

Eventually, Väinö pulled the pin from the extinguisher,

squeezed the nozzle at the panels in front of him and hoped for the best.

It was pointing in the wrong direction. The burst of carbon dioxide missed Väinö's face, but Juhani got caught in its wake. He fell down, coughing and spluttering, due to the lack of oxygen. Väinö quickly corrected his error and pressed on the nozzle, this time actually spraying in the vicinity of the controls. The small flames and occasional spark were soon put out.

Gasping for air, Juhani propped himself up and managed to breathe again. Väinö looked on in devastation at the blackened control panel. The system had indeed shut down like it should have. But the damage done had likely set themselves back by at least six months.

'I guess we weren't as ready as we thought,' he said with a sigh.

'Finland's dropped out!' Jones looked anxiously at Edward and Anne, as one of the lights in front of her stopped blinking its illumination.

'Just like Eurovision all over again,' Birch said wryly.

'Any chance they'll join us again?' Edward bit his lip.

Anne shook her head, after a quick look at the panel in front of her. 'Doesn't appear likely. Seems they've gone kaput. Must have had a blow-out of some description. That was always going to be the danger with these untested telescopes.' She gave him an apologetic look. 'Push too hard and something was bound to give.'

It was a worrying development, but Edward remained hopeful. 'Is everyone else still okay? Transmitting the wave?'

'Yes.' Anne and Jones responded in unison, looking at the equipment before them.

'Then I hope it's just a stray thread that doesn't matter; one that you can easily cut off and not worry about.' Edward tried forcing a smile. 'Or maybe we've been transmitting long enough?'

Birch then said the one thought no one else had been willing to voice. 'Let's hope we don't lose another station. Otherwise, everything really will start to unravel.'

There had been the barest flicker of movement in the eyelid. Almost imperceptible at first. Gradually, it became a flutter and then resembled a blink. The eye within opened and registered something it hadn't seen in years. Light. The brain connected to it was quite groggy and tried to comprehend the stimulus. As the signals travelled as impulses from the retina to the brain, long unused parts of the grey matter were suddenly triggered into action.

'Hey, that one's opening his eyes!' Gary pointed excitedly.

Barnett leapt up from his chair. What he was hearing was almost too good to be true. He had to see it with his own eyes. The soldier was definitely stirring. He was trying to comprehend where he was. As minutes passed and his eyes grew more accustomed to the light, he tried moving his mouth. Only a guttural sound emerged.

'Gary, get this man some water, quick!'

The young photographer quickly rushed to the sink and was soon holding a cup to the man's lips. It was clearly a struggle as he tried to ingest the water.

'Hate to think when he last did that,' Barnett murmured. 'He's only had this all these years,' he noted, nodding at the drip. 'Take your time,' he told the newly-awakened soldier. 'There's no rush.'

Gary held the water in front of him, letting him sip gently as his body rediscovered its senses.

Once the initial shock of the first man waking had passed, Barnett felt slightly on edge. Particularly when he finally noticed the others were waking up as well.

Gary was completely focused on his job at hand, ensuring water was provided as necessary. Barnett couldn't believe what was happening – a man being brought back to a proper life – after all this time. Tears welled up in his eyes.

He was waiting for the moment when someone would lurch from the bed and start screaming. It would be a brutal reminder of what he had seen during the war. But that moment never came.

Barnett quickly motioned for Sergeant Ward's men to help give water to the others who were awakening. It was going to be a slow-but-steady process of getting to them all, making sure they got the required hydration and whatever else they needed.

The former captain was racing around so much he didn't fully take in what was happening until he was sitting on another bed, copying Gary's earlier actions with the water.

This is it. These men are finally saved. Whatever they've done with the telescopes, it's working.

Barnett now knew what his purpose should be. He had to help these men recover… First from their extreme frailties, atrophied muscles and so on, then from the fact they were men out of time. He could help to integrate them back into a changed world. There was a long road ahead but that didn't matter. Barnett wanted to be the man these former soldiers could count on.

For the first time in more than two decades, Barnett felt a flush of pride in himself.

CHAPTER TWENTY
Back to Life

KEIBU KAZUKO Shimada lowered his firearm and dropped his shield. As squad commander of the police station and leader of the riot company, the chief inspector didn't quite know what had happened. The rest of his team were equally perplexed and not sure what to do next.

One minute they had been under attack; screaming men and women coming at them from across Ogimachi Park. All were completely bloodied, and some had insides which had been ripped open and were hanging loose. Shimada was about to give the order to throw tear gas, simply because they couldn't control the oncoming horde and he didn't know what else to do.

There had been previous isolated incidents, of course, but their manpower and weapons brought these strange, transformed citizens under control very quickly. Nobody knew where they came from – or wouldn't say anything if they knew. *Which is probably more likely*, Shimada had admitted to himself. The Emperor, Prime Minister and Ministers of State didn't keep everyone particularly well-informed. Shimada and his ilk were just given orders and expected to get on with it. Keep everything under control at all costs. That was the prime goal.

And now, before them, the advancing mass just stopped.

A strange silence came over the park, only punctuated by Osaka's traffic noises in the distance. The previously wild-eyed citizens looked completely bewildered, as if they had no idea what they had been doing or where they were. They were especially surprised to see the riot company bearing down on them. A minute or two passed and no one moved, neither police nor former wild, screaming humans. Then one fell to the ground. And another. Then another. But there had been no gunshots. Down they went like the dominoes Shimada's children played with. Soon half of the crowd were lying prostrate before him.

He cast an eye at the rest of his company. Some were doing their best not to be sick. It wouldn't do to be seen as weak while serving as a police officer. But some of the crowd in the park were also being sick, unable to contain themselves. Then Shimada realised what was going on. The strange injuries some of them had. Some were so severe, people had fainted almost straight away. Others then got sight of their own injuries and collapsed as well. The remainder had then taken in the injuries of those around them and had an automatic revulsion to it all.

The situation had changed, and Shimada needed to take the lead. It was time to call in the Fire and Disaster Management Agency for ambulance dispatch and try to provide first aid until they arrived. Osaka Police Hospital and City General were going to be busy.

Tama Latukefu wasn't sure where he was or what he was doing. He'd been in Christchurch with his rōpū and a friend of a friend from another Maori group, who said he knew a way for them to make some quick cash.

Something told him it was a bad idea, but he went along with it, anyway, because he needed some extra dollars for that month's rent and also had nothing better to do. He'd been drinking heavily before, so he only had the haziest recollection of being bundled into the back of a panel van, headed off to locations unknown. There had been patches of singing and more drinking, matched with bumpy roads and hitting his head on the van's roof, but it was all a drunken blur.

No one said exactly where they had ended up but there had been some yelling and some fists flying. How the argument started was anyone's guess, but he suspected it was to do with the promised money. Tama would be the first to admit he was a big boy – no one ever picked a fight with him – but in his alcohol-fuelled daze several unknown flogs had brought him down. Not before he got a few good punches in himself (he hoped). He did remember a massive blow to the head. Then passing in and out of consciousness on a bed somewhere.

There were some vague dream-like memories of getting up again and screaming, Tama recalled. But that was while he was knocked out, surely? But he couldn't shake the feeling that he'd been up and about, doing something.

Probably just the waipiro talking.

He felt extremely tired. As if he'd been pushing himself to

the limit, exerting himself as much as he could. Maybe it was an after-effect of the knockout punch?

Still disoriented, Tama looked down at his sizeable stomach. That didn't look too flash. His shirt was blood-soaked. Had he been in a knife-fight? He hesitated, but slowly pulled up the shirt to take a look. *That's some sick stuff, bro,* he told himself. Tama couldn't quite comprehend how he'd been injured in such a way.

The original fight was a punch-up, as best he could recall. Had he drunkenly broken into the Orana Wildlife Park? Maybe he tried tackling the park's lion or gorilla? Tama just couldn't see what could have made the gashes across his stomach. Normally, he had a strong resolve but this was a bit too much. He started feeling woozy…

He needed to get back to Cleo. She would look after him.

'Do you remember those three patients in Ward Four?' Nurse Irina Usikova had managed to stop Dr Lebedev, who looked particularly annoyed by the interruption. He was extremely methodical about doing his rounds in Minsk's City Clinical Hospital of Infectious Diseases and didn't like anything that threw him off his routine.

'Unless a patient is dying, you should know very well not to bother me at this time.'

Nurse Usikova always hated his brusque manner. No people skills whatsoever. He could show a bit more compassion to those he was supposed to care for. She tried to make up for it whenever she could, to make the patients feel a bit more at ease, but it was difficult when she was walking on eggshells. She found Dr Lebedev intimidating. The nurse decided to get to the point as bluntly as possible so he would take notice.

'The coma patients!' she said excitedly. 'They're waking up!'

She had never seen the doctor look surprised before. He was usually unflappable and completely no-nonsense about everything. The nurse wished she'd had a camera at that moment to catch him with his mouth open. It was only a split second, and she was the only person to see it.

'What are you talking about, Nurse?'

'Come see for yourself!' She led the way.

It had been a mystery as to how the patients had ended up in this condition. They'd been delivered to the hospital in the middle of the night under armed guard. Efforts to find out more from the Armed Forces of the Union of Soviet Socialist Republics and Brezhnev's cronies in the Council of Ministers had been fruitless. The hospital was left only with the instruction to 'look after them' and that's all they were ever told, despite Lebedev's attempts at finding out more.

From that point on Lebedev had little choice but to care for them, just like any other coma patient. If the nurses, doctors or any other staff started asking too many questions, he gave them short shrift. Nurse Usikova had taken a special interest in the patients, doing her best to keep her eye on them when her duties didn't require her elsewhere. She was just as intrigued as everyone else.

Now, Usikova tried her best to maintain a sense of professionalism, especially given Dr Lebedev was briskly walking behind her. Entering the ward, there was no denying what Nurse Usikova had claimed. The three patients definitely had their eyes open and were trying to speak, although their mouths were so dry they only managed guttural sounds.

'Nurse! Water for these men, quick.'

Dr Lebedev went over to inspect one of the men as Nurse Usikov hurriedly provided water to the others. He pulled back the man's eyelids and looked into his pupils, then took the man's pulse. The patient eventually got his share of water from the nurse and managed to speak, ever so quietly.

'Privet.'

Nurse Usikova wanted to squeal with joy. For the second time that morning, Dr Lebedev was dumbfounded.

'By Dostoevsky's grave,' he started. 'This is truly remarkable.'

Private Jack Miller still couldn't quite believe he'd made it to the Madhouse. He'd heard so much about it in the months since he was assigned to the Fifth. And it was everything he had hoped – not that he'd had the chance to see much of it, yet. But he was here, and that was something.

Once Captain Miles and his team had secured the warehouse, it was decided most of Werwolf's victims would be taken to the nearest hospital, where they would be kept on close watch. Fifth troops who had been infected, however, were airlifted back to Scotland and placed in the care of Captain Lindsay. Miller was reassigned to clear-up duty in another location, but he'd argued in favour of staying at Bishop's side.

Miles wasn't too impressed by the argumentative private, although he was soon persuaded otherwise when a corporal had vouched for Miller, and explained that Miller's actions at the warehouse had probably kept Bishop from turning into one of those creatures. Miles quickly approved Miller's trip to the Madhouse.

And that was why he now sat beside a bed in the Madhouse's sickbay, one of many beds containing strapped-down soldiers from the Fifth. Captain Lindsay was at his desk, busy writing reports while they all waited on the results of Professor Travers' plan.

A collection of gasps filled the sickbay, and Miller snapped his head around. Almost in unison, the restrained men let out a brief yell, then relaxed. Lindsay was on his feet immediately, rushing from patient to patient, checking their vitals and responses.

Miller looked down at Captain Bishop.

'What's happened to me?' he asked, looking around groggily. He noticed his restraints and the bandages covering his wounds. 'Was I attacked?'

Miller grinned. 'Yes, Captain, you were attacked. Rather badly.'

Bishop looked around. 'The Madhouse... What's the situation? Where's Anne?'

'She's busy with Professor Travers,' Lindsay said, finally reaching Bishop. 'Saving the world.'

'Again,' Bishop said with a sly grin.

'Quite. You're lucky to be alive, Bill. Miller here kept you safe in Newcastle, hasn't left your side since.' While he spoke he checked Bishop's vitals.

Bishop looked surprised, and Miller couldn't blame him. He and Andrew hadn't made the best impression during their mission in Newcastle.

'You need rest,' Lindsay said, removing the restraints. 'I don't think these will be necessary any more. But you'll rest until I'm satisfied the infection is no longer in your system.'

'More tests?' Bishop asked.

Lindsay smiled broadly. 'Always.' He walked off.

Bishop took a deep breath, and looked at Miller. 'I owe you my thanks, Private.'

'Least I could do, sir.'

'Yes. Well...' Bishop closed his eyes. 'Good job. We'll make a soldier of you yet.'

Miller remained there for another half hour, just to make sure the captain was okay. And all the time he found he couldn't remove the smile from his face.

This is for you, Andrew, Miller thought, thinking of his dead friend.

Anne, Ted, Birch and Jones all looked at the control panel, not really sure what to do next. They kept Nuffield's output going for as long as they could, as had the other telescopes around the world, but eventually the associated power grids couldn't keep up with the electricity demand. One by one, the telescopes shut down and the delta waves stopped transmitting.

'Do you think it was enough?' Anne was worried. She hated to think it might have all been for nothing. Especially given there was no real plan B.

'We can only hope, until we hear otherwise,' Ted replied, apologetically.

Birch and Jones didn't say anything. The awkwardness was palpable. Anne hated having to sit and wait but there was little else they could do. She didn't want to suggest checking the equipment and repairing any damage just yet. Somehow that seemed liked defeat, even though she knew it was nonsense.

Eventually, they heard steps on the metal ladder outside. Anne held her breath. The other three looked anxiously at the door. As it opened, Anne was still surprised, even though she'd had a good inkling of who it would be.

'Brigadier!' she said, rising to her feet. 'Any news?'

The second she saw his moustache start to curl into an almost-smile, she knew the outcome.

'You mean–?' Ted was taken aback.

'Well done, Professor. I mean, all of you. It appears we've neutralised the effects of this ghastly sleep experiment business.'

'All around the world?' Birch asked.

'That's what all intelligence says,' Lethbridge-Stewart said, almost miffed there was any doubt. 'Amazing effort. Just about the whole world coming together. Not sure there's ever been anything quite like it.'

'Should be more of it,' Anne said.

'Yes, well… quite. Certainly, something we should be aiming for.' Lethbridge-Stewart looked cautiously at Anne. 'You never know what threats the world might face in the future.'

Ted removed his glasses and rubbed his eyes. 'What about those comatose men? The ones at Maidens Port?'

'They woke up,' Lethbridge-Stewart said, then quickly added, 'No ill-effects, from what I've been told.'

Anne smiled warmly. 'Captain Barnett will be pleased.' She surveyed the room. It was the first time she could really take a moment and allow herself to breathe. 'I've been so caught up in everything and focused on the task at hand… I dread to ask, but how's Bill?'

'The Madhouse reports all patients are recovering, including Captain Bishop. In fact, Anne,' Lethbridge-Stewart said, motioning for her to leave the small control room, 'I've arranged a helo to take you straight there.'

Anne couldn't quite believe it. Obviously, she knew that if the patients had awakened in Maidens Port, then Bill would be okay too, but… Knowing and *knowing* were two entirely different things.

She said goodbye to Drs Birch and Jones, and turned to Ted. She still wasn't sure where things stood between them, but for a while, it felt good to be working with him. Almost like old times, in fact.

'We'll speak soon,' she told him.

Ted beamed, surprised despite himself. 'I would like that.'

With a final goodbye, and a gentle hand placed on Lethbridge-Stewart's arm in thanks, Anne left the small control room.

Every part of him ached. Bishop would be lying if he said it didn't. Despite the abundance of painkillers, the barest movement caused him to flinch at the soreness. The dizziness didn't help, either. He'd had a few hangovers in his life and been knocked out more than he cared to remember but that was nothing compared to the pounding in his head right now. Sleep would be a welcome relief, but he just couldn't get past the horrible sensations in his body.

The flicking fluorescent light added to his general quagmire of anguish. He could feel bandages wrapped around his torso and knew that's where the majority of his problems lay. Again. Lindsay assured him the infection and the actions it brought on hadn't done any severe damage to his previous wounds – both those external and internal. He would heal just fine.

His thoughts were interrupted when he heard a sound at the doorway. He managed to turn his head slightly, despite the throbbing aches, expecting it to be his own Florence Nightingale in the form of Miller, but he was instead welcomed with the best sight in the world.

Anne rushed across the sickbay, barely acknowledging Lindsay.

'Oh, Bill!' Her smile quickly disappeared, replaced by tears.

As she slumped over him, sobbing, Bishop gritted his teeth at the pain she was causing. This time, he managed to muster a few words. 'Anne… good to see you.'

Anne rose from her position and looked at her fiancé with tear-filled eyes. 'When I first heard…'

'It's okay,' Bishop told her, taking her hand in his. 'Lindsay says I'll be fine. No permanent damage done.'

She squeezed his hand and leaned over to kiss his forehead. 'I'm glad.'

'I don't know how long I'll be in here, but you'll be the one helping to change my dressings when I get home. I don't remember a lot.'

'You probably don't want to,' Anne said, moving to get him some water from the bedside table. 'Actually, you might want to take up gambling. Somehow you beat the odds to make it through.' Tears welled up in her eyes again. 'So many people didn't make it.'

'I know. We lost a lot of good men out there. Including Private Christiner…'

'No, I mean…' Anne frowned, and fresh tears formed. 'Oh god, Bill. It's Samson, he's…'

Anne couldn't bring herself to finish, but she didn't need to. Bishop closed his eyes and took a deep, painful breath.

'How…?' He shook his head. 'No, it doesn't matter how. I…'

'I know.' Anne forced a smile. 'He was a good friend. To both of us.'

'How did the Brig take it? They've known each other for years.'

'You know Alistair. Stiff upper lip. I'm sure he's broken inside, but for now he'll carry on.'

Bishop nodded. 'Yes. He's got Fiona, she'll get him to open up.'

'And we've got each other.'

She smiled that smile again. The one Bishop thought made her face light up like a pinball machine.

MILITARY MANOUEVRES MYSTIFY MOST
Story by GARY MERRIN
Photospread by GARY MERRIN

Authorities are remaining tight-lipped about recent military operations in Maidens Port and here in Newcastle.

But *The Newcastle Evening Chronicle* can reveal for the first time evidence of two major incidents involving hundreds of soldiers.

Newcastle residents living close to a disused warehouse were originally evacuated due to what they were told was a gas leak.

But enquiries made by this newspaper found gas was not actually supplied to the area in question with the majority of properties connected to the main power grid and running on electricity.

"It did strike me as odd when I thought about it later," resident Ida Macdonald said.

"But two burly soldiers came to my door and told me there was an emergency and that I had to get away from my house and my street.

"With a young child on my hip, what else was I going to do?

"Protecting young Kim is my number one priority and when someone in authority tells you to evacuate, you don't argue with them."

About the same time as the Newcastle incident, soldiers were deployed to Maidens Port on the coast.

Maidens Port, previously known as Maidens Point, was the home of a former naval base used as a code-breaking facility during World War Two.

Seemingly abandoned since the war, the base was also the focus of recent military activity with a variety of trucks and jeeps bringing armed forces to the area.

"I have to admit there were a lot of soldiers about the place," Mr Levene, a visitor to the town, said.

"Certainly more than I've ever seen gathered together at one time.

"If there was something going on, I'm sure the locals would have liked to know.

"It made me stop and think about my future, at any rate."

The Chronicle was prevented from taking photographs at Maidens Port but is able to show some of the action in Newcastle, as duplicates of the original negatives were made.

They highlight a vast array of weaponry in use and civilians among the soldiers, some who appeared to have weapons of their own.

Brigadier Alistair Lethbridge-Stewart, in charge of the Scots Guards Special Support Group, dismissed both incidents and simply described them as "training exercises".

"It's standard practice for the military to be ready and we

need to play out real-life scenarios for our training to be at its most effective," he said.

"Some things just can't be learned from a textbook or on a training field where the shooters fire at mannequins – they don't shoot back.

"By creating a situation with real people to interact with, using rubber bullets, it gives our recruits more of an insight into what they might be up against with any potential enemy.

"Obviously, I can't go into too much detail given the majority of our military intelligence is classified but know it's all in aid of protecting Great Britain, the United Kingdom and our allies around the world."

Lethbridge-Stewart would not be drawn on the extent of the training operations, nor whether they were occurring elsewhere in the country.

EPILOGUE

PAPERWORK WAS a fact of life. Lethbridge-Stewart looked at his mountainous in-tray. Given the oft-secret nature of his work, it couldn't be palmed off to some junior. Especially after the most recent events. The higher the rank, the more administration you had to do. Lives had been lost, chaos had ensued – but the bureaucrats wanted their reports in triplicate just so they could file them away and mark them 'classified'.

After the worldwide collaboration on the delta wave solution, Lethbridge-Stewart had strongly advocated for a unified system that could undertake a global approach when necessary (and quickly, depending on the threat). The powers-that-be had listened patiently and Lethbridge-Stewart was then told to 'put it in writing'. *As if I don't have enough to do,* he thought glumly, reaching for another paper from the pile.

At first, he thought it was just another report of a soldier's death. But this one made him pause as he read the name… It was Sergeant Ward's report on Samson.

He took a deep breath, and reached into his desk drawer to pull out the bottle of whisky and two glasses. He poured two measures into each, placed one on the table opposite him, and raised his own.

'Cheers, Samson.'

He took a sip and closed his eyes.

There was still much to uncover about Werwolf – and his top people were on it, including both Anne and Professor Travers. They'd get to the bottom of everything, find out what that weapon was. In the meantime…

Lethbridge-Stewart would have to contact Samson's grandparents – as far as Lethbridge-Stewart knew, they were Samson's only living relatives. And he was seeing that girl… What was her name? Lethbridge-Stewart couldn't remember, and smiled slightly… Samson seemed to have a new girl on the go every month. Samson and he had often talked about settling down, especially after Lethbridge-Stewart's engagement to Fiona, but Samson was of the mind that such a life was probably not for him.

Not now, at any rate, Lethbridge-Stewart thought sadly.

He finished his whisky and looked at the rest of the paperwork. Which would always be there. Lethbridge-Stewart decided the bureaucrats' sense of urgency was somewhat different to his. When the world was under attack, *that* was the time to drop everything. Pen-pushing could wait.

Packing up his desk, he resolved to take a break. To be somewhere and with someone who mattered. He'd lost a friend and right now he needed to be with the woman he loved.

Driving home, Lethbridge-Stewart focused on simple pleasures, such as the joy of being outside and taking in the passing scenery while a pleasant tune played on the radio. In what felt like next to no time, he arrived at his domicile. Fiona greeted him at the door, her face beaming. As he entered, the aroma of roast lamb welcomed him further, aided by what could only be rosemary.

'Knew I couldn't keep you away,' Fiona said, as she embraced and kissed him. Then with a touch of cheekiness added: 'Glad you remembered who I am.'

After showering and indulging in Fiona's efforts in the kitchen, Lethbridge-Stewart, now in his dressing gown and slippers, rested on their two-seater sofa. Fiona snuggled up next to him.

'I'm sorry to hear about your friend,' she said again, and kissed him gently on the lips. 'I liked Samson, and his girlfriend… Oh, what was her name?'

Lethbridge-Stewart smiled softly. 'Do you know, I can't recall. Sam was never one for settling.'

Fiona snuggled up closer. 'Unlike you.'

'Well, I wasn't sure about that, either. Until I met you,' he added, pecking her on the cheek.

'I love you,' Fiona said.

'And I you, dear.' He beamed at her. 'Very much.'

'You have good taste.' A beat. 'Alistair…?'

He looked down at her with a satisfied smile.

'About those wedding plans…'

Lethbridge-Stewart smiled. *Of course, life goes on.*

'Yes, we better get on with that,' he said. 'Can never be too prepared, eh?'

Fiona looked at him suspiciously for a second. 'It almost sounds like you're happy to go about this? That you'd even enjoy it, maybe?' She positioned herself so they were now eye-to-eye.

Looking directly back at her, Lethbridge-Stewart grinned. 'As long as you don't want anything too extravagant, like a wedding in Peru.'

'Maybe just a honeymoon in Switzerland.'

Shaking his head, Lethbridge-Stewart chortled. 'I'm sure we can work something out.'

VAMPIRES OF THE
NIGHT

MATATOV TRUDGED on through the snow, the flakes stinging his face a thousand times over as the wind blew harshly through the air. He was tired. He ached. He was hungry. *Curse being a lowly* peshkon. *Curse the Red Army of the Workers and Peasants. Curse the Great Patriotic War. Curse Stalin. And curse Hitler, too.* He sighed inside. Matatov was lost and he knew it. He should be cursing his own stupidity. The Motherland needed to be protected.

The pack on his back weighed heavily on him. He wasn't even sure he was still in the Soviet Union. Had he possibly advanced over the border into Poland? At least he was alive. That was more than he could say for his comrades. Ambushed from behind. The continuing blizzard meant such poor visibility that the Nazis had had the upper hand. But how they had managed to see was anyone's guess. Maybe they had invented some advanced device to improve vision?

And Matatov was still wondering how he'd escaped. He had fired back with his Mosin–Nagant as best he could. But he'd barely been able to see a metre or so in front of him. He was just firing wildly. Guiltily, he wondered if he had accidentally shot down any of his comrades. 'Fight to the death!' was the instruction from the Komkor. But some primal instinct had overtaken Matatov's body when he realised it was a lost cause. He ran, far, far into the night and snow, turning back to fire into the chaos. With his heart pounding, adrenaline racing and chest bursting, he didn't know where he was going – he was just getting away. To anywhere. Eventually, the sound of the gunfire and chaos stopped. That's when he knew. They were all gone. No one left.

He was sure the Nazis would be after him. But it was hours later. Did they think no one had escaped? It was hard to see, after all. But it wasn't like them to give up, either, if there was a chance the enemy was still at large.

Deep in thought, on edge, Matatov kept blindly stumbling forward. If he just kept going, he would come across something eventually. A fence, a road, a house perhaps? Unless he was walking in circles, of course. Which would be very easy to do, given the snow. But there was no other option. He had no rations and it was essential he find food before fatigue set in. He cursed again at his situation, his inner turmoil bubbling and boiling furiously. His boot struck something in the snow. A dead animal, maybe? Frozen to death?

A paranoid thought struck Matatov. *Could it be a Nazi soldier? Waiting to attack him?*

Shaking his head, he realised how stupid he was becoming – if it had been, the soldier would have heard him coming and shot him instantly. So, what was it?

Crouching down, he started to move snow away from the lump. His already freezing hands went instantly numb but he ignored it, shovelling into the ice. Eventually, Matatov had exposed enough to see it wasn't an animal. It was a body. Not a threat to anyone any more. But as he dug further, he realised something was wrong, very wrong.

No. *No. This can't be.*

He recoiled in horror, dry-retching as he stumbled backwards. This was beyond the horrors of an already horrible war. What in the name of Lenin could have done that to a human body?

Matatov had heard stories of what the Nazis were capable of. Even some sectors of the Red Army. But this was beyond abhorrent…

Overcoming his initial shock, Matatov took in the gruesome sight before him. The body was ripped open, all manner of organs and insides hanging out, frozen in time. Like somebody had cut the soldier open and torn out its innards completely randomly. Despite the (now-frozen) blood-soaked uniform, he recognised the man as a fellow comrade. But it was the placement of the body's frozen hand that bothered him… Could the solider have actually been gouging himself?

It must have been some form of torture. To hold a man at gunpoint, get him to cut himself open and then pull his insides out. He wouldn't have put it past them. But in the dark recesses of his mind, he remembered whispered stories from the battlefield. Shared among comrades late at night, on the rare occasion they weren't on the march. Some creature, going from battlefield to battlefield, ripping bodies apart and feasting on the organs within. Not differentiating between the Nazis or the Allies. Or any poor soul who might cross their path. 'Vampires of the night', they were called. But Matatov, like many of his comrades, had dismissed these stories as wild rumour. Rumours spread to show there was more to be scared of than the enemy.

Matatov knew there was little he could do with such thoughts. He had to focus on what was happening now. There was a very real possibility the Nazis who had killed his comrades might still be looking for him. It wasn't the time to focus on some vague horror story to help soldiers go into battle.

Freezing, starving, lost... survival was key. There was nothing left for it. Matatov knew what he had to do.

Trying to suppress his revulsion and gag reflex, he bent down to the frozen body and pulled out what he thought was a kidney. Closing his eyes, he brought it his mouth.

Survival, he told himself. *This is survival.*

Edward Travers wasn't sure what the Fourth Operational Corps had in store for him this time. Hence the briefing, he guessed. While he understood the importance of the war effort, of stopping the Nazi scourge, he couldn't help but think he was being used a little. Once again, he cursed Tobias Kinsella for dragging him into it all. He was pleased his background in science was being engaged – and the work *could* be stimulating – but it was as if he was being manipulated into using science for a darker purpose. At least he was being sought-after for his skills these days, rather than being mocked like ten years ago. And since Margaret's passing, he had to ensure Anne and Alun were provided for. *Wonder how they're doing in the country?*

Travers thought about the thousands of children that had been evacuated. *The Blitz, the Nazis, Hitler...* As he pondered the current state of the world, he arrived at his destination.

The Corps supposedly gave him *carte blanche* but, despite being a primarily scientific organisation, its military backing meant he had to follow orders. Travers walked down a stairwell, through a labyrinth of corridors, to find General Dornan in a concrete bunker, protected from the bombs. Despite the war, the efficiencies of day-to-day office life were still maintained.

'Glad you could make it, Travers.'

Is Dornan trying to be amusing?

'You asked me to come so I could be briefed on my next assignment.'

Dornan eyed Travers up and down. 'So I did. But anything can happen at the moment. You never know what loss or gain we will incur next. Sit down.'

Travers did as he was told. He noted the chairs were completely mismatched. It was a case of making use of whatever you could nowadays.

'The Russians have been up to something,' Dornan said, knowingly. His eyes met Travers'.

Travers had heard the rumours, of course. But they were allies… He responded with a raised eyebrow.

'You don't have to play dumb, Travers. Most people know we're allies out of necessity, not goodwill. Hate to think what they'd be like if we weren't working together against a common enemy.'

'The Baltic states again?'

Dornan shook his head. 'Atrocious. But no. More your line of work.'

Travers said nothing. How could his line of work ever be compared to whatever the Red Army may be up to?

'Don't be offended,' Dornan said, as if he could read Travers' mind. 'I'm talking about science. They have scientists too, you know. No matter what side you're on, technology plays a crucial role in assisting military might.'

Travers, once more, decided not to respond. Obviously, Dornan was warming to his theme.

'What do you think would help the war effort, out there on the battlefield?'

Presuming it wasn't a rhetorical question, Travers replied, 'Better weapons? More men?'

Dornan snorted derisively. 'We don't just need more soldiers, although that would help.'

'Then what?'

'More stamina. Specifically, soldiers with more stamina.'

'And how do we do that?'

'That's where you come in.'

Shuffling around his makeshift desk, Dornan passed over several files all marked 'Top Secret'. Taking the files, Travers couldn't fathom why they weren't just in plain folders. Indicating they were important was a red rag to a bull, surely? He started flicking through them.

'The orders have come from Churchill himself. I don't know where he gets his intel from. It's like he has someone in a box who can pop out on the other side of the world in a heartbeat.'

The comment triggered a memory in Travers. A vast snowy mountainside in the Himalayas… Det-Sen Monastery… The Doctor and his blue box… Some days he thought he must have imagined it. Or been hallucinating, due to the thin mountain atmosphere. But deep down, he knew it had been real. The silver sphere still in his possession proved it.

He studied the papers. It seemed the Soviet scientists had

been working on something to make their men last longer in the field. Possibly even to create the ultimate soldier. Sometimes the parallels between the Soviets and the Nazis sent a shiver down Travers' spine.

'Some sort of sleep deprivation experiments, it seems,' Dornan noted, trying to summarise. 'With less or even no sleep, think how much more an individual soldier could achieve.'

'But what about fatigue? The basic need to re-charge the body?'

'Our reports indicate the Soviet experiment has been bypassing that need somehow. We want you to explore a similar line of scientific enquiry.'

No sleep. Was it possible? Travers immediately flinched at the idea. The only way to find out would be to put a human through some horrible experiment. Surely that would make him no better than the Nazis or the Reds? He didn't mention that his expertise wasn't in the medical sciences, as surely Dornan knew that. Perhaps the General believed Travers' eclectic dabbling was enough? Certainly, Travers knew a few basics but, beyond that, other men were better qualified. The only motivation Travers could think of was that he was expendable, in the case of something going wrong. Despite his reservations, he continued to listen to what Dornan had to say.

'We've set up a base, out in the country. It's all ready to go – you need to go in and take charge of setting up the experiment. Then monitor the results so, hopefully, your findings can be used in the field. Everything we know about the Soviet experiment is in the files. We've replicated the set-up as best we can, based on the intelligence that has come back to us. Obviously, there are some gaps in the knowledge but, with your scientific mind, I'm sure you'll be able to piece it all together.'

If Dornan thought flattery would somehow bypass Travers' ethical misgivings, he was mistaken. But Travers also knew he was working for the military now and had to follow orders. So he kept his next question fairly tame.

'Who would be part of this experiment?'

Dornan coughed and looked straight at him. 'Several of our brave men have volunteered. Soldiers in the British army who are willing to do anything to stop this Nazi insanity.'

There was a tone in Dornan's voice, as if he was insinuating that Travers wasn't fully committed to the cause. He thought of asking more questions but knew it would be useless. A commitment to end the war, by whatever means necessary, was Dornan's goal.

Some good has to come out of this, Travers thought. *But can the end justify the means?* He was thinking like a scientist and, to a military man, science was simply a tool to be deployed. One of many strategies to be used. Nothing more. No curiosity merely for the sake of it.

'You have your assignment, Mr Travers,' Dornan said, clearly wanting to conclude the meeting.

'I see. And do I have the pleasure of Eileen Le Croissette this time?'

Now it was Dornan's turn to raise an eyebrow. 'No, Travers, you do not. You may have recommended her to the Corps, but the section officer is not your personal assistant. You'd do well to remember that.' Silence a moment, and then, 'You will be picked up, as per the instructions in the files, and taken to the location. You are not to be made aware of the location. You will simply be taken there, undercover.'

And with that final note, Travers left the strange underground bunker and was on his way.

So it was, on General Dornan's orders, that Travers found himself barrelling down an unknown stretch of road in a military vehicle. He hadn't signed up for the soldier's way of life – his hand had been forced, his own investigations and experiments re-directed into the war effort. At least it was still science. And there had been plenty of interesting twists and turns since he had become attached to the Fourth Operational Corps.

After what seemed like an eternity, they reached their destination. Travers was weary and tired. All he'd had to eat were some barely edible army rations that had done little to satisfy his stomach. A voice from the front of the vehicle cried out.

'We're here. Gerrout!'

Travers threw himself over the canopy at the back and landed on the ground with his belongings, not quite correctly. Before he had properly righted himself, the unnamed driver was off, and Travers was left in the pitch black of night.

Wise precaution, of course. Lights made you a sitting duck should one of the Nazis' Arados fly over. Unlikely out here, but you could never tell where the enemy might strike.

Gloomily, Travers trudged forward in what he guessed was the right direction. Was it not within the realm of even military logic to send someone to meet him, just in case he got lost? If this was such an important experiment, having the main scientist trip and break his neck before it even started might be difficult for General Dornan to explain to his superiors. Or even Churchill.

'Private Barnett, sir!'

As if reading his mind, a soldier had appeared out of thin air, frightening the wits out of him in the process. His heart pounding furiously, Travers noticed the soldier was still standing to attention, saluting him.

'At ease, Private,' Travers said, still trying to catch his breath. 'No need to salute me, I'm not official military. Just a scientist attached to it.'

'Respect all the same, sir.' Barnett quickly saluted once again.

Travers shook his head inwardly. 'Your eagerness is to be admired, but perhaps work on how you approach people in future.'

'Have to check whether friend or foe first, sir. Get the upper hand.'

'Quite. How about you take me to the base where I'll be working?'

'That's what I'm here for, sir.'

'How about you just refer to me as "Mr Travers"?'

'Yes, sir… I mean, Mr Travers.'

After a short walk in the dark, Travers realised he hadn't been very far from the base at all. But there was no guarantee he would have found it without someone leading the way. From what he could make out in the darkness, it was a ramshackle concern. Perhaps originally a couple of cottages with sheds then built up around them, using whatever the soldiers could get their hands on. Wood, old bricks, local rocks, canvas coverings… Metal was in short supply, of course. Travers sincerely hoped the medical and scientific equipment inside wasn't quite such a jury-rigged affair.

Private Barnett led Travers to a room, of sorts, presumably his quarters. No creature comforts but, at present, Travers didn't really care where he slept. He was bushed. He dossed down with his sleeping bag and fashioned his pack into a pillow. He hoped Anne and Alun were more comfortable with his in-laws. It took several minutes, but he was soon asleep.

When he woke the next morning, Travers immediately knew sleeping on the floor had done his back no good whatsoever. Grimacing as he stood, he freshened himself up and went to find if there was some kind of mess hall. He heard general chit-chat coming from one of the other… he didn't know what to call them. Rooms? Tents? He walked down the makeshift corridor to where he might find some form of breakfast.

Private Barnett stood up as soon as Travers entered but seemed to know better than to salute him. The other soldiers looked on with mild interest at the new arrival – but also mild indifference, given their breakfast was being interrupted.

'This is Mr Travers,' Barnett announced, unnecessarily. Surely they all knew that any new arrival would be the scientist posted to the base?

Travers tried to be cheery but only half-managed it. 'Good morning, all. Hope you saved some for me.'

A stout, muscular – if a little short – soldier motioned for Travers to sit down. 'Help yourself. Basic army rations. Best we can offer.'

'Thank you, Captain…?'

'Gampfer.'

Travers tucked in and put his breakfast away quickly. 'Now, who can brief me on the situation here? I assume you know what we're all here for, so if you can give me a status report on any scientific equipment and the volunteers we'll be using, it would be much appreciated.' He died a little inside when he thought of the people who would be subject to the experiment, but he had to move past it. 'I want to get this operation up and running as soon as possible.'

'All systems are go,' Gampfer replied.

'I'd like to give them the once-over. Just to check if there are any medical concerns with the volunteers.'

Gampfer eyed Barnett and the rest of the men. 'The experiment has already begun.'

Travers tried to hide his shock. 'Under whose orders?'

'Churchill's,' Barnett blurted out, as if Travers was some sort of imbecile.

'Obviously. But I was thinking a bit closer to home. Who was the commanding officer that gave the order?'

There was a general restlessness in the mess hall. As if

something was being discussed that shouldn't. Gampfer finally responded.

'I think you already know. General Dornan. He said you'd been fully briefed.'

Travers was irritated now. Someone was playing a game here and he didn't like it. Or someone was playing him. The experiment was going to happen whether he was there or not. They just needed a scientist to legitimise it.

'But the experiment wasn't supposed to start until I arrived! Anything could go wrong!' Even though he knew his protestations were fruitless, he felt he had to say something.

Gampfer looked at Travers. 'Everything is under control,' he said, steadily. 'Phase one is working well. There have been no major incidents.'

Travers noticed some of the soldiers exchanging furtive glances. 'Which might imply there have been some minor incidents? Anything you'd care to report?'

'Given you've finished your breakfast, I'm happy for Private Barnett to show you more of our facility – and what has been achieved so far.'

If he was honest with himself, Travers didn't know why he was so affronted. The fact the work had started without him? Or that he simply hadn't been told? Maybe it was simply the nature of the experiment that put him at unease. None of these soldiers, not even Gampfer – who seemed somewhat distant – had done anything wrong. But he had a nagging feeling something was going on. He didn't know if it was the war making him paranoid or... His mind was suddenly cast back to Det-Sen Monastery, all those years ago. Ever since then, he had always been wary.

'When you're ready, Mr Travers.' Barnett was stood at attention beside him.

Inwardly sighing, Travers got up, and motioned for the Private to relax and lead the way. As he was leaving, Travers thought he should say something to Gampfer and the men.

'I hope I find everything to my satisfaction.' He smiled. 'After all, we want to make sure General Dornan is happy with our progress when the time comes to make a report, don't we?'

Walking along the strange maze of annexes, canvases and makeshift pathways, Travers kept in step with Barnett, wondering what he would find. Did these soldiers know anything about the scientific method? Had they used a control? Or even kept detailed, quantifiable data? He knew they wouldn't let him start over, but he hated to think how much of the experiment had already been compromised.

Soon enough, they reached their destination, one of the cottages the base had been built around.

'Here we are, Mr Travers.'

There were a few other dead giveaways – medical equipment and the sterile air of the room. But perhaps the main one was the two patients isolated in their beds, clear plastic sheeting containing each of them.

Noticing Travers' reaction, Barnett spoke. 'There are more. We couldn't fit them all in here, so we made use of the other rooms in the cottage. Helps with the isolation.'

Maybe there was more to the Private, after all. Or he just could have been regurgitating what others had told him. Either way, the setup was intriguing, in its own piecemeal way. Travers decided to inspect the patient closest to him and call on his limited medical knowledge. He saw someone had been keeping notes, so all may not have been lost. Picking up the file, he gave the pages a cursory glance and looked at the man before him.

'Corporal Grayden?' At first, the Corporal seemed not to notice. He was staring off into the distance, eyes red with irritation. Then quickly, he snapped around and glared at Travers, looking like a wolf about to stalk its prey. 'How are you feeling?'

Grayden continued to stare at him but said nothing. An instant later, he threw himself over the bed and squatted down, huddled in the corner. Just like an animal, scared but ready to pounce.

Barnett didn't seem to have batted an eyelid.

'Are they always like that?' Travers asked. 'Do they ever speak?'

'Depends.'

'That's not the most helpful answer. Could you elaborate?' Travers was on the receiving end of a blank look. 'I mean, maybe you could tell me a bit more?'

'Oh right.' Barnett looked at Corporal Grayden. 'It all depends on how long they've been in here for. They all started at different times. This one's been here for a while now.'

Travers picked up on the use of 'one' rather than 'man'.

Given Barnett's nature, Travers thought he must have picked it up from those around him – another disheartening thought.

He looked back at Grayden's file. There seemed to be all sorts of stimuli used to keep the man awake. Lights, loud noise, spraying him with water, injections of goodness-knows-what... The rationale seemed to be 'keep him awake, no matter what'. Travers tut-tutted and shook his head. It was a hodge-podge of scientific process – if you could call it that – and, in many ways, simply an abuse of mankind. People couldn't keep blaming the war for these types of things. All he could do was make the best of a bad situation and see if he could bring both the science and humanity back to this experiment.

But if all the subjects were on edge, like Grayden, he'd have to tread carefully. He wasn't sure how he was going to deal with this man, given he was so cagey. He was mildly reassured the armed private was with him. Despite this, Travers was annoyed at Barnett's seemingly complete disregard for the patient and the whole operation in general.

'I must say, Private, the fact you take all this in your stride troubles me.'

'Just following orders.'

'Be that as it may, does this set-up not strike you as somewhat unusual? This patient could easily have been stationed with you. In other circumstances, he might have been someone you dined with in the mess hall.'

'I doubt it.' Barnett scratched the back of his head, for once showing signs there might be more than one thought in there.

'Why is that?'

'None of the patients are ever hungry. In fact, the longer we keep them awake, the more they refuse to eat.'

The comment gave Travers pause for thought. *What the blazes would cause that?* he wondered. If this was a test of stamina, then surely food and water would be necessary to help keep the body going. It would need fuel, even more so with little sleep.

He was suddenly pulled out of his ruminations by a piercing, almost inhuman scream. Some sort of horrible howling. Barnett was already legging it to another room and, despite his disorientation, Travers quickly decided to follow him. The howling continued, resonating through the cottage, as if it was penetrating Travers' mind. He almost ran into the back of Barnett, who had stopped in a doorway, rifle pointed at the ready.

Inside was another patient, contained in a similar fashion to Grayden. But this chap was far more feral and ferocious than Grayden had been. Haggard and unkempt, it looked like he'd spent several weeks in the wilderness. His eyes were red and wide, like a man barely clinging to sanity. The almost skeletal frame showed signs of starvation, the body using up all the reserves it had. The man's beard only added to the wildness of his appearance. And all the while, he was screaming – constantly screaming.

What could break a man down to such an animal level? And how can his fellow man just stand by and do nothing when he is obviously in so much distress?

'Does this happen often?' Travers yelled, trying to make himself heard over the din.

'More than you'd think,' Barnett replied, in his ever-so-unhelpful manner.

'So, how do you stop it?' The sideways glance from the Private and the itchy finger on his trigger spoke volumes. Travers knew he had to tread carefully.

'The threat of one of us here with a gun seems to quieten them down after a while. It's terrible when they all carry on at once. All hands on deck then.'

'How long before they settle down?'

Barnett considered Travers' query and replied in his most matter-of-fact manner yet. 'That's always the question,' he noted.

They had gone. Finally. One of the others had grabbed their attention. Whether by design or accident, it allowed Grayden to make his move. The screaming made him feel like he, too, wanted to explode with rage, to go wild. To rip open everything in a glorious rampage and make everyone feel his inner turmoil. He felt something primal stirring. But he hadn't given in yet. There was still enough of the old Grayden left, enough of his cunning and intelligence. If he escaped he could roam free and do whatever he wanted, beyond the confines of this so called experiment. He was a caged animal, halfway between man and beast, but soon he would be free.

Heart and adrenaline pounding, drooling at the mouth, Grayden knew it was time to go. Somehow, during the course of this experiment, his strength had increased. He didn't know how... but he did know that this cottage was so old that he could remove some of its stones easily, without bringing the wall down on top of him. When no one was looking, he had practised many times. But it wasn't until now he had felt the time was right. Whether it was because of the presence of the new arrival, the continued screaming from the next room or his body changing just enough, Grayden decided that this was his moment.

Now, in broad daylight, he removed the stones as he had carefully practised and wriggled through the opening. Within minutes, he was out and running – running like there was no tomorrow. Given the screaming noise throughout the base, all attention was elsewhere. The fresh air energised him even more. He was ready to do whatever his primal instincts urged him to do, with no sleep to hinder him.

And with that, Corporal Grayden was gone.

By now, Gampfer and the rest of the men had joined Travers and Barnett. Several were by Barnett's side, their sights firmly trained on the wretched, screaming man before them. It was something of a stalemate. And then, just as suddenly as it had started, the screaming stopped. The patient looked ahead at the soldiers before him and didn't move.

'Right, the situation's been contained,' Gampfer said. 'But, to be on the safe side, let's keep an eye on this one.'

Travers was both furious and dumbfounded. The whole situation would have been verging on ridiculous if the implications hadn't been so serious. They couldn't just keep watching the patients, aiming their rifles and hoping for the best.

'Captain, I demand you put a stop to this experiment at once. For the safety of these patients, for the safety of your men and, quite possibly, the safety of Great Britain!'

He was met with a cool gaze from Gampfer. Barnett, along with the other men, looked to their captain.

'Under whose orders? I am the ranking officer here.'

'And I am the scientist assigned to this experiment, and my order is stop it at once! Can't you see something is seriously wrong here?'

'It is a military experiment, based on Russian intelligence. Pushing the boundaries – and our men – to the limit and beyond is how we're going to win this war.'

'This is like something the Nazis would do to their enemies.'

'Or their own men, if it would help Hitler win.'

Travers wanted to throw a punch. Was Gampfer seriously likening the British fighting forces to the fascist regime currently holding most of Europe to ransom? It made him sick to his stomach. And yet he knew the way of the military mind. Gampfer's next comment was a foregone conclusion.

'We follow General Dornan's orders until otherwise instructed by him or another ranking officer.'

Knowing that saying anything else would be futile, Travers turned his attention to the patient.

The screaming and wildness had completely stopped. He was just standing there, staring into the distance. What was going on in this poor soul's mind that he could go from one extreme to the other in an instant?

'So be it,' Travers decided. 'If anything gets out of hand here, you and your men will be held fully responsible. I'll make sure of it.' Before Gampfer could speak, he continued. 'Don't worry, I'll play my part in this dirty little secret. But I'll be treating the patients as humanely as possible. Now, in the meantime, if you're going to "keep an eye on things", then I suggest whoever you station here gives me a full account of anything that happens, so I can add it to my observations. *That* is all part of the scientific method.'

Gampfer motioned for two soldiers to stay stationed in the troubled man's room. 'Barnett, stick with the "Professor" here. Allow him the access he needs, but don't allow him to breach any protocols. As you were, *Professor.*' Travers knew Gampfer was trying to get under his skin, so he made sure not to flinch in the slightest. With that, the Captain and the other men trudged away.

Despite Gampfer's attitude, Travers – and Barnett – weren't quite sure what to do next. 'Perhaps I should look at the patients in the other rooms?' Travers suggested. He had to do something, given Dornan had assigned him to the base.

Barnett started to move forward when a corporal ran into the room.

'Barnett! Mr Travers! One of the patients has gone!' Turning on his heel, the two of them followed the soldier. Barnett fell into step with the Corporal as they headed back to where Travers had seen the first patient.

But the empty bed and the hole in the cottage wall left no guesses as to what had happened. The tension in the air was palpable.

'Get Gampfer!' Travers snapped. 'We have an uncontained experiment. However shoddy this set-up was to start with, it's a thousand times worse now.'

Without thinking, Barnett saluted and left post-haste.

Travers shook his head, sighed and looked at the Corporal.

'Name's O'Brien, sir,' the officer said, gently. 'You might want to sit down. Given the situation, there's probably more you should know.'

While Gampfer and his men set out with a search party, Corporal O'Brien filled Travers in on everything that had happened during the course of the experiment.

Over the past few nights, some of the soldiers had gone missing. Gampfer suspected deserters, but O'Brien said the men involved were not the type. Worse were the stories that had come from the battlefields of Europe.

'The Russians talk about "vampires of the night",' O'Brien said.

'"Of the night", you say?' Travers noted drily. 'If you believe the legends, that's when vampires always do their bidding.'

'I don't think accuracy was on anyone's mind as these stories came about.'

'Go on.'

'It stems from lack of sleep.'

Travers pricked up his ears. It was like he had a few more pieces of a jigsaw puzzle, but still no idea how they fitted together, nor what the end result should look like.

'I'm sure you know this experiment is based on something the Red Army was doing,' O'Brien continued. 'But no one really knows what happened to their men. However, the Russians, French, English and Nazis all have similar tales of finding bodies ripped open, their insides mutilated and eaten. Soldiers see some terrible things in war, but, according to the stories, this was far beyond what anyone had come across before.'

Travers considered O'Brien's story. 'How do you know it's not just wild animals? Plenty of zoos have been shut down, and it wouldn't surprise me if a few animals had managed to escape being shot.'

'I've only heard this second-hand. But the damage to the bodies is nothing like an animal attack. It's as if someone had cut the bodies open and ripped out all the organs.'

'A new form of Nazi torture, then.' Travers was trying to

maintain an open mind while also being steady and methodical in his reasoning.

'Many have thought that. But these "vampires of the night" don't discriminate between Axis or Allies.'

'As much as I hate the idea, the Allies could simply be copying Nazi tactics. But how does this tie in with the Soviet sleep-deprivation experiments?'

O'Brien looked around, as if someone might be listening. 'General Dornan ordered Gampfer to remove certain pages from the intelligence files before you got here.' Then he shook his head. 'No idea what was on them. Something they obviously wanted to hide.'

'So they could avoid having the experiment shut down?'

O'Brien shrugged – but it was apparent he agreed with Travers' thought.

Something wasn't right here, Travers knew. He couldn't put his finger on it but he felt his initial suspicions had been warranted. He considered what O'Brien had told him. Just the thought of the experiment made his blood boil.

Travers stood and began pacing, anger fuelling every step. A realisation was starting to come to dawn on him. He looked at O'Brien.

'Did they not realise just how bloody dangerous this was?'

Looking sheepish, O'Brien replied, meekly, 'The experiment? It's to help against the Nazi menace.'

'Pfft… think man! Does it not strike you as odd that I'm assigned to this base the moment things start to go wrong? I don't think I was sent here to *oversee* the experiment.'

O'Brien looked puzzled. 'What, then?'

'I was sent here to fix it or contain it. My guess is the experiment has already got way out of hand. I don't think many of the volunteers are actually destined to survive.'

O'Brien didn't say anything but his face was a picture of guilt.

'I know it's not your fault, Corporal. I'm just angry at this bloody war. This is what we've been reduced to. Turning our fellow men into nothing more than lab rats, just to get the upper hand.'

'I never said I agreed with it.'

'Yes, yes, "following orders" as they say. Young and impressionable lads like you wouldn't know much different.' Travers sighed and sat down again. He was glad Margaret wasn't around to see that the world was going to hell in a handbasket.

Barnett had a growing sense of unease. He'd been in battle before and, certainly, he'd had butterflies — but this was different. This situation just didn't feel right. Whether it was the experiment, some of the comments Travers had made or Gampfer's constant manner, it all felt a bit amiss. Either way, he was being extra-cautious, even though he was on home soil.

Moving from tree to tree, bush to bush, Barnett kept himself covered. A piercing screaming rang out, not dissimilar to the one that had confronted him and Travers in the cottage earlier. He tried not to think about the lack of humanity in the screech. Could it be the escaped Grayden? Had he succumbed to the strange, wild nature like the others?

And then he saw it. One of the missing soldiers they'd been ordered not to tell Travers about. Stumbling through the woods, coming towards him. As the man came closer, Barnett could see he was ghostly white. There was a massive scratch across his face, and other wounds as well. Like he'd been cut open with a jagged knife. It was revolting yet fascinating at the same time.

Although he knew he wasn't the sharpest tool in the shed, Barnett had military discipline and he understood what he had to do next. Cocking his rifle, he swallowed decisively. There was no other option. The future of Great Britain was at stake. He took a deep breath and readied himself.

It was at that moment the injured soldier collapsed. The Private decided to chance it and ran over to where he had fallen. Looking at the body, Barnett saw that, close up, things were much worse than he'd thought. As the bile rose to his throat, it was all he could do not to expel that morning's rations from his stomach.

With what remaining strength he had left, the mutilated man whispered. 'Kill me. Kill them. Stop.'

This man is in agony, Barnett thought. *How is he even able to speak?* He could think about the soldier's words later. For now, he returned to his original plan.

Captain Gampfer and two of his men were busy searching another section of the woods. Nothing was said but they were ready to spring into action no matter what presented itself. As they made a steady, methodical sweep of the area, a gunshot rang out.

'Sounds like we have some action, lads. On the double!' Firearms at the ready, they quickly ran to the source of the sound, where they found Barnett with a body prostrate before him.

Running up quickly to the Private, Gampfer took in the situation.

'Barnett! What have you done? Were you attacked?' Despite his questions, Gampfer had a sneaking suspicion he might already know the answers.

'One of ours, sir,' Barnett said, indicating the uniform. 'He didn't have long. I don't know what could do this kind of thing… Do you think it's something to do with the experiment?'

Gampfer looked at him, the barest of flinches contained. *Do not speculate in the absence of fact*, he reminded himself. *Make sure you retain command. Whatever is happening, it is for the good of the war. Remain measured and calm.*

'It could be anything, Private. Yes, we have missing men but that could be due to any number of reasons. Our number one priority is containing the escaped patient and the experiment. Orders… Remember our orders!'

Motioning for his men to pick up the body, Gampfer resolved to take it back to base to let Travers give it the once-over. Despite being suspicious of the man, he knew General Dornan had assigned him for a reason.

'Barnett, you're with me now. We will keep up the search for our AWOL patient. Perhaps he just went for a stroll…' Gampfer might not have believed it himself but there was no way he could allow his men to be spooked. No more than they had been, anyway.

Meanwhile, O'Brien had led Travers around the rest of the cottage area, showing him the other facilities and the remainder of the volunteer patients. All were in various dishevelled states and gave them wild looks. But none had responded with the vile screaming they had experienced earlier. Begrudgingly, Travers admitted to himself the tools used for the experiment were up to par. It was just the method that left a lot to be desired.

Turning into one of the makeshift corridors, they could see out into woods surrounding the base. At the same time, both noticed two soldiers carrying what appeared to be another soldier's body. As they hurried outside, a wave of shock came over O'Brien.

'It's Davies! One of the missing soldiers I told you about!'

Travers wanted a closer look. 'Put him down.' As the men complied, he took in the atrocity that was before him. He looked at O'Brien.

'As sickening as they are to look at, do Davies' remains remind you of anything?'

'Vampires of the night,' a whispered voice blurted out. Everyone remained quiet. Travers, mulling over a hypothesis, finally broke the tension in the air.

'Get this body back to the cottage. I want to inspect it later. Then you're both coming with me to find Gampfer – and Grayden, wherever he may be. Corporal O'Brien, you seem to have more of a clue as to what's going on, so you're to remain here on guard. Whether it's guarding the patients, guarding against the enemy or guarding from the sheer stupidity of the military mind, I don't care. Do all three. Just be on guard.'

Traipsing through the woods and undergrowth, Travers had the soldiers spread out to cover as wide an area as they could. He knew their findings might be grim but at least the men around him were military-trained, ready with a crackshot and, he hoped, to deal with the sight of blood or whatever unknown terrors presented themselves. Travers hoped they would find Gampfer or some of the other men; at least then they could pool their resources and deal with the pressing situation at base. Maybe the latest developments would make Gampfer see reason, especially once Travers put his hypothesis forward. The thought of that dead soldier, ripped apart, was uppermost in his mind. He wished he had his hip flask – a quick nip might have helped to bury the unpleasantness for a while.

Aside from lack of sleep, Travers couldn't see what could possibly be causing the reaction in the patients. It was possible the process was irreversible – and Travers hated to think what that might mean, given the trigger-happy soldiers around him. But was he thinking about this the right way? Instead of searching for a cure, should he be looking for an alternative? *Containing* the situation, rather than curing it, might be the only option. Which was exactly what General Dornan wanted him to do.

He was just swallowing his annoyance at playing right into

the General's hands, when inspiration suddenly struck him. Whatever was happening, he couldn't cure it. Not in the time he had, anyway. But he could do the *opposite* of what had been done in the first place. Rather than forcing them all to stay awake beyond their means, he could force them to sleep. Some sort of induced coma. For the first time since he arrived, Travers had a little bit of hope in his heart.

Thinking too much, rather than being on the lookout, caused him to trip and fall. Something beneath the forest's foliage had caught his foot. Travers' heart started racing. Whatever it was, it hadn't felt like a stump or a fallen tree branch. Bracing himself, he called out, ready to investigate.

'Over here!' The two soldiers accompanying him were quickly on the scene. 'I think I've found something.'

Scrabbling about, they managed to uncover what Travers had discovered. All of them went pale. It was another body – another of the missing soldiers. If Davies' corpse had made them question the horrors of the world, then this was something straight out of Hades itself. They eyed each other, unsure of what to do next.

At the same time, out of the corner of his eye, Travers saw something move quickly through the trees. A dog? Unlikely. He considered the body before him. A wolf? That would explain the horrific injuries. Wolves had been feasting on the remains. But he could tell the difference between scavenging animals and the injuries to the body. There were no incisor marks. And the other-worldly nature of the jagged cut down the main torso had too much in common with that Davies fellow. Were there more escaped patients he hadn't been told about? And could they be capable of this? Travers knew his medical knowledge was limited but there was something about the injuries that didn't look quite right…

'Thought we heard something over this way,' said a voice in the near distance.

Travers looked around. It was Gampfer and his men, coming to join them. The Captain quickly looked down at the body.

'We found one like that, too. Ghastly.'

He certainly is the master of understatement, thought Travers. He was hoping these deaths – and the likelihood of similar finds – would sway Gampfer's mind about the experiment. But was Gampfer not telling him something? Or deliberately obfuscating details? Travers thought it was time to put his foot down.

'Will you listen to me now, Captain? Or will it take even more deaths to make you realise this experiment must be stopped?'

Gampfer smiled, meeting Travers' stare. No words were forthcoming.

'I'm not an imbecile, Captain. I know that you know the experiment is causing all this. Unless, of course, you believe there's some mythical creature on the attack, both here in Great Britain and all across Europe?' Travers was sure to emphasise the sarcasm in his last comment.

They continued to eye each other, each waiting for the other to back down.

Then the silence was broken. Screaming. More of that penetrating, horrible screaming, emanating from the base. Piercing their ears, almost shattering their eardrums. Despite an instinct to run away, they knew they had to go forward and face whatever was happening.

Collectively, they all headed for the cottage, where they immediately ran into another soldier. Or something that once had been a soldier. They stopped in unison, aghast at the sight. He was howling and scampering around the room, wild-eyed and unhinged. Back and forth he scuttled, knocking things over, looking up and around. The men looked at each other, uneasily.

But his piercing shrieks were not alone. There was a cacophony of screeching, bawling and squealing, as if somebody had set off a firecracker in a zoo and all the animals had been spooked in unison. The other patients had clearly gone wild, too – and there was no telling what they might be capable of. Captain Gampfer motioned for his men to be on standby, rifles raised and ready for action. Travers joined them, his gun drawn. All were slightly uncertain whether they would be a match for this abnormal threat. But there was little else for it...

'Barnett, keep an eye on...' Gampfer hesitated, unsure his next word would be correct. '*Him.* We'll go check what's happening with the others.'

'Best to keep someone here with Barnett,' Travers said. 'I'm not sure one man alone could withstand the brute force these patients seem capable of.'

Gampfer nodded and ordered a man to remain with Barnett. He indicated how his men should spread out into the other rooms. A trickle of sweat had formed on his brow but he seemingly remained oblivious to the perspiration. 'You're with me, Travers.'

Nodding his agreement, Travers followed the Captain into one of the patients' rooms, the endless wild screaming penetrating their skulls. Gampfer was barely a few steps into the room when he stopped suddenly and vomited on his own boots. Taken aback and reeling from the smell, he saw what had caused the man to be so repulsed – and it was all he could do not to follow suit.

Before him was a man. Just like the others they had found in the woods, his body was ripped open, with organs displaced and hanging out. But he was alive. Screaming like the others but sitting down, unable to stand any more. Travers realised the man had torn himself open, using whatever tools he could find. He had ripped out his own insides and was now eating himself, feral, voracious. Blood vessels streaked across his eyeballs. He only stopped shrieking when feasting. Growing paler and paler, the man continued to devour himself, oblivious to the damage it was causing.

It reminded Travers of the dancing plague of the sixteenth century. Then, people had kept dancing for a month without any rest, before dying from exhaustion. But there were no reports of the people involved doing such gruesome things to themselves. No wonder the 'vampires of the night' myth had spread throughout the soldiers. Even the most bloodthirsty veteran would be disgusted by this atrocity. Well, among the Allies, anyway…

His thoughts were interrupted as a shot rang out. Instantly, the disembowelled man in front of them keeled over, and all the screaming throughout the base came to an abrupt halt. Travers turned his head to Gampfer. He still had his rifle in the air, looking aghast at the mixture of blood and vomit at his feet.

'You can put the rifle down now, Captain,' Travers said, softly. 'Before you ask, yes, you were right. As much as I hate to say it, there was nothing we could do for that poor chap. I just hope the others aren't as far gone. There might be some hope for them.'

Gampfer snapped back to his officious manner. 'The situation must be contained. Mass termination might be the only option if you can't find a solution quickly.'

Travers followed him. 'You do know I'm not a professor,

don't you, Captain? I've never taught in any official capacity. Nor am I a qualified medical specialist. Anthropology is my field.'

Gampfer snorted in response. 'Either way, you're smarter than the rest of us. Given the situation, you're our best bet.'

As they made their way to another patient's room, Travers found himself getting riled again. 'Are you sure you're not a member of the Nazi party? Treblinka would likely welcome you. The care factor for human life is about the same.'

'If the situation weren't so desperate, Mr *Professor*, I'd have you under military arrest for such treasonous remarks. I am simply doing what's in the best interests of Great Britain. Good God, man, this is war. We all have to make difficult decisions and take action we might otherwise be averse to.'

'I understand. But if there's a humane solution to be found, then give me the opportunity to find it.'

They arrived at the next room, where two soldiers stood guard, ready for anything. Travers looked at the patient. He was still contained in the plastic draping, similar to Grayden's set-up. Travers couldn't see any signs of self-mutilation.

'This one stopped screaming at the same time as the others. Just went to being as you find him now,' one of the guards reported.

Travers looked at Gampfer square in the eye. 'You have to let me find an alternative option to terminating everyone.'

'I don't know how long these patients will stay calm for. Or when they might start eating themselves.' The Captain's manner was so deadpan it would have been comical if not for the seriousness of the situation. 'I'll keep my men at the ready but time is definitely something you don't have on your side.'

Don't I know it, Travers thought. Proper scientific method and process could take years. But necessity was the mother of invention. Look at how far radar had come during the war, especially the monopulse technique…

'I'll go back to your original records – what there is remaining of them,' Travers said, giving Gampfer a pointed look.

It was hours later and getting dark. Travers had been over everything – his original briefing, the experimental records held at the base and the various bodies and remains. There had only been one outburst of screaming in this time but, fortunately, it had only lasted ten minutes, and Gampfer and his men had managed not to shoot anyone.

'Are you certain this will work?' Gampfer looked sceptical. Travers, injecting needle in hand, gave him a withering look.

'Nothing's certain when it comes to experimental science, as I'm sure you're well aware by now. But with limited time to test everything, this is the best chance we've got. Now get your men to hold the patient down while I administer this serum.'

Five men had gone underneath the plastic drapes to ensure the patient did not move. He had struggled and screamed for a short while but now he was simply breathing rapidly, his eyes darting about. Travers injected the upper arm. Immediately, the patient cried out and started writhing, his body convulsing wildly. Travers was worried at such an adverse reaction. But after a few minutes, the patient went limp and his eyes closed.

'*To sleep, perchance to dream.*' Travers said, with a touch of sadness. He knew this wasn't a solution. The best hope was to keep the men alive until a better medical answer could be found. 'We just have to do the same to the others now.'

Gampfer grunted an affirmative response. 'But how long will it last? For all we know, it could wear off in a few hours.'

'I've used something that will ensure an induced coma. They can only be aroused by a similar means. I'm hoping that, in time, a more permanent solution can be found, to be administered before someone chooses to wake them up. We need to move these patients somewhere more hospitable but also out of the way.'

'General Dornan isn't going to be pleased about this.'

'Then you better make sure you give him a full report, just as I will be. Your biggest concern now is finding Corporal Grayden and any other missing men. Unless, of course, they've succumbed to tearing themselves apart like the others. Find them, Captain. We want to keep this situation under control.'

'I'll get my men onto it.'

'By the way...'

'Yes?'

'Don't just shoot them because it's easier.'

Gampfer glared at Travers but said nothing. 'We will do what is required in the name of Great Britain,' he said, avoiding the accusation.

'Good,' Travers replied. 'I don't know whether the General will keep me assigned to this case or move me onto something else. But just promise me this, Captain…'

'Go on.'

'Look after these patients. They are British soldiers. Your fellow men. They deserve to be treated well. I wish I could snap my fingers and cure them but this is the best we can manage at the moment. Give them a chance. If the positions were reversed, you'd want them to do the same for you.'

As Gampfer went to leave the room, Travers' words hung in the air.

'I'll get Private Barnett to organise another search party.' And with that he was gone.

Travers stared after him, then looked back at the patient. A thought occurred… how many other similar experiments were taking place across Europe right now? Or even the world? With a heavy heart, he left the room, wishing, like so many others, that this calamitous war would soon reach its end.